ALSO BY KATHRYN K. MURPHY

The Firemark Series

The Secret About Time
Simply A Matter of Time

The Sisters in Sirens Series

A Touch of Healing
A Touch of Fire
A Touch of Truth

THE LAST LOYALIST

KATHRYN K. MURPHY

Caraway Press

ISBN-13: 979-8-9933081-1-1

Cover design by K.B. Barrett

For everyone who's ever loved history.
And for Kevin, who gave me the inspiration for this story.

CHAPTER 1

H arlem Heights, New York
September 16, 1776

THIS WAS no place for an orderly fight.

Captain Nathaniel Harrington gritted his teeth as another branch snapped nearby, the sound too loud in the fog-laced stillness. Mounted on Nelson, the redcoat felt like a target—vivid and impractical in the thick underbrush. Around him, the light infantry detachment struggled to keep formation, their usual precision dissolving in the tangle of trees and smoke.

They'd chased the rebels uphill after the skirmish—mocking horns sounding, jeering jests—but it had turned quickly. Too quickly.

"They're flanking us," he barked, sword flashing in the mist as he pointed left. "Wheel about! Hold this line!"

But his voice was swallowed in musket fire and shouts. The Colonials fought like thieves, appearing from behind

1

trees, darting in and out, never giving a clean target. It wasn't by the book.

Nathaniel narrowly avoided riding into a tree as a ball struck just behind him, bark and splinters biting his cheek. His heart pounded. This wasn't supposed to happen—not after Brooklyn. Not here.

Through the smoke, he saw a familiar soldier fall. A private—barely out of school—clutched his stomach, his face twisting in disbelief.

"Fall back! To the rear! To the rear!"

It was chaos. The line had broken, and men were struggling to stay in the ranks as the Colonials shot from the trees, edging them back the way they came over the rocky hills, or rather out from them, seemingly appearing out of the fog.

He was able to fire a few rounds off, but the rebels were moving too quickly, darting in and out.

Nelson whinnied and strained against the reins as another shot cracked from their left.

The gray gelding rounded his neck to escape the sound, ears flattening against his head.

Nathaniel spurred him away from the shot and cracks behind him, keeping with his men, who tried to reload while moving toward open land where they could hope to regain the advantage.

That opportunity never came. Hours of guerrilla fighting ensued as the rebels followed them back, picking them off as they retreated away from the woods and into open ground.

After the battle, the cheers of the rebels could be heard for the first part of their journey to where they had camped on a hill in the pastures around the Van Cortlandt House, a Georgian home owned by a merchant.

While Major John Maitland went inside the merchant's house, Nathaniel and the others worked to organize the camp and check the horses for the night. The barn would be used to hold the tack and serve as shelter for the men. Others were near a few graves farther off. He followed them and found a quiet corner in what appeared to be the family cemetery.

He slipped his hand into the haversack and pulled out the crumpled letter that had arrived a few days ago. He had been eager to purchase his colors and make his mark in the world with a military career, but today's fight and this letter had cured him of excitement. There was a hollowness in his chest that only death could bring. Gone was the innocence of a new soldier. Death had brought a fragility to life he hadn't known before.

He knelt, aching with soreness and exhaustion. There in the muddy ground, he buried the gold watch before saying a final, private goodbye to a boyhood dream. She hadn't wanted him to go, and wouldn't see him return even if he survived this war. He murmured the Lord's Prayer while thinking of her sweet smile. When he was done, he sat back on his heels and gazed up at the night sky, hoping for stars. It was dark and heavy with clouds.

"Lord, let me be elsewhere. Anywhere but here," he added before peeling his aching muscles up to get back to his duties.

Nathaniel checked on the soldiers nearby and was making his way to his blanket when he noticed movement to his right.

Ensign Benny Coldwell stumbled away from the others, down the hill.

"Ensign," Nathaniel said once, before following. The kid had looked young when he volunteered for the regiment, but now, under a thin sheen of sweat with a gray look, he seemed even younger. Nathaniel's lips tightened a little as he walked down toward Benny, who was favoring his side but trying to hide it.

"Sir?" he asked through labored breathing.

"Got some business to attend to out there? The wind's picking up."

"Want to see about my horse, sir. Front hoof felt like it might be going lame." Nathaniel had always liked this kid. He had a soft spot for his horse, and that showed a lot. Even when Nathaniel knew that damn side must be killing him, Benny didn't complain and wasn't putting his work on anyone else.

"I'll come with you. Need to check out mine as well," he lied.

"Thank you, sir," Benny said, nodding once before turning toward the hill again.

Nathaniel had just started walking with him when a loud group of voices all erupted in protest from back inside the barn. He told Benny he'd catch up before walking over to where a small mob had taken up under the loft. Finding the source of the problem, Nathaniel swore under his breath. Not only had Elias claimed the loft, he had pulled up the damn ladder. Sitting like a cat, Elias dug into his pack and bit into what looked like some sort of hand pie, no doubt looted from the kitchens. Judging by the sounds below him, the mob's anger was past simmering and heading toward a boil.

Nathaniel saw an opportunity to kill two birds with one stone.

"Lieutenant!" The mob of angry men now looked on in a predatory silence, anticipating sweet justice. "Lieutenant! Get you and that damn mouth of yours down here now. You're needed outside. We're checking the horses." He turned on his heel and strode out, hearing the bouts of jeers in his wake.

The men drowned out any protest from Elias.

The corners of Nathaniel's mouth turned upwards when Elias had no choice but to comply with the jeers of the men who clamored up the ladder, but the slight smile of satisfaction left his face when he saw how little distance Benny had made toward his mount.

Nathaniel looked up at the sky while he listened to the rush of the trees being swept by the breeze. Black clouds swirled overhead, and distant thunder sent chills down his spine. A few of the horses snorted and stomped with unease. They hated wind, as did he. It was picking up, and a storm was coming in.

Something about storms had never sat right with him. Nathaniel had been far too old when he stopped running to his mother as a boy. His brother William's taunts had been the thing that broke him of the habit, after which he took to pulling a blanket over his head.

While the actual event was unsettling enough, Nathaniel particularly didn't enjoy the sounds of an approaching storm, as the anticipation made the final experience so much worse. A few raindrops hit the coat he hadn't yet been able to take off. Nathaniel fastened the buttons with an eye on the dark rolling clouds moving in fast, high above him.

He strode forward toward Benny, who was studying the swollen withers of his horse. The boy's cause was admirable, but the time had passed, and they needed to get back to shelter.

"Ensign—"

A thunderclap boomed over his head, drowning him out. Benny didn't look up, only limped forward with grim determination to see to his animal before he rested.

Nathaniel took a second and spun around to find Elias twenty yards behind, slowly making his way out of the barn.

"Lieutenant! Get over here!"

Nathaniel didn't watch to see the order followed through. He ran toward Benny to drag the damn kid back inside.

Looking at this weather, it would take both him and Elias to move Benny in before the worst of it.

Too late. With a downward rush, the sky opened. Sheets of rain poured over them, cloaking the landscape. From just a few yards away, Nathaniel lost sight of Benny and could make out nothing but the shapes of what he knew to be horses nearby. He clambered in the same direction, hoping to run into him.

The wind raged and carried off his useless voice as he tried to yell above its howling. A bolt of lightning burst through the sky above. Nathaniel saw the familiar landscape illuminated around him in an odd light before plunging back into chaotic darkness.

He'd seen a figure waving to him and fought the gusting wind to make his way in that direction. Arms outstretched, Nathaniel groped for something to guide him but felt only the piercing of rain spray into his face.

"Benny!" he tried again. "Elias!"

Another deafening explosion rocked the sky above and the ground below. The wind now roared in his ears. Nathaniel turned, trying to find the barn for himself. Panic bloomed when he couldn't. Blind, he searched again, desperate for anyone or anything to help. The small, terrified child from his past screamed inside him.

The last thing he heard was a loud crack above him before it all went black.

CHAPTER 2

B ronx, New York
July 13th, Present day

IT WAS ALREADY DARK when Melanie Reyes boarded the bus
for home. It had been another long day of meetings, paperwork, and hearings, but that didn't stop her from working on
her phone during the ride to her apartment.

Graduating from college, then law school and passing the
bar had been a big deal for her, and an even bigger deal for
Abuelita. It had been her dream to become a public defender
and stand up for the most vulnerable accused.

Seven years later, no matter how late she stayed, she felt
guilty about the dwindling time she could spend with each
client. The system needed to change, but all Mel could do
was put her head down and try to help the people in front of
her one at a time. They needed her, and she couldn't afford
to get bogged down or overwhelmed.

Reaching her building, she jogged up the five flights of

stairs, keys in hand, and had to do a little dance with the lock before she shoved her hip into the slightly dented, abused door that led to her would-be paradise. It wasn't the most expensive apartment complex, thanks to student loans, but at least it was clean-ish and had decent soundproofing between the walls. Still, Mel hoped that she could get a nicer place with better security in the future. Once inside, she tossed her bag on the floor by the little entry table on which sat an old picture of her parents in a pink glitter frame she had made as a kid. Mel kicked off her shoes and headed straight for the bedroom, undressing and tossing her black dress into the hamper.

Mel hit the bathroom to scrub off the day before returning to the kitchen and opening the fridge. She grabbed one of the few bottles of water inside and studied the mostly empty space. A few pieces of fruit, leftover salad, and some Chinese takeout stared back at her. With a sigh, she opened the freezer to pull out a pint of ice cream, which she set on the counter to let melt, and popped a diet, frozen meal for one in the microwave to cook.

This was a downside of being on her own. Abuelita's fridge was always full, even when money had been tight. She had moved out two years ago, when she had turned thirty. It was just the two of them for so long that it had felt right until she got her job and Abuelita encouraged her to find an apartment, which was code for date more. They were still in the same borough, and she went over weekly. The other six days, she was on her own for food.

Ten minutes later, the destroyed contents of the little plastic tray that had claimed to be a fettuccine Alfredo were cast aside while Mel ate chocolate peanut butter ice cream out of the carton and watched *Bridgerton* for the millionth time.

A buzz from her phone made her reach for it while

looking at the clock on her TV and thinking it was too late for Abuelita to be up.

Patrick was calling. Again.

Mel wrestled with the idea of picking up and finally caved.

"Hello?"

"Mel? Hey, it's Patrick," came the smooth voice on the other end.

"Hey. What's up?" Mel asked, hoping it was quick. She could almost feel his smile on the other end, and the idea made her squirm. She didn't know exactly why she didn't like him, but something about him had always rubbed her the wrong way.

"I just wanted to see if you were free this weekend. We could go grab coffee, lunch, or dinner."

"Oh, thanks for the invite, but I promised to spend the weekend with my grandmother," she lied, but made a mental note to make it a reality.

"I'm free next weekend too, you know? I'll make myself available anytime you pick," he said, his voice oozing charm, which probably was supposed to turn her on. She watched as Colin and Penelope walked together.

"Patrick, listen, I really appreciate it, but I'm just so busy with work right now, and I'm not ready for anything like that."

"I'll put a word in Tabby's ear about freeing you up. I know there have been some cuts, but she shouldn't overload you like that—"

"No, Patrick, it's fine. Thank you, but I just—"

"Consider it a personal favor. For a friend," he added. He hadn't been working there much longer than she had, but did seem to have a rapport with Tabby, the Chief Public Defender. She oversaw all cases and managed the personnel.

"Really, I'm—"

"I'll see you tomorrow, Mel."

He ended the call before she could respond.

Well, shit.

In and out of the courtroom, Patrick always seemed to try to name-drop and one-up anyone in the close vicinity, but there was something else. She couldn't put her finger on it, and maybe it was unfair, but she had a gut feeling that he had slept with plenty of the people she worked with, and maybe —scratch that—probably clients, though she had no way to prove it. The guy walked around clearly thinking himself a savior to all women, and she wasn't buying it.

After a string of uninteresting dates, she had met one man fairly recently but ultimately broke it off. She felt bad about having to do the whole *let's be friends* thing, but he really was a great guy, and she wasn't the person for him.

She watched the meet-cute on *Bridgerton*—where they bumped into each other in a crowded room—and she sighed, wondering again what the hell her problem was. Maybe it was her job addiction, and Abuelita had told her many times she was too picky, but shouldn't she be picky?

Watching the love scene pour out on her screen, Mel sat and wondered if and when she would be someone's diamond. So far, no one had ever been able to compete with her work obsession, and if they did—Patrick popped into her mind—they weren't a good fit in other ways.

She worked a little more before bed, reviewing the case she'd pick up tomorrow before setting her alarm for an ambitious five o'clock.

She eyed the melatonin bottle on her nightstand and glanced out her window. Ominous gray skies swirled low. Mel had always hated storms, especially after what had happened to her parents. She decided to pop a pill and hope for the best.

She drifted off until a loud thunderclap had her jumping

up in a hazy fog. The room flashed white like a strobe, illuminating outside so it looked like day for the briefest moments. Another punishing crack came out of nowhere and sounded right on top of her apartment, rattling the building.

She reached over to flip on some music and hugged her other pillow, squeezing her eyes shut.

Mel had no idea how long she was up or when she fell back asleep, but five o'clock the next morning didn't happen.

"Shit!"

After a quick shower, detangling the dark nest of curls that was her hair, and throwing on a dress—black, of course—Mel eyed the clock on the stove, weighing breakfast against the bus schedule, opting for the latter. Soon, she was out the door and cursing the summer traffic while mentally adding up how late she would be if she got a coffee on the way to the bus stop. There was late, and then there was late.

When Mel finally walked into her office, she had no coffee and was ten minutes late, which wasn't that bad considering. She regretted not stopping for coffee to be at least fifteen minutes late, but then with her luck, it would've turned into twenty. Good news was that Tabby wasn't one to be picky as long as the job got done. Recently, she had been more focused on a special investigation that required most of her attention anyway.

"Morning, Mel. You just get in?" Patrick asked her at the door.

He wore a dark suit today with an expensive blue shirt.

"Yeah, traffic was horrible, as usual." Maybe if she kept it brief, he would move on.

No such luck. Patrick sauntered and sat opposite her desk in the little chair for clients.

"You alright these days, Mel? I'm getting worried about

you. You always seem overworked and never come out with us for drinks."

"I don't drink," she said automatically as she made a show of finding the case file that was already on top of the stack on her desk.

"Okaaaaaay," he said. "My offer for dinner still stands. Maybe just dessert," he added in a low tone with a smirk.

Enough was enough.

"Patrick, now's not a good time." The tone was firm, and she gave off plenty of signals she did not want to be messed with. The idea of turning him in for sexual harassment danced in the back of her mind.

Message received.

He held his hands up and said, "Fine, fine. Just trying to be friendly. I can't help that I'm a people person."

Mel eyed him with a cool stare and said nothing.

"I'm in court today, but let me know if you change your mind." With that odious proposition, he was gone, but the scent of his overpowering cologne lingered in her office.

CHAPTER 3

Nathaniel felt like his head had been kicked by a horse. He opened his eyes and rolled over with the pain. Trying to catch his breath, he lay on his side, dragging his hand over his eyes. Memories floated in and out of his consciousness—horses, storm, running for the barn. He considered that maybe he had been kicked.

A groan reached his ears. He croaked out a call, but his throat felt like gravel, and no sound came out. Another wave of pain rolled through his head. Turning onto his side, Nathaniel strained his ears for any more sounds that would give him a clue to where he was. None came except for a distant call of a crow. Nathaniel let his breath escape slowly while he listened. The crow called again, and a slight breeze swayed the trees.

Another distant groan reached his ears, then a cough. He wasn't alone.

Nathaniel pushed against the hard ground beneath him. Pain bloomed again in his skull, but his arms held him up. He worked his eyes until the blur wore away and he could make out the blades of grass beneath him. Sure enough, he was under a small tree. Leaves swayed again with another breeze in the morning sun. A scatter of raindrops sprinkled down onto him from the foliage above.

Nathaniel rolled over onto his back and struggled to stand, remaining still until the feeling of dizziness passed. Many more trees surrounded him in neat rows. He ran his hand over his skull and felt a bump on the back, but nothing other than that. He pulled his hand away. At least there wasn't any blood on the outside. He blinked a few times and looked around.

The buzz of a distant bee matched the setting. Maple trees sheltered him from the morning sun, which glowed without burning heat.

A creak from behind had him turning toward the barn, or what had been the barn.

Nathaniel staggered back, his mouth parted at what he was looking at.

The barn was gone.

Grass, hip high, swayed in the breeze where the middle of the barn had been.

Nathaniel rubbed his head again and turned, looking for the barn everyone had slept in last night, because they hadn't gone that far. He started walking and looking for everyone. It made sense that in the wind, he had been turned around.

"Nathaniel?" a voice called out. He turned and saw Elias walking toward him, looking considerably worse for wear. "Have you seen any of the horses?"

"Not a one. Must've run off into the woods. We'll round 'em up."

"What about the men?"

"Haven't seen them either."

"Indeed." Nathaniel watched as Elias sat down, rubbing his head and rummaging in his haversack for something to eat or drink.

"I'll have a look," Nathaniel said.

"Suit yourself. Hey, walk slow, would ya? I'm content to sit here for a bit after last night."

Nathaniel began walking up a hill, thinking that if they had been downhill from this wood, the men would have seen it and sought it out before the storm.

He didn't see any slaves or farmhands working the land, and considered that perhaps they had fled the coming armies when they got wind of the campaign's movements.

Such a shame that a good field would go to waste. He made a mental note to send a message off to the major about this location, which promised good hunting and unspoiled wood to rest.

He thought he must have run farther last night than he remembered because he still had not seen any sign of the men or any evidence of the camp. All branches were intact, and the grass flowed freely without signs of being trampled. The lines of trees stretched before him, and he turned to go back when he heard a rustling to his left.

Nathaniel froze.

Another rustle caught his ear, and then a low whimper. Nathaniel walked through the rows, ducking under and avoiding branches as he went.

"Benny!"

He was face down in the grass, leaning on his bad side. Nathaniel rushed forward and murmured words of comfort, but he didn't know if they were for Benny or for himself.

Benny's face was frozen in agony. His breaths were shallow and inconsistent. His side was stained with brown, which Nathaniel knew to be old blood. When he peeled back the flimsy linen, though, it wasn't brown that he saw.

"Come on, let's get you out of the sun. I have you," he grunted as he pulled Benny up, trying to be careful of the side. Benny whimpered and groaned again with the movement.

Nathaniel reached for his belt for a canteen, but felt only his sword and pistol before he remembered it had been on his saddle back in the barn. Swearing, he leaned down to look at Benny's face. His eyes were fluttering now, working to open.

"Elias!" Nathaniel yelled.

He leaned Benny back into the crook of his arm. "Elias!" he called again.

"What do you want now— Son of a bitch, Benny!"

"Stop shoving food in your mouth for a damn minute and get over here. Benny needs it."

Together, they hauled Benny under a tree and sat him upright. Elias broke some old bread, which Benny refused. They dribbled the remains of Elias's canteen into his mouth.

"We'll need water."

"I'll go find some," Elias said before heading down the hill.

Benny's breathing was labored but calm, as he let the tree support him and closed his eyes. The sheen of sweat covering his pale face was not a good indication. Nathaniel stripped his coat and covered Benny. The red wool against his face made him look even more ill.

Elias returned with a bucket that Nathaniel had never seen before and an odd look on his face.

With more important things on his mind, Nathaniel said, "Good then, set it here. Took you long enough." Nathaniel began splashing water on Benny's face and trying to wake him so that he could drink more. He noticed Elias was quiet, which was a less-than-rare occasion.

"What sort of bucket is that?" Nathaniel asked.

"I dunno. You've got to come and see this."

"What the hell is it?"

Elias shrugged and added quietly, "I dunno."

"Well then, it can wait." Benny's eyes fluttered, and another groan escaped his lips, but this one was stronger. "Benny! Benny."

"I brought these too," Elias said. He pulled a cucumber out of his bag and started cutting it up into small bites to hand to Nathaniel. Benny was now trying to wake up. His face scarred with pain, his eyes opened and blinked as if trying to see who was with him. Benny began to thrash around with panic, but he was weak, and Nathaniel could hold on well.

"Stop, you fool. Do you want to hurt your side again? It's me. It's Nathaniel and Elias. Stop fightin' us."

Benny calmed down, but a fresh sheen of sweat had broken out over his skin as his body clenched against the pain.

"We need to get him back to camp and find a doctor," Nathaniel said while feeding Benny pieces of the cucumber. "Elias, go look for the others. I'll stay with Benny."

"I found the barn. The well pump was near it, but—"

"Great, go tell the major—"

"That was what I was trying to tell you. There's no one there."

"Elias, now's not the—"

"I'm honest. There's no one there, and it looks like they left a long time ago. There's no trail of them or where they went."

"Elias—"

His voice hardened. "Nathaniel, they're gone."

"Go look again."

"That's not the only thing." The odd look was back on his face.

"What now?"

"I've never seen anything like that barn before."

Nathaniel looked at him and thought this man must

surely be an idiot. He had always known him to be hard-headed, a lover of good drink, and a cheat at cards, but now he realized that all of that was overshadowed by the fact that this man was sitting here rambling about a barn when they had larger issues at hand.

"Elias—" he began.

A low rumble started to their left. The noise was gradual and sounded like a distant carriage, but one that was getting nearer.

"Be ready," Nathaniel said, drawing his pistol.

The noise got louder. Rushing air like a wind through an old barn drowned out the bees. Sticks cracked under the weight of something heavy. It was getting closer now. While he wondered what it could be, Nathaniel saw Elias grip his knife and revolver. Nathaniel threw an arm around Benny and dragged him back as much as he could, only a few feet, before it appeared.

Branches bent to make way for some sort of carriage. Nathaniel looked at the ground again to confirm what his eyes were seeing. It was unlike any carriage he had ever seen before. There was more glass and an open back full of shovels and odd farming equipment. The wheels were large, and they moved without horses. Nathaniel read the green lettering on the side to himself.

NYC Parks. It made no sense.

Benny moaned again, his face now losing color. Nathaniel stood and waved to the man getting out of the carriage, but he froze.

A black man wearing an odd light-blue shirt with a strange patch on the shoulder came out.

"Oh shit, what are you doing here?"

Elias grabbed his pistol and aimed it at the man, who immediately raised both hands.

"Take us to your command. We have a soldier who needs help."

The man's eyes darted to Benny against the tree and back to Elias.

"Are you guys reenactors or something? You need a permit, and firearms are prohibited in all parks."

"I said, take us to your command."

"Uhhhh… Look, man, I'll call for help."

Elias gave a cold smile. "Yes, do that."

The man backed away toward the carriage, picked up a black box, and talked into it before getting inside and backing the carriage away.

Elias, frozen in place, kept his pistol aimed at the carriage as it backed down the way it had come, as if trying to make sense of what he saw.

Nathaniel halted next to Benny, who, thankfully, hadn't noticed whatever that was.

"Elias," he started, carefully, "what did you see?"

"A barn unlike anything I've seen before."

Nathaniel's eyes went to the bucket. It was blue. It wasn't tin, and it wasn't wood. He didn't know what it was made out of.

Gradually, his brain worked to make meaning of what he was seeing, but he found that he couldn't.

The rumble from the woods below was the same now. A white carriage with blue lettering appeared farther away, drawing closer.

"Hello? NYPD. Heard you need some help?"

A Spaniard in a blue uniform with a silver badge approached with his right hand on the butt of what looked to be like a pistol.

"Our man's been shot; he needs a doctor."

The blue soldier leaned over to eye Benny in his red coat, before putting a black box against his mouth.

"Central, I need a bus at Van Cortlandt Park. One male down, conscious but bleeding from a reported gunshot wound. Requesting EMS."

A second man, larger than the first, came out of the carriage, with the sound of another carriage coming toward them.

"How'd he get shot?"

"Are you daft? During the battle."

"There's no reenactment here, and you all need to drop your guns."

"I'll do no such thing," Elias said, drawing his own and pointing it at the soldier in the chest.

Something was very wrong.

"Elias—" Nathaniel said in a low voice, urging caution.

The soldiers opposite both drew their pistols, small and black.

"Drop it! Now!"

Crack. The blue soldier went down. Hit in the arm, he began to scramble back behind the carriage.

Elias aimed again, firing off another round.

But Nathaniel dove instead and reached for Benny, dragging him away from the fight, cutting back through the rows of trees.

Shots rang through the trees, multiplying in the orchard, each crack ricocheting off the trunks. He laid Benny down and waited. There was nothing to do. Those men were fresh and well-rested. Whatever that carriage had been, it was more proof than Nathaniel needed to know that this wasn't a fight they would win.

He looked at Benny and thought of putting the poor kid down lest he fall into the hands of the enemy. Nathaniel gripped his pistol, ready. The gunfire behind him stopped, and there was quiet. The gunfire had silenced the nature around them like it always did.

It was now or never.

He should make it quick. The boy was too young, too weak. Better to die here than suffer in the hands of the enemy. Nathaniel sent up a prayer as he turned Benny onto his side, exposing the back of his neck—

"Freeze. Drop your weapon. Hands up or I shoot."

Too late.

Nathaniel sighed and let the pistol fall from his hand before he threw down his sword. With a last glance at Benny, he turned and lifted his hands in surrender to his captors.

Another soldier stood across from Nathaniel, with his barrel pointed squarely at Nathaniel's chest. This was it, he thought, but no shot came.

"Put your hands where I can see them!" he shouted at Benny, who was too weak to move under Nathaniel's coat.

"My friend is wounded and needs help. Please."

The soldier eyed him before focusing on Nathaniel. "Get on the ground! Now!"

He did as he was told and felt his hands being put into shackles behind him.

"You have the right to remain silent—" he began.

Nathaniel hit the ground, face-first into the dirt.

CHAPTER 4

It had already been a long, hot day when Mel got to the new Bronx Detention Site. She parked and grabbed her oversized bag, overflowing with files.

Law school had always been her steadfast plan since she was a girl, but she hadn't fit in at NYU School of Law. Most of the students' affluent parents were paying. Mel had loans. There was no way her grandmother could cover that on Social Security. Raising Mel after her parents died had been a stretch.

Representing the underprivileged still drove her as a public defender despite the influx of new people daily and budget cuts that weren't making life any easier.

Like everyone else, today's new client needed her best. She wanted to make sure they got it. As a child, she had wanted to be a prosecutor to help serve justice and protect the innocent. When she grew up, she saw the injustices in her community, and many needed help navigating a situation that may not have been their fault at all.

When she and Abuelita served in the food drive ministry, cooking and making peanut butter sandwiches, she saw firsthand how people suffered and struggled to regain their lives.

With one tug, she hefted her bag to reposition its weight. She clawed the wayward curls out of her face and tugged at her black dress, which was already wrinkled with sweat, defeated by the day.

Mel pushed through the heavy doors to check in. Officer José Gutiérrez raised a hand in greeting.

"Sup, Mel? You look cheery today." He'd been a corrections officer for a while and was one of the few people Mel liked here.

"I'm always cheery. How's Mary? Getting excited?"

"Yeah, you know it. One more month to go, so it's getting down to the wire. I told you it's a girl, right?"

"Yep. No boyfriends."

"Damn straight. So what's up?"

"New client. Nathaniel Harrington. I got the file last night."

"Yeah, ICE got done with him. They don't think he's illegal, but—" He gave her a look.

"No papers?"

"Not a one. He might be ex-Amish, that's what I heard, or some crazy reenactor guy. You know the ones who think they're Jesus? Clothes weren't your normal run-of-the-mill."

"Yeah, and that would make sense with the whole antique weapon thing. At least he isn't accused of killing anyone."

Gutiérrez's easygoing attitude cooled. "That other one fucked around and found out."

Mel nodded, then frowned. This had perplexed her since she opened the file. "Amish can't carry guns."

He shrugged. "He's probably one of the crazies."

"Where's the other one? There were three."

"At Jacobi. Injured when they found him. It's not looking good."

"Why? The file didn't say." She leaned against the check-in desk. Gutiérrez leaned back in his chair.

"My cousin's wife works over there. The guy was shot with an old bullet. Plus, get this, he tested positive for small-pox. Damn anti-vaxxers. As a precaution, we put your client in isolation after the medical screening."

Mel shook her head and hoisted up her bag. "Show me the way."

He buzzed her through security, where she dropped her stuff before heading back, then sat in front of the thick window waiting for her client to arrive. The name he had given was Nathaniel Harrington, but a quick search told her no such person existed, so he was lying or undocumented. To pass the time, Mel made a note to email Stella, the social worker, to get the ball rolling on a Social Security card once she got her phone out of the locker. Electronics weren't allowed inside the facility.

The door opened on the other side of the window. Nathaniel Harrington walked through and sat down. His cheekbones jutted out under eyes that flicked over her. Eyebrows rose with mild surprise. She knew that look. Wouldn't be the first time she had a client who was against women, and a Hispanic woman to boot. That made her want to prove him wrong even more.

She laid out her files.

"Mr. Harrington, my name is Melanie Reyes, and I've been appointed by the court to represent you." She flipped open a file. "You've been charged with criminal trespass in the third degree and criminal possession of a weapon in the fourth degree, both of which are misdemeanors."

She glanced up at him. "Now, there's some debate over whether your pistol qualifies as an antique under New York law. If the court determines it can still be fired, you could face a felony weapons charge, including concealed.

Right now, it's listed as a misdemeanor, but that could change."

She leaned forward. "These are serious charges. You could face up to a year in jail or probation, plus fines if convicted. However, if we can argue that you had no criminal intent and that your weapons were strictly historical, there's a chance we can negotiate a better outcome."

Bright blue eyes stared back at her.

"Do you have any questions about these charges?" she asked in her most professional voice.

"What happened to Elias and Benny?" he asked in a British accent.

Mel concealed her surprise. Whatever she had expected, it hadn't been that.

"The two men who were with you?"

He nodded.

Mel took a breath before delivering the news. She hated this part. "Elias was shot and died at the scene. I'm sorry for your loss."

Nathaniel closed his eyes tightly and looked down before nodding once.

"And Benny?"

"He's at the hospital being treated for his injuries and smallpox."

Mel paused. Something in his gaze pushed her on.

"I'm afraid it isn't looking good."

This time, his lips thinned slightly. He looked down, the left side of his face undulating as he chewed on his cheek.

Back to business. Mel clicked her pen and began to write.

"Where was the sword when the police showed up?"

"Tucked into my belt. Next to my pistol. They took that as well."

Mel looked down and saw that he had a flintlock pistol listed on his paperwork that the police had confiscated.

"So they were both visible from the outside when the police arrived? Even on your belt?"

"I assure you, madam, I did not conceal the sword."

So formal. Not what she typically saw as a public defender.

"Okay, good, so you weren't trying to conceal it. That will help in court. Were you coming back from hunting or a camping trip?"

"We weren't hunting."

"Camping then?"

"We had made camp that night."

"Okay, that'll work. Tell me how you ended up in the park."

"I don't know."

"Is this your first run-in with the police?"

He frowned. "I've never seen those men before."

"Okay, good. Did you see any signs that marked a restricted park area?"

"No."

"Alright." Mel made a note to drive out and see if there were any posted signs around the park, and moved on to explain the procedure. While she studied him, she went through the rote words she always said when meeting a client. His eyes looked like someone far older than his listed age, which wasn't unusual in her work. Calluses covered his hands, which appeared rugged and tanned by the sun, while the kind of dirt that didn't come out with a quick wash had set up shop in the lines of his knuckles.

"You don't have ID or paperwork of any kind." Mel hadn't phrased it as a question, but still sat waiting for an answer to tell her more.

He shook his head.

She waited.

"Okay, I've already gotten a jump on starting the paperwork to get you some documentation and ID. Without documentation of legal presence, ICE can hold a person charged with a crime, so I won't be able to get you bail."

Nathaniel nodded again.

"I think we can get the weapons charges dropped, and I will work on the trespassing charges. Alright,"—Mel shut her folder—"do you have any questions?"

He muttered something while looking down.

"I'm sorry. I didn't hear you."

Those eyes met hers, and he said it again.

CHAPTER 5

Mel's third cup of coffee sat on the desk, cold and untouched.

It didn't make sense.

According to the police report and notes from the doctor, Nathaniel Harrington and the two men had no dental work, no vaccines, and were treated for intestinal parasites. When she had called the hospital to get information on Benny, who was going to be charged as well, if he came out of that place alive, Mel had learned that in addition to smallpox, evaluation suggested minimal medical treatment at an early age, as well as extreme vitamin deficiencies. All of the evidence suggested some ex-commune situation or ex-Amish.

"I submit myself to the court's mercy."

That was a phrase she hadn't expected to hear when she walked into work today, or any day for that matter.

Something was off here. Way off.

The text flashed on the screen. She shoved her hair out of her face and leaned over her keyboard, searching. Mel punched in his name and waited, drumming her fingers on the desk.

There were a few Nathaniel Harringtons on Facebook, but none matched the face she had just met.

She Googled him again, this time adding British. Nothing came up except some Revolutionary War soldier. Odd.

Mel leaned back.

"Hey, Reyes, late night tonight?"

Jeff wheeled a large trash can into the room and emptied her small one.

Mel pulled her eyes away from the screen in front of her, and glanced at the time.

"Hey Jeff," she said. "Yeah, I guess so. Didn't realize what time it was." A dull ache was starting to throb behind her eyes.

"I hear ya. I've got about three more hours tonight. Man, I tell you what, I'm tired. Tryin' to get me another lotto ticket after work. If you don't see me, you'll know I won." He winked.

"Figured that was still the policy. I'll pass along your goodbyes."

Jeff laughed as he pushed the trash can out of the room. "Imma be back to vacuum later."

"Thanks, Jeff," she called back, computer screen beckoning her tired eyes again.

Mel didn't know why she was bothering. If ICE hadn't found anything, her chances would be close to zero. People came and went in the world, and even with so much technology, some still managed to sneak through the cracks.

She hadn't seen any undocumented people from England, but she was sure it had happened before. Mel eyed her keys, tossed on a desk calendar cloaked in almost illegible appointments. She debated whether this was worth a trip to the Amish communities. Didn't they have an accent? Maybe it was the same.

Mel tapped her pen to a tune from her old drumline days

in high school. A decision was made, and she tossed the pen down and leaned into her keyboard.

The Amish may not have records, but in today's world of social media, something could end up online when they stepped out in their teen years. Her fingers tapped in a quick search, now adding the Bronx as the geography, revealing more hits than she expected.

Mel's eyebrows raised and lowered as she leaned in to skim. She sat back, checked the clock, and rubbed her eyes before giving it another go.

The top hit was from the New York Historical Society, which had a line about the Battle of Harlem Heights and Captain Nathaniel Harrington.

Mel's heart dropped into her stomach, and her chest felt too tight. Smallpox, a weird pistol, and a sword?

Nope. She was not entertaining this. He was probably a reenactor who took it too far. Maybe the historical society would know him? He had been wearing a red coat. That was easier than calling the Amish, and they would probably know someone who liked history in the area.

She grabbed the phone she rarely used off its cradle, and punched in the number. She hadn't expected to reach anyone, so she left a message and shoved her files in her bag to head home.

The next afternoon, after a sleepless night and one hell of a day, pills rattled out of the little white bottle and tumbled into Mel's palm. Taking a large gulp of her massive, iced coffee, she swallowed them down and stepped off the bus, hiking up her big bag and heading inside to meet with the curator.

Sleeping had been a joke, and her focus was way off its game. All day, the possibilities had been tugging her exhausted mind and clouding her thoughts. It was like a puzzle she couldn't solve, and it was pissing her off. Typically, she had an excellent sense about people and where they fit in this world. She couldn't get a read on him.

The New York Historical Society wasn't far. Thank God the archivist returned her call and agreed to meet with her today so she could get this over with. Pain throbbed in her temples, and she took another pull on the straw of her iced coffee, praying for relief.

Mel walked into the cramped lobby, thankful her shoes weren't making any noise on the slate floor. She didn't think her head could've taken it.

"Hi, how can I help you?" asked a cheery college student at the welcome desk, surrounded by pamphlets.

"I'm Melanie Reyes, and I called about the reenactor posing as Nathaniel Harrington."

"Oh, right. I'm sorry, but we haven't had any reenactments here since before the pandemic."

Damn, this was a crazy dead end. Mel pushed down her frustration for coming out here when they could've told her that on the phone. "Oh, okay, well then, thank you anyway." She turned to leave when the college student stopped her.

"Our archivist is eager to meet with you and is all set up in her office. I'll call to let her know you're here."

Mel checked her phone. Dead ends were not what she needed with her schedule today. "You don't have to do that."

"It won't take long. They've already pulled everything on the person you were asking about."

Mel thought about it. Well, she was already here... Curiosity got the best of her.

"Well, okay," she said before roaming around the lobby and finishing her coffee. The interior of the building was spacious and light with tall arched ceilings that felt more like a cathedral than a museum. Mel had expected some dark, dingy stacks without any sound, except for the gentle turning of pages. It felt fresh and old in a way she hadn't expected.

What the hell was she thinking? She had a million things to do and would have just gone home to nurse the pounding in her head. Nathaniel Harrington was an interesting client, but he was just that. A client. And one of many. Ordinary. Average. Completely normal.

Still, she had always been nosy, and at least if she knew who he was pretending to be, maybe it would help.

"Ms. Reyes?"

A woman in her midfifties walked up. She wore a black top, large earrings, and slacks, with a fiery scarf tossed around her neck. "Sorry to keep you waiting. I'm Lorraine Williams."

"Thanks for seeing me so quickly." Mel shook her outstretched hand, which had a large, wooden bracelet dangling on its wrist.

"Glad to help. I've pulled everything on Nathaniel Harrington as you requested. Please," she said, indicating the elevator. Hitting the button for the second floor, she asked, "Is he your ancestor?"

"Oh no. No, he's not my ancestor. It's related to a case of mine. I was hoping you could tell me more about him."

"Of course." Mel followed her into a two-story library lined with columns. They walked to a small room in the back where a black case sat on a table. "Please have a seat."

Mel sat and watched as she pulled on blue plastic gloves, opened the box, and laid out a portrait the same size as a small postcard.

She had to blink twice. A chill washed over her arms.

It was him, or someone who looked very much like him.

Mel stared at the picture. Harrington sat, staring back at her with a haunting gaze. He was dressed in a vest under a coat that was open at the chest. He looked healthier and slightly younger, but for all intents and purposes, the portrait, or whatever it was called, could've been painted six months ago. "What information do you have on him?"

"I'm so glad you asked. Researching the Battle of Harlem Heights is a personal interest of mine. No one has ever requested this specific portrait before. It was donated about eighty years ago by a British woman cleaning out her family's estate before they renovated. Captain Harrington was her ancestor and the second son of the Duke of Harrington. According to the notes that the archivist at the time made, this woman was Mrs. Leticia Humphrey, and she reported that the family remembered him as a barrister who purchased a commission into the British Army in 1776. This portrait was painted just after he joined and before he came here to fight, where he went missing at the Battle of Harlem Heights."

Mel blinked a few times while digesting this information. "Has this picture been on display before? Anyone seen it?"

"Not according to the records I have."

"You're sure?"

"Yes, ma'am. Why do you ask?"

"My client is pretending to be from the Revolutionary War, and was caught trespassing in Van Cortlandt Park. There is no paperwork, but the name he gave was Nathaniel Harrington."

Lorraine's eyebrows went up a little. "This has never been on display, but perhaps they did their own research. Some people take reenacting very seriously and can develop whole personas. We've received mail from people who refer to themselves as their ancestors, including their rank. It's rare, but not unheard of."

Mel pulled her mouth tight and let out a breath slowly. He hadn't seemed crazy, but everything was pointing to that.

"Can you tell me what Captain Harrington was doing when he went missing?"

"I could look, but I'm not sure I'll find anything. There isn't a list of everyone who went missing and was never recovered—"

"Really? They didn't have records?"

"Not accurate ones, no, and so much of the fighting was —" she paused. "Well, sometimes remains were often difficult to identify."

Mel nodded, appreciating Lorraine's honesty. It was almost like speaking to a detective or fellow lawyer, just one who worked in the past, piecing stories together with clues and logic. "What else do you know about him?"

"Let me look him up." Lorraine opened a laptop sitting nearby and began to type. The light sound of the keys reached her ears as Mel stared at the picture.

The similarity was uncanny.

It definitely could not be him.

A small voice in the back of her mind wanted to wonder, what if...

All of the facts of the case started to swirl in her head, racing around and bouncing off her skull. The sword, the clothing, no vaccines, smallpox, a pistol, malnourishment—

"Alright, so we have that he was a captain in the light infantry. There's more on his brother and father, which makes sense since the title went with them. That's all there is, I'm afraid. After the war, his family continued to search for him, but never found any information."

Mel nodded and asked a few more questions about him, which came up empty before she stood and thanked Lorriane for her time.

Lorraine smiled and thanked her for coming in, offering to email her copies of anything else she could find.

Mel waved to the college student on her way out and

found her mind continuing to work the puzzle that was Nathaniel Harrington.

Everything in her wanted to deny it and write him off as crazy. Considering that her client could be the same man who had vanished during the Revolutionary War? It wasn't possible.

There had to be a mistake. This was either an elaborate scheme or a freaky coincidence. Mel had never encountered a client who had concocted this much of a cover, but such instances were known, and there was a first for everything.

Lorraine's words came back to haunt her. No one had seen this picture before it came out of storage today, when she had requested this appointment. No one had seen a portrait of Captain Nathaniel Harrington.

No one had been interested—

Mel shook her head and tried to get her thoughts in order.

Her client was not from the eighteenth century, and the next time she talked with him, she'd get to the bottom of this puzzle.

CHAPTER 6

Nathaniel knew something was wrong, but didn't understand anything about the world around him.

Shuffling in line in a sort of barracks painted blue, he took in his surroundings again. He had an idea of what might have happened to the three of them, but of course, that idea was impossible.

The other prisoner, who had already been in the cell when Nathaniel arrived, hadn't expressed any interest in him. He had simply lain on his bed facing the wall, looking up only once. When Nathaniel nodded and muttered a "Hello" to his cellmate, the man hadn't responded, other than letting his head fall back on the pillow. His tanned skin was roped with rough black tattoos in words Nathaniel could read, but didn't understand. Nathaniel welcomed the silence, though, as he had much to think about.

Hungry for information, Nathaniel kept a low profile and always watched everything around him. Every night when the lights went out, Nathaniel lay awake and thought of his family and whether or not this was a dream.

As days went on, though, the impossible began to emerge

as the only option. Nathaniel continued to wake up in the same cell, so to preserve his mind, he focused on small details around him and found them all fascinating.

It was clear that he was in jail, but everything was brighter. The lights were far superior to the candles he was familiar with. It was daylight, as long as the warden wished.

The first time he was pushed into the large common area, the sights and smells that assaulted his senses had almost been too much. Men of all different colors were in one room, shouting, moving, and sitting down with trays filled with food.

Overhead, there were frames with pictures that glowed and moved. One held a woman talking about the rain for the days ahead. Nathaniel couldn't look away as he tried to comprehend what he was looking at.

A man shoved him from behind. "Move it, asshole."

So he walked and sat down, where a tray had been shoved toward him. Men were eating around him with abandon, complaining about the food and how it wasn't enough. The options in front of him had transfixed Nathaniel. He tasted fruit that he had not seen before and found it delicious. The meal was warm, the coffee was strong, and milk and cream readily available.

When he had looked on, awestruck at the abundance, he heard a voice to his right. "They give us real cream because the fake shit is flammable. I would know." A man with a dark goatee and a tattoo at his temple grinned. "Ain't totally a fuckin' hellhole."

The next few days had been the same routine of eating, sleeping, and sitting in his cell. The chamber pot that emptied with water was foreign to him, although from what he could see, it operated pretty much for the same purpose.

It wasn't until the second evening that he realized the temperature inside the jail did not match the outside. In the hallway, he had been hit by a cool breeze. Searching for the source, he found a grate in the wall that appeared to go to the outside, but the wind was pleasantly chilled despite the blistering July heat.

Nathaniel knew the weather, following what he learned to be weather predictions. One night, he found them to be correct when a large thunderstorm could be heard raging beyond the walls, and when he checked the clocks, it was right when the woman in the frame had said it would be. Like before, he closed his eyes tightly, then opened them and tried to study the bricks on the dark wall to distract himself. When that didn't work, he imagined himself reciting Latin from his lawbooks back at school.

All of this was a marvel, and every day brought a new experience.

Throughout all of it, though, Nathaniel remained silent. Absorbing. Waiting. Thinking.

What had happened to him was surely impossible. It was something he had never even considered possible. Every morning, he questioned his sanity and whether this was some purgatory meant for him and his sins in war, but no matter how he tried to test himself, he found himself to be as he always had. But then he considered that the insane would think that way, wouldn't they?

Much to his surprise, he was allowed time out of his cell, and to his further surprise, found that there was a library filled with books on legal codes, presumably for the inmates. He found the man with the goatee reading a book on appeals at one of the circular tables in the middle. Nathaniel roamed around the room with various titles on display. A few inmates came in and went to the desk where a woman sat wearing a multicolored scarf with a smile. Signs advertising a book club hung on the ends of bookcases about waist high, along with large pictures that advertised various book covers.

Goatee turned and with a nasty snarl hissed, "Fuck off. I was here first."

Nathaniel backed away but didn't leave. Instead, he went to one of the nearby shelves and paced. None of the titles were familiar, but the content was, for the most part. When he turned to leave, Goatee was watching him with an odd glint in his eye and a smile that made Nathaniel back away without question.

He had seen smiles like that from men who had joined the army and liked the killing a little bit too much. Nathaniel left the library empty-handed and felt those odd eyes on him the whole way.

The education continued when Nathaniel saw others head for a bath, which was not a bath at all. It was rain.

A tiled room contained a bank of what looked to be well pumps protruding from the walls. Men would enter with someone they were talking to or alone before they stripped and turned on the pump, which rained water continuously over them. Once he had seen it, Nathaniel grabbed the provided towel and headed for the room. He had chosen his time carefully after a few days of watching for when it was least busy. It wasn't that he was ashamed—the army had taken care of that—but he avoided everyone until he learned what happened to him.

The spray surprised him initially, but the true luxury became apparent when the water warmed. It wasn't that he had gotten used to it like he usually did, but it truly warmed. Nathaniel couldn't remember the last time he had washed himself in warm water, and thought it must have been when he was a child. For a moment, he just stood there with his eyes closed and let the warm water wash over him.

A hand yanked him back and spun him around, slamming

him into the tiled walls. "Guess who," Goatee said with the same evil smile from the library.

Nathaniel didn't answer, but grabbed the man's arms and flipped them off his chest before shoving him back and pushing off the wall himself.

He went to leave, but Goatee blocked the exit and pushed his face close.

"You got a problem, bitch? Huh?"

Nathaniel didn't say anything, but made a move to go around him.

The man grabbed him by the shoulder. "Nah, man, I asked you a damn question. You gonna answer or not?"

"I am not looking to quarrel with you," Nathaniel said. He was still naked, and Goatee had some clothes on, but not much. Still, it was an advantage in a fight Nathaniel didn't want.

"Fuck me, you ain't, Fancy Boy. Circlin' around me and shit in the library. Can't you see I'm in there trying to read? I can't read with you up in my shit."

Nathaniel swiped the water from the warm spray out of his eyes and tried to change tactics. "If you're reading on your case—"

"Oh, and now you're putting your damn nose in my business?"

"Maybe I could help," Nathaniel offered, thinking it best to get on his good side. Perhaps if he had something to offer...

"You think you're smarter than me? And you wanna act like we're cool? Get the fuck outta here before I beat your ass."

Well, that hadn't gone as he had hoped. Intelligent behavior wasn't welcome.

Nathaniel shrugged and went around him, trying to figure out when he could return to the warm water.

"That's right. Run, motherfucker. Little bitch-ass pussy."

Enough was enough. He didn't know where he was or how he got here, but he had tolerated enough. All of the emotion came out at once.

Nathaniel swung around and grabbed Goatee by the throat. He slammed him back into the wall where the water still ran, before dropping him on the floor. The tattooed inmate clawed at his throat as he went into a coughing fit. Anger at everything pumped through his veins. Nathaniel's nails bit into his palms. He wanted to beat this man into the ground with his bare hands and see blood circle the drain at their feet.

He should have been shocked, but that innocence had left long ago, and the stress of the situation had reached a boiling point. He backed away to leave, not wanting to turn his back on the man, but to his surprise, between the coughs, came bouts of laughter.

"You got me, man," Goatee choked out, sitting in the spray. "You alright."

Nathaniel glanced behind him with a careful eye before watching. Maybe he was in an asylum and had lost his mind, for this man surely had. Nathaniel left and only visited the showers when a guard was nearby from that time on.

The next day at breakfast, the glowing frame he had heard others call a TV was telling him what should have been in a newspaper. Nathaniel sat mesmerized.

"Thank you, Stacey. It'll be a scorcher today."

"That's right. Remember, today's one of those days when pets should be inside."

"Will do, thanks. Alright, today is July 15th, 2026. Let's take a look at your top headlines."

The date came onto the screen. Bold, white letters told him what he had been fearing.

Nathaniel read it repeatedly until it disappeared, and the

screen flashed back to the woman talking about a new attack in a distant place on the map.

The truth hit him like a punch in the gut. He surely must have lost his mind. Traveling to another time was impossible. Frantic, he looked around the common area only to see all the other prisoners as they were. Ugly, hot panic bubbled in his stomach.

He had to do something, but unsure what, he turned to the man nearest to him.

"What is the date?"

"Dude, you just saw the date in the damn news. Why are you asking me?"

"So that year was correct?" Nathaniel hissed.

"Man, how long have you been in here? Yeah, it was. Jesus." The large man shook his head and returned to eating.

The white thin fork in his hand clattered against the tray. When he looked down, he realized his hand was shaking. His mind reeled with questions, spinning out of control.

A deep sorrow hit him when his mother came to mind.

His family. Would he never see them again? What would happen to his men? Was there any way to tell them what had happened? His breath quickened along with his heart, and he tasted bile in his throat that he swallowed back down. Nathaniel looked left and right, but for what he did not know.

Prisoners continued to mill about, unaffected by the desperation he now felt. None of them knew him. None of them cared to.

He was truly alone.

CHAPTER 7

Mel swore as a bus cut her off while spewing black exhaust everywhere.

"Asshole," she muttered under her breath. Her knuckles tightened on her phone and bag as she stalked her way across 187th. A couple of kids were playing with a fire hydrant. Older residents watched from the side in doorways and stoops, escaping the heat with T-shirts draped over the back of their necks.

As often as Mel had shown Abuelita different properties and apartments in the suburbs, she remained steadfastly unmoved. Mel couldn't blame her, though. Abuelita had lived in this part of town for over fifty years and was not planning on moving anytime soon.

"*Porque?*" she would say. "St. Elizabeth's is three blocks over, and the bodega has expanded. I can get everything I need right here. No one bothers me, and I know where everything is. No, I don't need all that trouble moving when I have everything right here."

They weren't that different. While neither of them

discussed it, staying where her parents had lived before they'd been killed was an unspoken truth that they both silently kept like a vigil. Neither wanted to move on. It's like the pain of the memories kept them company; without it, they'd be lonely. There were two sets of growth marks scraped on the doorjamb. One was her father's and one was hers.

Everyone seemed to gather back here for birthdays, First Communion, dances, confirmation, and after funerals. There were so many memories, it was hard to imagine home anywhere else.

Still, they had both agreed Mel should have her own place, but it wasn't really home. It was independence. Home was where Abuelita was.

Even when her work schedule got busy, Mel visited weekly.

Fifteen minutes that should've been five later, she jogged up the stoop of Abuelita's building. This group of buildings had yet to be reached by the gentrification bubble and held a variety of young immigrant families and a melting pot of old-timers that had been there for decades and didn't plan on moving.

Mel bounded up the stairs and dug out the key to let herself in. Inside the foyer was a cramped landing with one room to the left and a hallway leading back to the main living areas and other bedrooms beyond. Mel kicked off her heels and dropped the impossible bag on the table in the entryway next to an old picture of her parents before following the smell of something divine into the kitchen.

"You're late."

Abuelita was a short, sturdy woman with hair that had been gray for as long as Mel could remember. With her usual neat-as-a-pin bun, Abuelita was facing the stove, stirring the source of the tempting aroma, wearing the housecoat she always wore whenever she cooked or cleaned, which was almost all of the time.

Mel leaned around Abuelita's shoulder to kiss her cheek and scope out the food.

No fool to her tricks, Abuelita said, "It's been ready, but I've had to add more water, so it needs to cook down again." Ouch. She wasn't just late; she was *late*.

"I'm sure it's delicious," Mel said, opening the cabinet over the coffee pot to pull out a bottle of aspirin. She shook out two pills and got a glass from another cabinet before heading to the sink.

Abuelita didn't say anything as she watched Mel swallow down the pills and head to the small dining room to lay out the plates. The blue placemats were already laid out, telling Mel how long Abuelita had been waiting.

Ever the traditionalist, Abuelita was the type who moved the centerpiece on the table for mealtime to make way for the place settings. Before the leftovers had even cooled on the stove, once everyone was finished, the plates were cleared, dishes were cleaned, and the centerpiece restored to its rightful place.

This month's centerpiece was a bowl of fruit from the Carter era, but it was meticulously clean. In September, it would change to leaves, then pumpkins, which her abuelita left out for October and November because she liked them. All of this led up to the Nativity, which was out from Thanksgiving until Easter.

It was easy here. Everything stayed the same, but not in a bad way. There were dozens of pictures of Mel in various stages of her life arranged on the wall of the hallway leading to the back bedrooms. Seeing as Mel hadn't had any boyfriends, they focused on education and the sacraments, of course. It was surreal to see herself holding a degree, grinning, right next to the picture of her grinning at the altar of St. Elizabeth's for her First Communion.

Abuelita walked in and set down a salad and a basket with a blue dish towel that contained warm bread.

Mel followed her back into the kitchen to get the glasses, which she filled with ice and brought back to the table with a pitcher of iced tea.

"Alright, now we're ready," Abuelita said before beating the spoon on the rim of the caldero pot she had gotten as a young bride.

Plates came down from the cabinet and were filled with pernil and habichuelas guisadas. The pair retreated to the dining room and took the seats they'd had as long as Mel could remember.

"Bendícenos, Señor, y bendice estos alimentos…"

While Abuelita recited the prayer with devotion, thoughts of her day crept into Mel's mind. Something about the picture to her seemed authentic, but that must be what he wanted her and everyone else to think—

"—Amén. I made the good bread today," she said, taking out a roll and offering it to her. Abuelita only did that when she could tell Mel's day had been a rough one.

She took it and inhaled the scent of warm, homemade bread. No one could bake bread like Abuelita, especially when she did it in the old way rather than the healthy way. Every restaurant Mel had been to paled in comparison with their alleged "homemade" and "fresh" bread.

"You come with headaches too often." Like everything with Abuelita, this was a factual statement that cut right to the heart of an issue.

"Work's been crazy."

Abuelita served herself some salad and said, "That's what you said last time."

"I know."

"And it's your fault. You can't live on coffee, aspirin, and frozen food." The latter was spoken with a grimace.

"I can't eat like this all the time either," she countered. She forked a mouthful of the pork into her mouth and wanted to cry at its perfection.

Abuelita made a noise of dissent that didn't equate to a word, but communicated her thoughts flawlessly. "You were raised on this food and turned out beautiful."

"You have to say that."

"Lying is a sin."

"You go to confession."

"You *are* beautiful. In fact,"—Abuelita served some salad onto Mel's plate—"I ran into Marguerite and her son—"

"Her son's a creep."

"He has a good job."

"I see we agree then." Mel was quick enough to catch the hint of a smirk on her abuelita's face before she continued. "No, I know. It's just I landed a lot of clients and we're short-staffed."

Abuelita made a tsking sound in her throat. "They don't appreciate you. You work so hard. So smart. You could work in a big law firm downtown with a nice new office." Abuelita looked over and eyed her plate. "You've barely eaten. Have more."

Mel knew better than to complain when more rice and pork appeared on her plate, so she picked up her fork and took another bite because she knew eating would make Abuelita happy.

"I don't want a big fancy office. I want to help people who need it most, not the guy with the biggest wallet."

"You are a good girl—"

"I hear a 'but' coming."

"—but you are a tired woman. All you do is work."

"I don't have time for anything else."

"You'd be surprised how that works. You'll make time for something else one day before you know it happened."

Mel tried not to think of her trip down to the historical society, but a sigh escaped her.

"Yeah, I spend a lot of time working. I don't want to take time off, and besides, what would I do with it?"

Abuelita pointedly buttered a piece of roll. "You could come to mass with me, or join a ministry. The food bank needs help."

Mel pushed around the last bits of rice with her fork. "Yeah, maybe."

They cleaned up and sat down in the small living room's recliners, each with a piece of Abuelita's specialty—chocolate coffee icebox cake.

Mel settled into the light-blue recliner to watch a rerun of *María la del Barrio*, and felt the tug of sleep pull her down. She didn't stay here often, but knew that if she did tonight, her bedroom would have the same crisp white sheets with eyelet that she had always loved.

Her mind wandered back to Nathaniel Harrington, his blue eyes staring back at her from the painting. Mel went through the thought process she had in the bathroom earlier that afternoon. There were two possible solutions—time travel, which was impossible, and a long plot to impersonate. So, really, there was only one solution.

With her mind settled again and the TV droning in the background, she tried to give way to the sleepy feeling of being full and truly at home, but those eyes continued to pull her back and beckon to her.

"If you would stop thinking, you would fall asleep," Abuelita said, all-knowing.

"I can't."

As a rule, they had never spoken specifics about her job, for the privacy of her clients, but also because she didn't want Abuelita to know exactly what her day-to-day looked like. It was easier that way even though they both understood that Abuelita knew way more than she admitted.

CHAPTER 8

"Looks like you're a woman on a mission," José said. He checked his watch. "Early too."

"Just getting a jump on things," Mel answered as she signed in. Her head hadn't stopped hurting, she had barely slept, and she was ready to get this off her damn plate.

"When my wife says that, it usually means I need to stay outta the way."

"Good thinking," she said and hauled her bag over her shoulder.

"By the way, that new client of yours?"

A chill went through her. "Yeah?"

"He's an odd one. Doesn't seem to fit in, but maybe you can get some answers out of him," José called after her as she walked away.

Damn straight she was going to get some answers. Mel had stayed up late, but not by choice. Every time she closed her eyes, she anticipated what Nathaniel Harrington would say when she showed him the copy of the picture from the historical society. Would he try to lie? Fake like he had never seen it? What would be his tell, and more importantly, what in the hell would she do with this information when he did come clean?

Mel couldn't wait to figure out what was happening and put it behind her. Her other work was piling up and she needed to get some serious shit done, but something kept tugging her back, to this case and the mystery that was her client.

The fluorescent buzz overhead and the green linoleum reminded her of an old gym locker room, but with more chemicals on the floor to fight the odor.

Mel crossed her legs and crossed them again the other way, impatient. She was antsy, exhausted, and on edge. Come on, she thought, looking at the file in her bag with her evidence. Mel rehearsed the lines in her head for if he didn't cop to pretending to be a dead guy. Today's goal was to get his real information and move past this sham. Honestly, if he wanted insanity, this was not the way to go about it.

The door across from her opened, and he walked through before taking a seat.

Mel didn't speak but instead studied him. She wanted the silence to be uncomfortable for him, to put him off his game and make his tell easier to pick out.

He sat across from her, watching her. That was just fine with her. Let him see, she thought, let him see that I know his secret. *You're impersonating a dead man.*

Mel crossed her arms and leaned back. Confidence personified.

He was thin, but not in a way that suggested chemical dependence. His hands were in his lap, so she couldn't see them, which was unusual from her other clients. He wasn't relaxed, so much as resigned. Interesting.

"Mr. Harrington," she began. He looked up, and once again, she was struck by the ice-blue eyes that met her own.

A shiver went over her as she thought of the copy in her bag. Facts, she told herself. He wasn't the redcoat in the painting.

"Do you understand that I am your legal representation?"

His mouth tilted up just a little, as if it was funny. "That much I understand, yes."

"Do you understand that it is my responsibility to ensure you have a fair trial?"

"Yes."

"As your counsel, I need to have all the facts in order to give you the fairest case possible."

He nodded once.

"All of them."

There was a muscle spasm in his right jaw, but he nodded again.

Bingo. She flopped open her folder and put a printout of the painting on the table.

"I know you said you weren't a reenactor, but finding you in a redcoat's uniform with a pistol looks like the opposite. 1776 ring a bell? You look a little young to be impersonating this man. If you are trying to plead insanity, I need to know."

It was as if he had turned to stone. In the fluorescent lights, a green pallor tinged his features. Mel watched, waiting for a response.

Nathaniel didn't move.

"In order for me to help you, I must be in possession of all of the facts. Especially those pertaining to your identity."

"You don't need to know who I am to put a guilty man in jail."

"True, but I don't think you're guilty."

"I've already confessed."

"Fine, so let's say we go into court and say just that. You serve jail time, maybe six months to a year, if I totally slack off, and then what, Nathaniel?" She paused and watched him look away. She had met many clients who thought jail was the best shot at a roof over their head, a bed, and steady meals. He didn't strike her as one of them.

"If you tell me who you really are and what has happened to you, I can help get you into some program. Take you off the streets. Get you a job and a roof over your head, so that this kind of thing won't happen again." She leaned in more. "I know you're British. There can be a process to get you paperwork if you need it."

He didn't raise his head.

"Tell me."

"And what good will that do?" he said. "You'll never believe me."

"Try me."

He took a deep breath. It almost shuddered as if it was painful for him to say his next words out loud. "My name is Captain Nathaniel Harrington. I was in the light infantry and fighting in New York. There was a storm one night, and I woke up in the wooded area where they found us."

Mel had to give him points. She was almost convinced. A small voice reminded her of the photo. Told her to consider—

"Okay. Now I want the other truth."

Nathaniel looked up at her. "Pardon?"

"You told me what I expected, now I want the other truth. You know, the real one."

He stared.

"You know you're good at this, but I want the one where you're impersonating a dead guy to escape the past behind you." Mel pointed at the picture again. "It's just us. Tell the truth."

His eyes flicked over the photo, widening. "Where did you get this?"

"I asked you first."

"This is me."

Mel sighed.

"Where did you get this?" Nathaniel leaned forward, his hands against the glass, like a starving man tempted by food.

"The truth, Mr. Harrington." She wanted him to crack.

"This is me! Look at it. Do you not see it? I commissioned this portrait after I joined and sent it home to my mother. Have you heard from my family? How are they? I need to—" He let his sentence hang in the air as if he ran out of steam.

"This Nathaniel Harrington is dead, and going by the fact that we're now in the twenty-first century, he's been gone a long time."

"Damnit, woman, it is me!" He banged his fist on the glass.

A guard down the hall looked at Mel. She shifted and gave the thumbs-up.

"Mr. Harrington…" she began, her voice calm now.

"Ask me anything. I'll prove it. This is me. Please. Tell me what happened to my family."

Mel made a note to email the social worker about a consult and evaluation. This wasn't going anywhere.

Nathaniel must have seen her because when she looked up, he was reading her notes. Mel moved her hand to cover them.

"You don't believe me?"

"I need the truth to help you, Mr. Harrington. I've already told you that."

Nathaniel said nothing. He looked back at her in disbelief. His shoulders dropped, the fight gone out of them.

He stared hard at the floor, and then in a low voice said, "I was in the light infantry, under Lieutenant Colonel Thomas Musgrave of the 42nd Regiment of Foot."

The hair on Mel's arm raised. "Mr. Harrington—"

"I joined after my father died. He left me five thousand pounds, and the rest to my brother, who became the Duke of

Harrington. With nowhere to go, I trained as a barrister at Middle Temple for income, and I thought the commission would help advance my social standing."

"And how do I know you didn't look all of this up?" she asked, her voice low, but steady.

He didn't answer, but instead continued on.

"That's not the original portrait. Mine was on a canvas"—he held his hands about two feet apart—"about this big. The artist was George Romney in December 1775 at his home in Cavendish Square. On the back of the linen, I wrote 'For mother and all.'"

Mel hadn't checked the back of the picture because she wasn't sure if she could've picked it up, but intended to call Lorraine to verify.

Nathaniel continued. "Before the storm, we were in a field with a new barn. I was trying to help Benny with the horses when the wind picked up. Something must've knocked me out because I'm in the storm and then I'm waking up. The barn is nowhere to be found, and everyone was gone except for that bastard, Elias, and Benny."

Mel was afraid to breathe or move. This was insane.

"That is my truth." His eyes dared her to doubt.

"It can't be," she whispered.

He looked at her now, his blue eyes flat and serious.

Mel felt the earth shift and caught herself to realize she was sliding in the chair. That she was even considering his story was anything more than that made bile rise up her throat. She looked down at her notes and tried to clear her head. The conclusion in front of her was impossible.

"Please tell me about the picture," Nathaniel said in a low voice. The desperation was more than clear.

Defeated, she thought. He sounded defeated and—she studied him through the glass— lost.

Mel sighed. "I went online and did some research. I saw the original."

"Where?"

"The historical society downtown." Mel debated about what to say next and decided to go for it. "The archivist told me that no one had seen this in eighty years other than a few staff members."

Nathaniel's eyes fixated on her. Rapt with attention and hanging on every word.

Mel pressed on. "It was donated by a..."—she flipped back a few pages in her notes—"a woman, Mrs. Leticia Humphrey, who said this was her mother's great great-uncle."

"Do you know her mother's name?"

"No."

"I had two sisters apart from my brother."

Mel blew out a breath. "I can't believe this."

Nathaniel smirked without humor. "I believe I share that opinion."

CHAPTER 9

Mel was in court for the next few days and had almost caught up enough on her work to forget the exchange with Nathaniel Harrington—until now.

The evaluation from the social worker was opened on her computer screen. Elements of trauma from violence and loss of family, and showing signs of possible PTSD, but otherwise no further signs of mental illness. The paperwork to get some form of identification had been filed.

Short and sweet, just like Stella's notes always were. She was a year or two younger than Mel, so pretty new to the job, but that worked to her advantage. The evaluations Mel had called Stella for in the past were spot-on and held up in court. Mel had found, too, that they were almost always in line with her own opinion.

She hadn't told Stella what she had found at the historical society. Mel hadn't told anyone that little tidbit. She tugged on her dark hair as she considered the implications of Stella's report and the follow-up email from Lorraine.

Mel opened the email again.

"Ms. Reyes, I've attached a scanned copy of the portrait, including the back."

Mel opened the first attachment without bothering to read the rest of the email.

It was his face, alright. The eyes and cheeks gave it away.

She leaned forward again now and opened the following image. It was a stretched canvas, yellowed with age, with some writing in the corner. Mel had to hit zoom a few times to make out the text. She skimmed everything once, then twice, and then slowly read it a third time.

All of it matched exactly as he said it would.

"Hey there. Tough nut to crack?" Patrick said, leaning on her doorjamb.

"Why do you say that?" she asked and then immediately wished she could take it back.

Dressed in a gray suit with a yellow tie, Patrick oozed into her office with the fog that was his cologne.

"You're sitting like a grad student." He flopped into her guest chair. "Figured it would be about a client, unless there's someone you're hiding from me," he added in a mock coy voice.

Irritation sparked. "When do you get your work done?" It had come out harsher than she wanted, but Patrick didn't give a hint that he took the slightest offense.

"Oh, here and there." He waved his hand.

"I'm drowning over here, and I haven't even looked at the email from Tabby with the new list for my caseload."

"I was CPR certified in high school. Lifeguard," he said, giving her a thumbs-up.

"That's a good line, but I'll pass."

He barked out a laugh. "Listen, I'd be happy to help take a look at your cases. See if there's anything I can do. Paperwork and all that."

"I just gotta get through it," she said before adding,

"thanks, though." The last thing she needed was Patrick claiming to have come to her rescue.

"You wound me, Mel."

"You don't look that hurt about it," she pointed out.

"It's deep." He slapped his fist right against his chest. "Right in the heart."

Crap. How the hell did she get him out?

"I think I'm going to finish this up at home tonight."

"You sure you don't want me to take a crack at it?"

"I'm good," she said while making a show of packing her bag.

He got the hint, stood, and ambled out of the cramped space. "Well, my offer stands. Both of them."

Both? Oh, right, dinner. Not anytime soon.

"I'll see you tomorrow," she said, grabbing the printouts of Lorraine's email and shutting down her computer. She closed her office and made a beeline for the exit. Though she didn't dare look back, she had a feeling Patrick watched her the whole way.

Mel had breezed through town to get to her apartment, since she had left early. Pushing through the door, she headed straight for the medicine cabinet, trying to ignore Abuelita's face in her mind and the good, healthy dose of guilt and denial that came with the take two and call me in the morning trick.

It wasn't like it was serious pain medicine. Hell, it wasn't even a prescription, and she took far less than the recommended dosage and far less often.

Except when it came to this case, a small voice in her head pointed out. The puzzle of Nathaniel Harrington that she couldn't step away from.

Mel changed out of her work clothes and into her emotional support hoodie before she eyed her bag and pulled out the pages she printed on the way out of the office.

Though it was impossible, unheard of, and probably made her a fool, she was considering the possibility Nathaniel Harrington had traveled through time. God help her.

The picture was too odd, and when she finished reading Lorraine's email, she confirmed that no one had requested this portrait since its donation. Also, it had never been on display and had effectively been "waiting in storage," as Lorraine had put it.

Mel didn't understand the implications that this could have, and she didn't want to think about them anyway. Abuelita had raised her to have faith, and in her heart, Mel had faith that Nathaniel was telling the truth.

Besides that groundbreaking realization, his case was relatively straightforward. Mel had to laugh at herself as she made her notes on his charges. It was ridiculous, but the fact remained that she was his attorney, and she would do her job just like she would for anyone else. Whether or not he had gotten lost in time didn't matter in the courtroom.

A knock on the door made her jump. She checked her phone for the time and frowned. Mel shoved her papers to the side of the coffee table and stood, wrapping her hoodie around her. She walked over and peered through the peephole to see a deliveryman holding a bag.

Knowing full well she hadn't ordered any food, she flicked her eyes over to confirm that the chain and deadbolt had been thrown on her door before she called out, "Wrong place."

She watched through the peephole as the man checked a receipt. "Reyes? Beef and broccoli, wontons, spring rolls, and extra cookies. Diet Coke?"

The hairs on her neck rose. Working in law had made her extra careful. You didn't know when a past client or family member could call wanting to get ugly. It was the nature of the job to consider those uninvited as a threat. What made it strange, though, was that it was her exact order.

"Uh…a Mr. Patrick placed the order. Phone number ending in 5692?"

Mel inwardly groaned. "Okay, thank you. Give me a minute." She dug out a couple of bills for a tip, took the food, and retreated to the couch, where she found a text on her phone from Mr. Prince Charming himself.

"Thought you might like this," she read aloud. Damn the bastard. He knew her exact order. She peered into the bag to get a whiff. It was a sin to waste food, and Mel considered it worse to waste fresh Chinese takeout. She supposed she didn't mind him getting dinner, as long as he wasn't here to bother her. Still, she'd make a point to return the favor, so they could call it even.

Half an hour later, the remnants of the takeout boxes were scattered over her coffee table. Mel picked at the crumbs of the first fortune cookie, which had said nothing helpful.

Though she hated to admit it, the food had helped her headache a little, which meant Abuelita had been right.

No surprise there, she thought, opening the second fortune cookie.

The shocker of the evening was that Patrick had been genuinely thoughtful and had, in the process, hit the nail on the head. She leaned over and grabbed her phone to text him, thanking him and saying she would see him tomorrow.

With that done, she gathered the trash and noted the fortune.

Even the person who looks wrong is right sometimes.

Nathaniel. Nope. Not going there.

Her black leather bag had spilled over the rim with her notes and onto the couch, becoming her go-to habitat. Mel puffed out her cheeks and let a breath escape before she dove in, absentmindedly chewing on a fortune cookie while a rerun of *The Golden Girls* played out on TV.

Maybe Abuelita was right. She was working so much, it was like she wasn't living. Shit, she didn't even have a diary or a cheesecake in the fridge like the belles of Miami. Mel vowed to try to figure out a hobby as she finished the spring roll. Maybe after Nathaniel's case was closed, she'd take up history. The historical society had been nice.

Before she fell asleep, surrounded by crumbs that would make Abuelita start praying in Spanish, Mel had worked through almost her entire bag. The one file left behind contained a photo of the man in her dream.

Mel was on the verge of sleep, or maybe she was waking up, when she walked through high grass and felt warmth on her face. The sun was setting, and the sky had a blush-orange tint. Trees swayed around her. Nathaniel Harrington was sitting under a tree in the British uniform from his picture.

"I was wondering if you would come here," he said.

"Why does it matter if I do?"

He shrugged and went back to picking his fingernails with a knife. "Guess it doesn't to you, but you're the only one who knows about me."

"I still can't believe it."

"But you do."

"I believe you enough."

"And your friend Stella?"

"Yes, I believe her too."

"So you don't think I'm crazy?"

"I don't know what to think, but I don't think you're crazy."

"I'm not so sure." He had a rueful look about his face as he focused on his hand, which had dirt—at least she hoped it was dirt—caked into the creases.

"I'm working on your case," she said. With everything else done, it could now have her full attention.

"How does that help me?"

Mel frowned. "It'll get you out of jail."

Nathaniel turned to her with his wide eyes, as in the picture. "Then what will happen to me?"

She stammered. "You'll—you can get a job."

He let out a sardonic laugh. "With what skills?"

"I'll help you."

"You don't fully believe me, so how can you help?"

"I'll talk to Stella—"

"My life is gone."

A wind picked up, but colder and harsher than the breeze. Dark clouds loomed overhead.

"We can fix this."

"Tell *them* that."

All the trees around her had now turned into soldiers from the Revolution, wounded, deceased, decaying, each one staring at her with a bored expression, resigned to his fate.

"There's no fixing the damned," Nathaniel said, getting up and walking away from her.

"Stop! I can help."

Overhead, a crack of lightning brought her awake, thrashing, drenched, and out of breath. A storm raged outside. Mel took a few deep breaths and swept back the hair stuck on her damp forehead.

The glow of the TV gave the otherwise dark room a blue hue. *Little House on the Prairie* was on now, which meant it must be late. She rummaged around for her phone, knocking trash and a throw pillow to the floor. Finding it, she checked the time and groaned for two reasons.

One, it was late, and two, Patrick had answered her text.

"Anything for a friend."

It would be so much easier if she liked him back. This

could be good, simple, and yet...she had just dreamed about Nathaniel. He was like a puzzle she couldn't walk away from.

Mel just smiled to herself, and it remained, as she heaped her stacks of files onto each other and shoved them into her bag with her laptop.

Being the dutiful granddaughter of Maria Reyes, Mel straightened the couch before dragging herself to bed, where she mercifully slept without dreams.

CHAPTER 10

Nathaniel sat in his cell with a book on American history. Once he had figured out what had happened to him, he realized how far he was behind those around him. Little things that they found simple, ordinary, and of no consequence were mysteries to Nathaniel.

Much of his day was spent navigating new information and technology he didn't understand. Thank God he had always been a quick study.

The library's section on American history had fascinated him. Since he had arrived, the one thing he had understood was the first three chapters of this book, all of which covered the general history through the beginning of the American Revolution.

He hadn't followed the movements of the crown and the colonists prior to purchasing his colors. He had heard of trouble in the colonies, but most everyone in England had been focused on France. That the colonists had organized in such a way was surprising.

Nathaniel was mildly surprised to learn that the colonists had won. The number of men they had and the condition of the land they were fighting in were not suited to their training. Clearly, George Washington and the other leaders simply had to outlast the British, which they did effectively.

He wondered what life would've been like for his family after the war. From what he had read, the British were back at war with France, now an empire. The duchy of Harrington had been well-established, but a significant portion of the estate relied on imports from France and the Southern colonies.

At one point, Nathaniel had to stop reading, as all he could think of was his poor mother and her already weakened state. Losing his father, him, and then the family's savings—it would've been too much.

If he had been able to go back, he would have tried to convince his brother to reduce spending and plant new crops on their land in advance of the changes, but he wasn't sure when or how to do that. He hadn't even figured out why he was here.

From that point on, the readings got a lot tougher to understand. It was his country, but the technologies in the wars that followed horrified him, while those in the farming industry he studied to understand how they worked. Everything became more difficult when new countries were mentioned. In 1871, the states of the German Confederation unified to form a country called Germany, which proved to be an enemy to much of Europe and the United States.

Nathaniel read everything he could about what had happened since he left. Often, he would have to reread a chapter the next morning just to ensure that he understood the content.

Other than reading his books and studying the weather, his days were routine, and he kept to himself since the incident in the showers. A woman who had introduced herself as a social worker had asked him questions and told him she was working on paperwork to get him legal presence documentation. The more he read about the events of the 20th century, the more he noticed an increase in such administration. He knew that even if he had access to all of his records from his past life, he would have none of the papers that were required now.

Miss Reyes, his attorney, hadn't come back, but did send a letter. It stated that she was working on his case and wouldn't see him until his trial, as it was close and she had everything she needed to prepare. Nathaniel used the letter as a bookmark.

He had lost his interest in trying to prove himself to her. She had all of the information and more. Nathaniel had thought back to the picture she had of him. If she didn't believe him…and hell, why should she? He barely believed it himself. But if she didn't believe him, no one would. No sense in exhausting himself. There was nothing else to do but try to fit into the new world.

Nathaniel entered the common area after getting his tray of food and went to sit in the corner, alone, as he had since his arrival. Today the weather was supposed to be hot, and according to the TV, farmers had called in, presumably on the telephone—a term he had recently learned from his book — to complain about the lack of rain. As he tore off some of his brown bread, he considered that some things were the same no matter what time you were in.

A tray clattered near him, and Goatee sat down before sliding over. Nathaniel made a move to get up, but he said, "I have a question I need to ask you, England."

Nathaniel eyed the guards watching them and figured they would get involved if something were to happen. Hopefully. "Yes?"

"I got to thinking that maybe I was a bit hasty in the library. You know about this law shit?"

"A little, but that was in England," he said hesitantly, remembering what had happened the last time they had spoken about it. After that incident, he had offered advice to another inmate they called Big Rich, who had promptly told him to go fuck himself. That time, the guards had laughed to themselves, and one even gave Nathaniel a sad, grim smile.

"He doesn't even listen to his own lawyer," they had said.

That had been weeks ago, and since then, Nathaniel hadn't said much. The next time he spoke to anyone was to Goatee in the showers, which, of course, had gone about as well as a mule through a brick wall.

Goatee shoveled more food in his mouth before he said, in between chewing, "I got me a lawyer."

He kept chewing, so Nathaniel said, "Good."

"Yeah." He swallowed and took a drink of water. "But it's court-appointed, obviously. Shit, that's what most of us got. Anyway, I'm trying to get an appeal."

"Why are you here?"

"This time?" Goatee said, eating more bread. "Armed robbery and second-degree murder."

Nathaniel schooled his face to hide his grimace. He had suspected as much.

Goatee leaned over his tray, eating his potatoes while he spoke. "See, the thing is, though. It wasn't me. Well, the murder wasn't, at least."

Prison wasn't much different from war, Nathaniel thought. Here they were talking about killing a man over lunch as if they were talking about horses or crops. It was a fact of life. An ugly one, but still a fact of life.

"I was there, and it was my friend, Tooth." He took the last chunk of his bread and mopped up some gravy around the beef. "On the camera footage they had, I ran out before Tooth shot the guy." He drank some more. "Dumbass. We already had the money and shit."

"Anyway, Tooth could run faster than me, and he took off into the bushes. Jumped a fence like a damn rabbit. We both were in hoodies, but I'm the one who ran out first on the tape. I think they're just after me cuz I got me some priors. You know what I'm sayin'?"

Nathaniel nodded as he had gotten a pretty decent picture despite the vernacular. At least human nature hadn't changed.

"Well, anyway, I told my lawyer that I wanted an appeal, but I don't know about it. Never gone that high, and I'm trying to learn about my situation cuz I ain't paying the lawyer, so I want to make sure I get what's right. Seeing as you know about that shit, I was hoping you could help me out?"

Nathaniel sat, watching him lick his fingers one after the other, while Goatee's napkin sat on the tray neatly folded. He took a breath and started to explain what he knew about writ of error, hoping common law from over two hundred and fifty years ago was something close to what they had here and now.

CHAPTER 11

Mel fiddled with her phone while she waited outside the pre-release center. With every client that was released from jail, Mel tried as hard as she could to meet with them on the morning of their release day and wish them good luck.

It was a joy to see these men and women on the day they would get their lives back. Some were going home to see their kids for the first time in months or years, and others were just happy to be free. Of course, sometimes, despite her best efforts, Mel knew in her gut that many clients would struggle, but still, release day was a happy occasion.

She wrote thank-you emails to witnesses and other places, including Lorraine Williams for her help with the research.

The trial had been quick, with the judge finding Nathaniel guilty of trespassing and sentencing him to half the maximum of forty-five days, with time credited for what he had already served. The weapons charges were thrown out, as she had made a strong case for them putting on a living history display without a permit before everything had gone tragically wrong.

Mel winced at the memory of that moment in the courtroom. She had been pulling out her prepared notes on Benny's medical condition when the district attorney had updated all of them that Benny had died earlier that morning. When she had turned to him to apologize, Nathaniel's lips had been drawn into a thin line, his eyes closing for a few beats.

"I am too. He was too young for all of this," Nathaniel said, opening them again.

As Mel checked her phone again, the ethical question of public safety popped up in her head, but Stella had found him to be perfectly sane.

Just like those people who believe aliens have abducted them, she thought with a thin-lipped smile—perfectly harmless crazies.

But she didn't think Nathaniel was crazy, and as she boarded the merry-go-round of overthinking again, she came to the same conclusion that she believed him. God help her—and she would keep this secret until worms sucked on her bones—she had started to think Nathaniel Harrington had traveled in time.

Which inspired a lot of questions. The main one being—now what?

It wasn't as though he ever was going to get life, she thought as she grabbed her bag and headed inside.

"It's a big day," José said, when she came through. "Congratulations. He might be a weird one, but he was good."

"Thanks," Mel answered slapping her bag on the belt for the routine security. "I'm worried about him a little though. It'll be hard to adjust to life on the outside."

"It always is," José answered, passing her bag back to her.

Mel tilted her head to one side. "True, but I don't know, I think this one might be a little more lost than usual."

"You going to help him out a little with services and shit like normal?"

Mel smiled back at him. "Always do."

He extended his fist, which she bumped with her own. "You're a real one."

"I wish everyone did the same."

"Hey, look, you're not in charge of everyone else. You can only help the person in front of you."

"When did you get so wise?"

He shrugged it off and looked away but he was grinning. "Man, I got to get this fatherly wisdom ready."

"You already have it," Mel said, and waved goodbye.

Nathaniel was waiting for her when she signed in, as she had called ahead to make the appointment.

"Good morning and congratulations," she led with like she always did.

"Thank you," he said.

In the silence that stretched, Mel took in how much he had changed from the picture and from their first meeting. His cheeks were no longer hollow, and his shoulders seemed wider, now that he had eaten properly for a few weeks. She shifted her legs uncomfortably and cleared her throat.

"Did Ms. Smith give you the information on the programs?"

"Yes, ma'am, she did," he said. His fingers were linked loosely on his lap and damn him, he looked relaxed whereas she was wound tight as a drum. Mel couldn't fight the fidget. Shit, what did she usually say?

"I appreciate all that you've done for me," Nathaniel said. "I will try to compensate you for your time."

"No, Mr. Harrington, that's not necessary. I receive a fair

salary from the state for my work, though I appreciate the offer."

"That concept was new to me, but it is from Miranda V. Arizona, right?"

"Gideon V. Wainwright, actually, but you're close. Miranda has a few more bits to it. Informing the accused of their rights and charges upon arrest and avoiding self-incrimination."

"That's right, I've been getting the names mixed up."

"Lots of people do." The silence stretched.

Mel almost sighed with relief when Nathaniel continued to speak. "I've been reading a lot of American history."

"That's good. I always liked history—more modern stuff —but I'm a political science person through and through."

"That's fascinating."

"Why?"

"You're a woman."

Mel felt her hackles start to rise. "And?"

"I was just reading about the civil rights movement last night. It's a shame I'll have to leave the book here. There's so much—" He paused and shifted. "There's so much in which I find I have an interest."

Mel nodded slowly. "There are libraries outside, of course. You'd be eligible to get a library card and check out books. I think you need some paperwork, but the first would be a bill or a piece of mail."

"I think I'll do that soon." The silence stretched again. "My sister would have had a wonderful success in business had she been allowed the proper schooling."

Mel didn't know what to say, so she nodded again.

"Again, I appreciate you representing me in court."

"That's my job, and I enjoy it."

"You've found your calling." He smiled at her, but his eyes

had a sadness in them that she caught before he dropped his gaze.

"Thank you. So what else do you plan to do with your freedom, Mr. Harrington? Did you secure lodging somewhere?"

"Ms. Smith gave me the information on a few shelters nearby. I'll go there first and then look for a job. She explained that I needed paperwork for most jobs now."

"Yes, that's correct. I think you'll find everything will fall into place once the paperwork comes through."

"Ms. Smith has had a hard time verifying a few things, but I'm sure it will work out in time."

In time. Wasn't that an odd statement for him to say, she thought. Mel dug into her bag and came up with a card.

"Here's my number." She wasn't sure what to say, so she figured when in Rome… "My telephone number, so you're welcome to call me if you have any questions, or if I can assist you in any way. Are you familiar with a telephone?"

"I've read about it, but have not touched it myself. I don't know anyone." Nathaniel shifted in his seat and looked through the glass at another inmate passing with some guards. "I've seen others do it, though."

The feeling she couldn't pin down this morning rose in a tremendous wave that no one, especially a cradle Catholic, could mistake.

Guilt.

He couldn't even use a damn phone, and what broke her otherwise usually professional reserve was that the man sitting across from her didn't have a soul on earth to call. No one, and now that Benny was gone, there was no one like him here. No tether to the world from which he had come.

Somehow, giving him a card seemed insulting instead of helpful—a pathetic use of charitable and kind words to substitute for action.

He sat across from her, studying her card, when a guard came into the area behind him.

"Harrington? We're ready for you. You can come and sign out your belongings."

Nathaniel stood and turned to Mel and inclined his head once. "Thank you, Miss Reyes."

Typically, she hated being called miss and would've had no bones about correcting someone immediately, but today she nodded once and turned around to leave. She was halfway to her car when she turned around and headed back.

Years later, Mel would remember this as the most idiotic and important decision she had ever made.

Shoes clipping on the sidewalk, as if her body was not under her control, she marched out of the front of the building just in time to see the glass doors slide open and Nathaniel Harrington walk out.

Mel felt her jaw drop.

He was dressed like the picture. Nathaniel Harrington looked like a British soldier coming out of jail. His coat was a crumpled red wool that hung down past his waist over filthy pants that may have once been cream colored. Nathaniel held a few papers and an evidence bag that she assumed carried what had been on his person when he was arrested, but everything else matched.

It shouldn't have startled her. She knew and had structured her whole argument around him being a reenactor without a permit. Still, seeing him in real life on the sidewalk in the Bronx was jarring.

He didn't see her at first and walked forward, stopping under the flagpole he looked up at for a minute before looking left and right, clearly at a loss for what to do.

Mel felt the guilt ease away. She had made the right call, whatever her logical side told her. Mel stood up and jogged over. She had been telling herself that if it were a ploy, surely he'd have somewhere to go, someone to call, but yet, here was the final proof. Human behavior. He was lost.

"Mr. Harrington."

He turned to face her. "Hello, Miss Reyes," he said, eyes a little wider than they had been inside. It was small, but there seemed to be a sense of relief at seeing her.

"It occurred to me that you may need assistance immediately upon your release."

A wry laugh escaped him. "Yes, I believe that would be a correct assessment."

"So this is all you have?"

He looked down, back up, and nodded, unsure what to say.

"I think we need to make a few stops," she said, eyeing his clothes up close. Not only did they look old, but they also reeked. Abuelita wouldn't use the white shirt he was wearing for a cleaning rag, and the pants looked less comfortable than carpet.

"Right," she blurted out. Shit, she thought, what the hell did I get myself into? "Okay, let's go."

Nathaniel didn't ask where to, which she thought was odd until she considered that he had no other option. Her heart broke again as she glanced at him while they walked along the sidewalk.

He looked like an orphaned puppy as he followed her. Everything interested him. She started to wonder again if he had a concussion or special situation, but all of the reports had come back perfectly sane. The warmth she felt at this decision burned off any remaining unease about the situation. One thing was for sure—Mel didn't feel guilty anymore. It felt good to be helping someone else, not just in the courtroom, but in life.

"This one's a Ford," he said, looking at a beat-up truck a few spaces over.

"Yep. Sure is," she said, not seeing what he was getting at.

"I read about this automobile. Henry Ford."

"Oh yeah, well obviously that was a long time ago—" Nathaniel raised his eyebrows. "I mean, like relatively a long time ago. About a hundred years, I think."

She walked over to where she had parked Abuelita's old Civic. Technically, her grandmother had given it to Mel when she graduated from college, but they still shared it. It wasn't anything fancy—just a well-worn sedan with surprisingly low mileage. Since Abuelita's building had a parking garage, they maintained it for flexibility, whether for meeting clients, getting out of the city for the weekend, or driving Abuelita to her church retreats.

"I'm starting to believe you more," she said, pulling out her sunglasses and cranking over the ignition, which made him jump back in his seat a little.

"You believe me?" The excitement in his face seemed to light him up.

Mel held up a hand before she shifted. "I don't know how much I believe, but I've never seen anyone look at a Civic like you just did. Oh, wait, you gotta put your seatbelt on."

"My what?" He looked down and around, trying to figure out what he had done wrong.

Mel pointed over to his strap and lifted her own. "See? It just clicks…yeah, like that, and when you want to get out—right, yeah, the red button. Don't worry." She laughed when he looked totally uncomfortable. "Henry Ford didn't have those. Nothing bad will happen. I'm a very safe driver."

She fluffed her hair in the mirror, shifted to reverse, and K-turned out of the space. When they hit the main road, she nearly gave her new passenger a heart attack and slowed down. His head went very still as if he was trying to focus on the road and not show panic.

The radio came on before she could turn it down, with a woman talking about the latest pop star's love interest.

"What—what is that?" he asked, almost indignant in his British accent.

"Radio," she said, figuring Bluetooth was a step too far. "Was that in your book?"

"I think so—Marconi—but I didn't understand that part."

"Most people don't know how it works," she said, getting up to speed. "We just kind of accept it. Basically, you now know as much about it as I do. You push the button and sound comes out. Well, actually, there are different channels, so if you don't like this music, you just flip to another channel."

"I've heard that word before. The other prisoners talked about changing the channel."

"Yeah, but I doubt they got the choice. José and the other guards like to keep things consistent. Routine makes life easier."

"I liked the weather," he said.

"Really? Huh, I never watch the weather myself. Usually, I hear about whether a big storm is coming or something like that from somebody else."

Mel noticed out of the corner of her eye that Nathaniel was sitting as stiff as a board, and his grip might break her door handle.

"Too fast for you?"

"I've never gone this fast before."

"I'll avoid the highway this time," she said.

"You can go faster?"

The car in front of her tapped its brakes for what must have been the tenth time, even though literally no one was anywhere near them. "I'd love to go faster," Mel said through gritted teeth. "Traffic can be hell around here."

"Traffic?"

"Yeah, like, you know, uh—congestion? Too many people are trying to go to the same place at once. Everything gets bogged down, and God help us if someone gets in an accident, or heaven forbid, it starts to rain. Then everyone goes super slow so they can get a glimpse or just because, and it takes me an hour to get home."

"Why are so many yellow?"

"Those are taxis. They take you to anywhere in the city, but the farther you go the more it will cost."

"There are a lot of them."

"Yep. There are even more people under the ground on the subway. It's a train that goes through tunnels under the city."

"I read about trains, but not underground."

A siren started wailing through the streets before a loud horn blasted a few times. "Good God, is it always this loud?"

"That's a firetruck or ambulance. I can never remember which one sounds like which. They usually go together to an emergency. The siren is so you can get out of the way."

"When that automobile came through the trees—"

"You can call it a car or truck depending on what it looks like," she said. "But yeah?"

"It looked like the Ford."

"Probably was one too, actually. Ford makes the police vehicles now. Anyway, that is a truck, and this is a car, but yeah, go ahead."

"Well, when the truck came down the path, I thought it was a carriage, but I kept looking for the horse, and there weren't any."

Mel drummed her fingers on the steering wheel while she waited for a light to change. "You weren't far off. We haven't used horses in a long time," she added, fully aware that she actually might be insane as well.

"I did read about them during the wars."

"World Wars?"

"Yes. I don't understand how so many people dying is acceptable."

"There's been nothing like it since," she said. "I mean in terms of scale. There hasn't been any conflict that large since then, although did you read about—" She didn't know what to say and turned into the shopping center while she tried to reword her thoughts.

"My war? Yes, I read that."

Mel glanced over at him. He sat still, looking out at all the cars around them, in her Civic, wearing his clothes from the Revolutionary War.

The weirdest thing was that once she had stopped trying to figure out how and why, and instead focused on what was next, it all didn't seem so odd.

Nathaniel sat next to her, quiet and content with wherever they were going and whatever they were going to do. He was happy just to look around at his surroundings. Whereas Mel thought her Civic was filthy, Nathaniel was amazed. She smiled to herself as she wondered what he was going to think of their destination.

CHAPTER 12

Mel parked and grabbed her purse from the back. "Okay, come on. Let's get you some new clothes."

Nathaniel looked down briefly before getting out of the car. "Uh, I appreciate the offer, but I don't have any money. I mean, I do, but—" He reached for his wallet.

"Yeah, anything you have is good for an antique dealer, and that's about it. Don't worry about it. I got you," she said, walking him into the store. "God, it feels good in here. I can't wait until this heat leaves. I'll get a cart." When she came back, Mel found Nathaniel in the dollar section, slowly walking through and studying all of the cheap, bright little toys.

"What is this place?"

"Target. It's pretty great, unless they don't have enough lanes open." He nodded slowly and turned to look at the checkout lanes, where a woman was buying groceries that beeped across the scanner, while her kids begged for a pack of gum.

They started walking back toward the jeans, and Mel

said, "Sorry, that's not a very good description, is it? It's a superstore."

"It's huge. I've never been in a building this big. How is the roof held up? There are hardly any columns." His neck craned back to study the roof above.

"I dunno." Mel shrugged before she turned the cart into the section. "I guess it's steel or something. Never crossed my mind."

"This is incredible." He wandered around. Born again, she thought as she watched him feel the fabric of every item.

Yup. She was totally doing the right thing here.

"Okay, so you'll need a pair of pants... Ooh, they're on sale. What the hell, I never buy anything anyway. Ah, you don't happen to know your size, do you? That's a dumb question—"

He shook his head.

"I've never bought men's clothing before."

As Mel studied the label, she was aware that he was looking at her instead of ogling everything else. "Nope, not married, no boyfriend."

"I didn't mean to—"

"Do you know your waist and length?" she asked, cutting him off.

"No, but these," he tugged on his waistband. "They were loose for a while, but not this morning."

No wonder, she thought. He had definitely filled out after being in jail. The sad thing was that she saw that often in her line of work. Men would be underweight or average upon arrest, but they had leveled out by the time the trial came around.

Maslow's hierarchy of needs was one of her favorite subjects during her undergraduate studies. When people couldn't access regular food and shelter, everything else seemed to fall apart. Humans needed a foundation to thrive, and her clientele weren't thriving.

"Go ahead and try these on, just to make sure. Do you think you'll gain more weight?"

"I've never thought about it."

Mel sighed. "Oh to be you," she said wistfully. "Dressing room is back there; I'll pick out a few more things." She turned to a rack and flipped through a few shirts.

"Ah…" Nathaniel was blushing. "I do not believe my underwear will fit."

"Oh. Yeah. Um…" Crap, she hadn't thought of that, had she? This guy needed everything. "Well, I tell you what, just throw them in the basket and we'll try them on later. If they don't fit or you don't like them, I'll take them back. No big."

"I truly appreciate you doing this."

Mel flipped it off with a wave of her hand. "Said to call me if you needed assistance." That sounded bitchy actually. She turned around. "It's really fine. I enjoy helping."

"Thank you, Miss Reyes."

"Mel, well Melanie, but everyone calls me Mel."

"Thank you, Mel." He looked down at the jeans he was holding. "I don't know what I would've done if you hadn't come back or known about me."

She gave him a tight smile. Mel wanted to ask more about his past, but she didn't think she was ready for that conversation while standing next to packs of men's underwear.

"It's fine, really. What kind of underwear do you want?"

"I didn't know there were choices."

"Oh man, that's all there is nowadays." Did she really just say nowadays? What the hell. "I tell you what, just see what you like and throw it in." Holy hell. Mel tried to think about what else he might need. Toiletries? Shoes? The list was endless.

Nathaniel threw in a pack of white boxers, and she tossed

a pack of T-shirts in too. "Let's keep going. I think we'll have to make the whole loop around the store."

Close to an hour later, Mel needed an iced coffee, but surprisingly didn't have a headache. They had been around the store twice and had a cart full of everything from shaving cream to socks to combs to shoes. She had racked her brain trying to think of something she might have missed before she headed to the checkout.

Nathaniel had settled into the Target way. Every few feet, something caught his eye. What surprised Mel was that almost none of it was for himself.

At one point, he stopped at the jewelry section and asked her if she wanted to look at anything for herself, which, of course, she waved off. He did convince her to try on one scarf, though. It was just that he was so entertained and engaged with everything they came into contact with.

"There is so much here," he said in awe when they passed the children's section. The aisles of bright toys beckoned them both. In the beginning, Mel had agreed to wait while he explored, but ultimately she got sucked in too.

"Barbies were always my favorite," she told him as they walked through the shrine to all things pink and glitter. "Sometimes I walk in here just for me, but I never buy anything."

Nathaniel looked like he wanted to ask her something, but held back. Mel was about to encourage him to ask away when he saw what she liked to call the hall of electronics ahead of them. For the first time since entering the store, Nathaniel moved forward without her by his side to watch the annoying ad reel that Mel barely noticed on a typical day.

Nathaniel walked slowly and turned around a few times to study each of the various items behind the glass cases that Mel had never seen. He snapped out of it and waved her over.

"What are these?" he asked, pointing to the latest Switch, which people would fight each other over in November.

"It's a game for kids, and I guess some adults. I used to play, but that was literally years ago. Don't have the time anymore. You hold the controller like this."

Before Mel knew it, they were racing on Rainbow Road—he as Mario and she as Peach. Nathaniel struggled to drive and kept going backward or falling off the track. Of course, she won. It would be a disgrace to her generation if someone who held a controller for the first time beat a child of the video gaming era. It was like playing a toddler, and she wanted to be encouraging.

"Victory!" she yelled, like a ref calling touchdown with both arms up.

"How did you do that?"

"Practice," she said, grabbing the cart. "And lots of power slides. Don't sweat it. I'm sure you have skills I don't."

Nathaniel stayed quiet when that remark was made, and the pair started unloading all of their finds onto the belt.

The cashier was quick, but Mel was quicker and saw the flick of the eyes over Nathaniel.

"We're all set here," she said firmly, looking the cashier square in the eyes, daring her to say something.

She only said, "Have a nice day" when she handed over the bags.

She paid, and the two of them gathered up the bags before heading out the door. Mel figured she would hit her favorite drive-thru coffee place on her way home.

"God," she said, putting on her sunglasses. "It feels like the sun out here. Ugh." They loaded the bags, and she cranked the A/C on full blast.

"Miss Reyes—"

"Mel," she said, fluffing her hair in the mirror again

before backing out of the space. Nothing but frizz. Damn humidity.

"Mel, I don't know what to say, except that I want to pay you. That was an incredible amount of money."

"Like I said before, it's fine. Things cost more now, so don't worry. It wasn't that much in today's money." Nathaniel sat unmoving, studying the plastic bag in his hand. "Hey, it's going to be okay. I wanted to help you. It's a gift."

"It's just so different here."

Mel stopped the car right there in the parking lot. To hell with everyone else. They could go around. She waited until he met her eyes.

"It's going to take some time. Even if you were—" Don't say normal, don't mention time, she thought. "Look, everyone who comes out feels this way. That's why so many end up going back. It's okay to be overwhelmed. It's a lot."

Nathaniel nodded, but didn't look all that reassured.

Duh, she thought, she had only really talked about the surface problem, hadn't she?

"I tell you what. Let's go get a coffee and just talk. Would that help?"

He nodded again and gave her a very unconvincing smile, but at least it was something.

One thing was clear, though, Mel thought as she drove out of the parking lot. Dropping him off at the shelter like she had been planning to wasn't going to work.

CHAPTER 13

A flurry of pigeons abandoned their fight over a bagel on the sidewalk outside the coffee shop. Nathaniel followed Mel inside and found it different from what he had expected. People sat at small tables where they talked or watched small screens alone, while people in aprons rushed behind a counter. A few of them glanced up at him, their eyes scanning over his uniform, staring at the apparent oddity, before returning to what they were doing.

A large metal box hissed as a cloud of steam rose, and a young man with a beard called out, "Macchiato for Laura and soy latte for Karen."

He didn't even understand their words and wondered how something as simple as coffee could be so complicated.

Mel marched confidently to the line and barely read the specials board before turning to him.

"I'm dying for an iced coffee, and I've been craving one all day. When it's hot like this, I get a headache if I don't have it."

Nathaniel nodded, much like he had at the Target store.

"How do you take your coffee?"

"I'm not sure."

Mel raised one dark eyebrow into a perfect arch. "You gotta be kidding me."

He shook his head, but then thought better of it. "At the jail, I added a little cream. The sugar made it too sweet. But the cream was good."

"I think we're just going to go with a cafe latte then," she said to herself, stepping up to the bar to order so quickly that he couldn't understand what she had said.

When she paid using that little card again, Nathaniel tried to see the bill. He looked up at the board. Several dollars for a cup of coffee was shocking, but it was clear that people had no trouble paying it. There was even a jar of bills that read "tips" on the outside.

A group of young girls giggled in the corner, each with their cup of something fluffy and made of cream. At the end of the center table, a young man sipped out of a cup as he bent over a book with a stack of others next to him. An older couple sipped in silence as the man read a newspaper, occasionally showing something he had just read to his wife.

None of these people struck him as particularly wealthy, but they must be. As a duke's son, his inheritance of five thousand pounds had been generous, but it was clear even if he could've accessed it, it would not last long with these prices.

"Cool. It'll be ready in a second. They'll call us," Mel said, walking over toward two leather chairs facing each other by the window. Nathaniel followed and sat across from her when she flopped down.

Mel sat across from him, bare legs crossed in a black dress that fit well and would have sent his mother into a fit with its impropriety. Smooth tan skin without hair stretched over lean legs from the top of her exposed foot to her knee. As if that wasn't enough, when she took off her jacket, her shoulders and arms were also visible to everyone. Nathaniel had been working hard to pointedly not stare at her or anyone else.

It was clearly the fashion of the day, as the women on the TV at the jail all wore the same style, much to the prisoners' delight. They, like Nathaniel, had been equally enthralled by the weather, but only for one reason, which had nothing to do with rain.

"Skinny iced cafe latte for Mel and a cafe latte for Nathaniel," the bartender in the apron called out, sliding the drinks onto the bar for her to pick up.

"Alright, here you go. They're usually cool with making you another one if you don't like it."

He brought his own cup to his lips and tasted a velvety, smooth taste. It was strong, but with foam on top.

"Well?" Mel said, watching him. "Do you like it, or do you want something else?"

"It's good. It's very good. Different." Like everything, he added to himself.

Her dark eyes studied him as she took another sip from her cup. "How so?"

Nathaniel thought for a moment and took another sip. "It's smoother."

Mel sat, not moving, clearly expecting more. "And?"

"I can see what you mean about the coffee in the jail now," he ventured.

Her face lit up with a brilliant smile as she started to laugh. "I would have hoped this would be better."

"At least it was hot," they both said. Mel leaned back and laughed again. Nathaniel couldn't help but laugh.

Mel flicked some more hair out of her face and took another sip of her coffee. "That's funny," she said, still smiling to herself.

"Thank you again for all of the things you bought for me. I do intend to pay you back when I can."

She waved him off. "I told you before, don't worry about it. You have bigger things you need to focus on."

Well, that was the truth, was it not?

Nathaniel wasn't sure what to say, so he took another sip of the coffee, which was very good. The boiled chicory paled in comparison.

"So, what do you want to do now?" she asked with an odd look in her eye, letting him lead the conversation where he wanted it to go.

At least that was an easy answer. "I need to see if I can get back. I mean to my own time. I want to see my friends and my family." He took a breath. "I don't belong here."

Mel sipped her coffee, as if mulling over what to say next. "Do you know how it happened or if that's possible?"

"No, but I want to try. I don't know anyone here, and I have no skills. I can't even buy the clothes on my back."

Mel's lips pulled into a thin line before she said, "You don't need to feel bad about that."

"I was the son of a duke, a trained barrister, a captain in the King's light infantry, and now I have nothing. I'm ripped away from all of it. I thought I was in purgatory. Who knows? Maybe I am."

"My grandmother could tell you all about that," she said, almost to herself.

"Do you think she could help?" he asked, before realizing the truth of her meaning.

Mel's face fell as she winced. "Sorry, I just meant she's very Catholic."

"I wasn't a perfect man, but I cared for my family. I know they're gone now, but I need to know what happened to them." He started at the rim of the cup with the perfect smoothness that was somehow light but strong. "My mother was sick when I left."

"I'm sorry," she said.

"I wasn't sure I would see her again when I left, but I didn't think it would be like this."

"Maybe we could go and see the archivist who had your portrait. She knew about the person who donated it, so she might be able to track down your family."

"Yes, that would be nice. I want to get some experience and maybe return to buy my own property. I want to go back to my old life, but I don't know how. There was a storm after the battle, and I fell asleep. Maybe I could go back that way."

"I can take you to where you were found—Van Cortlandt Park."

Nathaniel's throat felt too small. He shouldn't be here, and even if he could go back somehow, he knew it would never be the same. "Yes, I would like that very much. To see if, maybe…"

"I'm not due in court today, so we can go now, if you're ready?" She stood and went to throw her cup away— a sight that was still foreign to him, no matter how much he saw it in jail. It felt wasteful.

Nathaniel stood and did the same with his own cup when Mel said, "I know you're trying to go back to, um, then, but it's a scorcher out there, and technically you're still on probation for trespass, so do you want to change here? You might fit in more that way."

Ten minutes later, Nathaniel left the men's room wearing fabric that was so thin, he didn't know how long it would last, though he welcomed the cooler fabric. He was used to his trousers, but the cotton denim was a nice change from the wool. The shoes on his feet were lighter and much more flexible than his boots. Not having leather up to his knee was also much cooler. Everything down to the underwear and socks was thinner and lighter. All of it, though different, he enjoyed.

On the way out of the room that read "Restroom"—though Nathaniel couldn't figure out why—he stopped at a board that held a series of cards and papers, each advertising a different business or service. Not wanting to hold Mel up, he read quickly, intrigued by what was there. It reminded him of the broadsides and he found that many of the postings were of the same ilk.

"Hey—woah, you look good. Did everything fit alright?"

"Yes, but"—he leaned into her and lowered his voice—"it's different. Are you sure this is decent to be going out?" Nathaniel pinched the fabric of his shirt, showing Mel how little material made up the garment.

"Yeah. Like I said, you look normal. Nothing weird is showing."

"I must admit it is a little strange."

"Yeah, apparently that's the theme of the day," she said. Her eyes left his and went to the board behind him. "Checking out the board?" she asked.

"Oh, yes. I've seen this back at well, home. It's different jobs, right?"

"Yeah. People put up these business cards. There's more than one, see? You can grab a few if you think the job or service is something you need. Go ahead. I'm going to start the car. Come out whenever you're ready," she said, walking toward the exit.

Nathaniel turned back and read quickly. Some jobs were familiar, while others were utterly foreign—dog walkers, babysitters, gutter shields, and a help desk. He recognized tutors, at least, but one stack of cards in particular caught his eye. For the first time, he saw an opportunity he understood. Glancing around, he grabbed the one that caught his eye and then one of every other offering on the board. Even if he didn't understand them now, information was the only way to make meaning of the world around him.

Slipping the cards in his new pocket, Nathaniel left carrying the clothes of his old life in a Target bag.

CHAPTER 14

As Mel followed the directions in the email, she kept her eye on Nathaniel. Before they had left the coffee shop, he had changed out of his, literally, old clothes, throwing them into a Target bag that now smelled like a gym locker mixed with a bucket of ashes. Dressed in jeans, a blue cotton T-shirt, and sneakers, Nathaniel looked like any typical guy riding shotgun.

But he was far from typical.

What gave away his difference was his fascination with the most ordinary things, from the disposable coffee cups to the sugar packets, and even how the cup fit perfectly into her cup holders. Nathaniel studied everything with a childlike innocence that did not detract from his age. More like an engineering student, or at least what she imagined them to be.

Mel had plugged in the information from his file, and they set off in the Civic. They sat in silence for most of the drive, broken only by Nathaniel asking a few questions about tractor-trailers, a motorcycle, and a plane overhead. His knuckles were white on the handle.

"Let me know if I'm going too fast, okay?"

"Of course," he said in a voice that was trying not to sound nervous.

The logical good-girl voice in her head was screaming warning signs that this was precisely how women died in the woods. She had just gotten him out of jail, so there wasn't any malice on his part, but still, she didn't know him well. Mel glanced over at Nathaniel again and knew that he possessed a knife and a firearm in the evidence bag, but having just come from jail, there was nothing else, except for what she had bought him. Once she parked in a spot at the edge of the park, she slid her hand down into the car door pocket and wrapped her fingers around her can of mace.

Though Mel was the last thing on Nathaniel's mind as he jumped out of the car and looked around.

"I recognize this place. I think I was over here." He hurried onto one of the paths heading back into the woods.

Mel stared after him for a full ten seconds. "Well, alright then," she said to herself, pocketing the mace she no longer needed to hide on the sly before punching the button on her key fob twice.

She had been here a couple of times over the years but didn't know the layout by heart. A few people walking dogs and jogging passed them both.

She didn't know how people did this for fun. She felt the sweat already begin to form at the base of her spine, but it was shady at least, and she could hear the birds in the trees. The path in front of her was spongy and easy to walk on, but her cute shoes might be trashed after this little jaunt. Nearby, kids squealed and giggled on a playground set back to her left while their parents sat using their phones at a few picnic tables.

After a few more minutes, she came to a fenced-in area, with the gate suspiciously open just enough for her to slide through. She made a mental note to remind Nathaniel of his probation terms and followed in to find him.

It took a while, but she headed up the hill and saw him standing by a tree with his hands on his hips.

His posture wasn't encouraging.

"I don't know what to do. We were there, over there, making camp after the fighting. We had wandered off, and then the storm came up, and now they're— "

"I know what it's like—"

His eyes were wide, crazed, like a rat caught in a trap. "Do you?" he asked. "Everyone and everything I know is dead." It was a statement of fact.

Mel stayed quiet, but gripped her spray in her pocket.

"You're the only one who knows about me, and you still can't believe me entirely."

"It's hard to. Any rational person—"

"You think any of this is rational or logical or makes some sort of sense to me?" His voice was rising with anger. Mel knew it wasn't directed at her, but she stepped back and gave him his space.

Nathaniel blew out a frustrated sigh and ran his hand through his hair, as the muscle in his jaw twitched.

"Nathaniel, I believe you enough to help you. It's hard—"

"You're damn right it is."

Mel pressed her lips tight.

"You have a picture of me. You have seen my clothes. I don't know how else I can prove myself to you."

"Why does it matter if I believe you one hundred percent? I believe you enough. You're asking the impossible." She let her hands fall away, exasperated.

"It matters to—" He stopped and looked over the landscape toward a large rocky hill near the Van Cortlandt House.

"I can prove it."

Now, it was Mel's turn to sigh. "Nathaniel, I don't need—"

"I need a shovel."

"This is ridiculous. You can't just dig up a city park. You're already on probation."

Nathaniel either didn't hear her or didn't care as he gestured for her to follow him toward a path shrouded in trees leading up the hill.

He only slowed when he saw a trash can and started digging through it. Two kids raced by on another path before a harried, red-faced mom appeared and followed, pushing the largest stroller Mel had ever seen.

"Hey. How ya doing?" Mel asked with a nod, trying to hide the obvious embarrassment as Nathaniel tossed a greasy McDonald's bag onto the grass.

"Hangin' in there," the mom said, throwing her full weight behind the stroller, which Mel could now see was over-flowing with everything but children. "Carly and Michael! I said wait! One! Two!"

Seeing another person was a big enough relief for her to lower her shoulders. As she looked back at Nathaniel, she also felt a connection with the frazzled mom.

A pile of trash sat on the grass, and a plastic bag drifted away from them like a tumbleweed in the wind. Nathaniel had emptied all the contents of the trash and was going through them by hand, analyzing each piece before tossing it away.

He came up with an empty can that smelled like a leftover tuna fish sandwich sitting in the sun at a landfill.

"Come on."

They climbed to the highest point of the rock, so Mel could see the city skyline, but barely hear the usual cacophony. It felt like a world away.

The large old house stood in a field adjacent to the rock they were on, but he didn't head that way. Instead, in what could barely be called a clearing, they came upon a small brick enclosure that read, "BURIAL PLOT OF THE VAN CORTLANDT FAMILY."

He didn't even hesitate.

Marching to an overgrown back corner, he studied it and started digging. Clumps of sod and long grass gave way, as he dug down to the soil with the filthy can. Clearly, the soil hadn't been disturbed in a long time. Beads of sweat started to appear on his forehead, right before the swearing under his breath began, but he was determined. Getting closer to whatever he sought, Nathaniel tossed the can aside and started tearing at the soil with heartbreaking desperation.

She didn't know what to do or think, so she stayed at the cemetery entrance and watched him. The desperation was clear. Whatever he was looking for, she hoped it was there for his sake.

"Look," he said breathing heavy. "There it is."

"It's a hole."

Mel couldn't be sure, but she thought he muttered "Christ" under his breath. He reached in again and pulled out a small clump of dirt before handing it to her. Mel leaned back, not wanting to get dirty, but he pushed it into her hands.

"There you are. Proof."

Gingerly, Mel swept some of the dirt away and found she was holding a small metal box.

"What—"

"Listen." He leaned in now and talked fast. "When I left home, there was a girl." He stopped and swallowed. "Her name was Emma."

Mel nodded, feeling the same tingle she had at the historical society wash over her as her stomach started to get all fluttery again.

"I just pulled that from the ground, and you watched me.

Grass was over it," he said, gesturing to the disturbed pile of sod and weeds. "When you open it, you'll find a pocket watch with a a lock of hair inside."

Nathaniel brushed his hands off and looked at her, waiting. He swept his arms wide. "By all means,"—he nodded at the box—"at your convenience."

When confronted with the impossible, the brain finds the easy solution to process the information, but Mel knew in her heart that it would be exactly as he said it was when she opened the box.

Though the age was apparent, Mel was surprised at how well the little tin box had held up.

"She and I…" Nathaniel paused and then said, "Well, she was sweet on me, and gave it to me when I went away." Nathaniel looked at the hole. "She wanted a husband, but I always thought of her as a little sister," he added to himself.

Mel held the box but didn't open it, her eyes on him.

"She lived a few properties over. Her father and mine did business. It would've been an excellent match for her, since he was untitled and my family was my family, but I…" His voice trailed off.

"You weren't ready," Mel said, her voice soft.

He shook his head and looked down with his hands on his hips. "A letter came from my brother the night before the battle, letting me know she had passed. It was a fever."

Mel's breath caught. "I'm so sorry."

"Thank you. When we stopped to camp, I buried it here in my match case. Thought it was a fitting way to honor her."

Mel's hands shook as she looked down at the filthy, rusted metal box. The lid wouldn't lift, but once she scraped the dirt away, it gave way when she slid it.

Inside was a golden pocket watch. When she opened it, s small hair clipping was curled over the face.

Mel looked up to find Nathaniel staring at her, waiting.

"It's impossible."

He leveled a gaze at her, filled with knowing and grief. "I know."

"And you can't go back?"

"We went to the same spot, and nothing happened."

He looked at her with a look of desperation and grief, pain clear across his face. Pain for the loss of his family, his friends, and, she realized, his whole life.

Her head started to spin, so she drew in a slow breath. "It's hard, but yes, I believe you."

"You humble me with your kindness," Nathaniel said. Mel expected more sarcasm, but there was none.

They walked back out of the park, Nathaniel pointing out various key elements of what he remembered before they slowly started returning to the car. The walk in the woods next to Nathaniel had been good. It had given Mel enough time to come to terms with what she had decided should be their next step.

God help her.

CHAPTER 15

"Alright, let's do this," Mel said to Nathaniel, grabbing her purse from the back. It was a good thing she usually had no reason to spend money because she sure as hell was burning through it today.

"Go grab a cart, would ya?" she asked him as she checked her email on the phone. "Yeah, the silver things. The big one is fine." Mel had sent a quick email at the coffee shop to check in and let work know she was taking a half day. Stella hit her back, asking if everything was okay, which pretty much confirmed that Mel needed to get out more.

"Got it," said Nathaniel. "What is this place? Some sort of market?"

"Dude…" she said, shaking her head. "Didn't you go shopping back, er, home?"

With a confused look on his face, he answered, "No, not typically. I think it was delivered to the kitchens. The cook managed all that."

She had to laugh. "Well, those of us without staff have to go out and forage."

Walking into a grocery store in late August wasn't quite

the same feeling. That large air conditioner fan over the door almost flattened Mel, and she relished it after the walk in the woods that had made her hair resemble a hedgehog.

"Alright, let's make the lap."

Nathaniel was staring at everything with his mouth slightly open. "There's so much"—Nathaniel paused and let his hands fall by his sides in awe—"of everything," he said in a reverent whisper.

"Yeah, I know. It's like the Target of food."

He looked at her, stunned. "But how can you choose?"

She shrugged. "I guess it's like anything else. Sometimes you try new things, and learn what you like."

"It's beautiful." He picked up an orange. "This is the most food I've seen in my life. How do they get these out of season?" Without waiting for her to answer, he moved on to pay his respect to each of the selections.

Mel had to smile despite herself. It had been a long time since she had ever regarded anything with the childlike wonder that Nathaniel was feeling now. And this wasn't even the biggest store compared to the ones outside the city.

"Come on," she said. "You can stare at everything while we walk."

When she looked at the produce section with him and through his eyes, she supposed it was beautiful. The fruits and vegetables were all without blemish and arranged in neat, colorful rows. Signs were handwritten on chalkboards with little drawings that were actually pretty darn good.

She stopped now and turned to him, unsure. "Uh…what do you like to eat? Nathaniel?"

No answer came. Mel turned to find Nathaniel by the dragon fruit and coconuts. "What are these?" he asked in awe when Mel walked over.

"I'm going to be honest with you and say I literally have

no idea. I've never tried it. That, on the other hand, is a coconut, which I also have never tried fresh."

"There's so much here. I don't even know—"

"I tell you what, why don't you tell me what fruit and vegetables you used to eat, and we'll go from there."

"Why?" he asked suddenly, zeroing in on her.

"Uh, so I can buy them."

"Why?" he asked again. With that striking blue eye color, the intensity with which he stared at her was a little unnerving.

Okaaaaaaay. "So you can have something to eat?" she added.

He frowned and kept looking at her. His eyes narrowed.

"There's no food at my apartment," she said, wondering why the hell he was frowning even more now.

"Wait. I'm supposed to be going—" He dug around in his new pockets for the card Stella had given him.

"If you want to, I can take you there, but I—" She shrugged. "I just thought things might be easier or whatever if you came to stay with me until you, you know, figure things out." She shrugged again.

Nathaniel's blue gaze was piercing now. "You'd do that? For me?"

Uncomfortable, Mel looked down and let her sarcasm out to fill the void. "Well, yeah, I mean I can't just let a time traveler sit in a homeless shelter." She paused and looked at the floor. "That felt weird to say out loud. If you don't want to…"

"You barely know me," he said, studying her in awe as if she were one of the rare fruits around them. It was starting to give her the creeps. Maybe he was right about this.

"Look, if you don't want to…"

"You believe me." It wasn't a question.

"Um, yeah, I guess I do." God help me, she thought. Next stop was the loony bin.

Nathaniel sucked in a hard breath and held it while he stared hard at her with rapt attention, like a starving man seeing food for the first time. He took her hand in his calloused palm. "Thank you. You honor me more than I deserve."

She squeezed it once. "You're welcome. So, what fruit do…er…did you like?"

"Currants."

Mel wrinkled her nose. "Alright, let's get some of those. What else?"

"We used to have apples. Oranges were very special, so I've only had them a few times before."

"Makes sense to me," she said, loading up the cart before she added some strawberries and a watermelon. Why not? She actually had someone to share it with for once.

"Alright, what about veggies?" She tossed a bowl of fruit salad into the cart as well. She couldn't help but smile when she envisioned him trying a kiwi for the first time. This might actually be kind of fun.

"Potatoes."

"Those are a starch, but yeah, okay."

"Carrots…" He rattled off a few more, all of which Mel grabbed and put into the cart.

"Okay, let's grab some meat and stuff."

Aside from her roommates in college and Abuelita, of course, who naturally had her own way of doing things, this was the first time Mel had been grocery shopping with another person—let alone a man. Maybe it was just because this particular man was enthralled with everything, but the experience was definitely a step up from her weekly pilgrimage to the figure-friendly, frozen microwave meal for one section, conveniently located near the ice cream.

When the two reached the meat section, Mel couldn't help but smile when Nathaniel almost walked into a display of day-old bread because he was too busy taking everything in to watch where he was going. She tossed some chicken, steaks, and a pork loin into the cart. Mel had some inkling on how to cook—she had been watching Abuelita for years—and besides, she had two degrees and a Wi-Fi connection. How hard could it be?

While they walked around the perimeter, Nathaniel kept asking where all of it came from and the agriculture of the modern age, which Mel could honestly say she hadn't thought much about.

The real fun started when they began going up and down the aisles.

Everything was fascinating to him. The soda aisle, which Mel had never paid much attention to, stopped Nathaniel in his tracks. He went from bottle to bottle to stare at the colors, asking her what the various ones were so much that for the first time since Mel had started watching her weight when she was in college, she plopped a multi-pack into the cart.

It was fun to treat someone other than herself. Seeing Nathaniel's wonder and interest was the most positive thing Mel had experienced in years, other than a client on his or her release day from jail.

Geez, she thought, doesn't sound too good when you put it that way.

The pair of them wound through the aisles, with Mel curating a cart of modern delicacies like Mac and Cheese, Oreos, Ruffles, Cheetos, Reese's Cups, and Ho Hos. In every aisle, Nathaniel wandered off and found something to study, even if it was just the packaging.

Meanwhile, Mel was having an absolute field day herself. It had been an age since she had bought the ingredients to make chocolate chip cookies and brownies.

Since she had been living alone, Mel had found that it

wasn't worth it or nearly as fun, though on occasion she fired up the microwave and "baked" one of the mug cookies or cakes. With a scoop of vanilla ice cream and a chick flick? That was her idea of heaven.

Walking toward the dairy section, Nathaniel's questions continued like an eager pupil. "How do the cows produce this much? How long does it last? How can they get this much? Are there more stores like this?"

"I've never seen a cow up close, so you're asking the wrong girl. I just buy it here and go by the date."

"The date?"

"See for yourself," she said, holding out the jug of milk.

"That's too long for milk," he said, frowning.

Mel shrugged as she pulled out some coffee creamers a couple of doors down. "I've never had a problem. Must be all the preservatives, I have no idea. I mean, you have to keep it cold, you know? Like you can't just let it sit out and expect it to last, that wouldn't work."

"That must be why they keep it cold," he said, looking back at all of the choices in the refrigerator.

"Yeah, that's a big part of it. What did you do before?"

Nathaniel looked at her for a second before he furrowed his brow, clearly going back in time. "We had a root cellar and a spring house. Those places were cool, but not like—" He nodded toward the glass doors next to them.

"Yeah, didn't think it would be. I think my grandmother used something like an icebox back in the day, but I don't know how that worked. I think it was kind of an in-between. Like the box was insulated, but you had to put the ice in, maybe? I don't know." Mel reached for a dozen eggs and checked the interior.

"Can you get ice?" Nathaniel hesitantly asked.

"Yeah," she said, distracted by the dozen eggs in her hand.

She thought better of it and traded the ones she had for the larger pack. It was funny, and not to mention more than a little sad, that she actually didn't know how much a man ate, but going by how Stella talked about her boyfriend, it apparently could be a lot. Abuelita surely would know, but Mel wasn't about to ask her. That conversation was a complication she definitely did not need.

"Sorry," she said with a wave of her hand. "Ice, yeah, I have an ice maker in my fridge. Why? You like it?"

"I've only had it twice."

"You can have as much as you want." They moved on with Mel grabbing a few things along the way; Nathaniel was still overwhelmed. "It refills automatically. I'll show you. Actually, it'd probably be good if you emptied it because now that I think of it, I never have, and I think you're supposed to at some point. Maybe it cleans it out or something? And before you ask me," she said, looking over at him, "I don't know how it works."

"But to get back to your question," she continued, "if you needed a lot of ice? You'd come here." She paused in front of the bags of ice stacked neatly behind the glass. "You can get it at any grocery store."

While he stared in wonder, the frozen food section beckoned to Mel with the bright lights and colorful packages.

"Have you ever heard of ice cream?" she asked Nathaniel, hoping it would be no, so she could really blow his mind. She felt herself deflate a little, though, when he started nodding.

"We didn't have it often, though."

"Well, be that as it may, I bet you don't know my two best friends, do you?"

When he solemnly shook his head, the innocence was so sweet that it almost physically hurt.

Mel resisted the urge to skip over to her favorite spot in the whole store. "Ta-da!" She stretched out her arms. "I give you"—she paused for effect, before saying in a voice filled with worship—"Ben and Jerry. You free tonight?" she whispered to the pints.

Nathaniel's face looked cautiously amused, as if he thought she might be joking, but wasn't sure what the joke was.

"It's literally the best ice cream I can get." Mel cranked open the door and grabbed her favorites without looking because hello? Muscle memory. "Now, you're never going to beat a good ice cream parlor, but this is pretty great stuff. We gotta move quick though because I don't want it to melt. Go ahead and pick out a few flavors while I stock up on some more cardboard for work." Mel grabbed a few of the microwave meals that didn't totally suck when she heard a swear before a hiss.

Without turning around or waiting for him to ask, she just said, "Called a freezer. Different from a fridge. Colder too, obviously."

Mel watched the frost form on her pints while Nathaniel agonized over the variety, before she finally jumped in to advise him. He liked nuts, so they headed to the checkout with some Everything but the..., Chunky Monkey—especially after he told her he didn't know what banana tasted like—and Chubby Hubby, which she had a feeling would be Nathaniel's favorite.

While he studied the magazines and the screen that did the math on its own, Mel had to admit that she herself was a little bit surprised as well. She watched the mountain of food —real, actual, honest-to-God food—go by on the belt and smiled to herself. This was the most food she had ever bought at the grocery store, so she and Nathaniel had that at least in common.

"Alrighty," she said, trying to inject confidence into her voice, when everything was bought and bagged. "Let's head home."

CHAPTER 16

As Mel drove the Civic full of food, Target bags, and one whole extra person, she wondered how the car had ever seemed large. She was also trying to shut up the voice in her head that still pointed out that this could be the worst and last mistake of her life.

Her eyes slid over to Nathaniel, who was analyzing the receipts like she had never seen before.

Mel thought through the idea of him in her apartment. Nathaniel was going to have to make do with the couch. Period. There was no way he was sleeping in her room. Conveniently, her bedroom door had a lock on it, so at least that was something. She'd also take her mace with her, so if something did go wrong quickly, she had some sort of defense with her.

After considering her immediate personal safety concerns, Mel wondered what she was going to make for dinner. She decided that some chicken was about the least complicated thing she could do, as was boiling a few potatoes and heating up some veggies.

Look out, Betty Crocker.

Then would it be ice cream and TV and bed, like always? Did that work with company? She didn't know. She had never had a guest.

Mel squeezed the steering wheel and focused on the road. She would not overreact just because this was the first person she'd ever had over to her apartment. Talk about no pressure to entertain, she thought, he'll probably spend an hour just looking at the ice maker. Easy peasy.

"So we'll need to put away the food first."

"Alright," he said when she parked the car outside her apartment complex.

Mel grabbed her keys and slid the mace into her purse. The two of them gathered up all of the bags and headed into the brick building. Once inside, Mel hit the lights and put the bags on the kitchen table, which thankfully was cleared off.

Nathaniel walked around the main room slowly, looking at her few items and pictures. Though Mel hated to admit it, having him in her space was unnerving, but not for the reasons she had expected.

For the first time, she noticed how tall he was, with such a broad chest. Even though the apartment had plenty of room, it seemed much smaller with him in it.

He stopped at her bookcase and read the titles, which ranged from some of her law books to photo albums to romance novels. While she grabbed the butter from the fridge, she noticed him pick up her Regency romance from the coffee table and read the cover and the first page before setting it back down.

"Is there anyone else here?" he asked.

The hairs on the back of her neck rose. "No one; it's just me," she said in what she hoped was a normal voice.

She didn't take her eyes off the chicken she was cutting up, but could tell he was looking at her. "Why?" she asked when he said nothing.

"You're a woman," he said. On instinct, Mel stiffened, bristling for a fight.

"And?" she said in a clipped tone.

"I thought you had your grandmother."

"I do, but she lives in a house nearby." Better to make it sound like she had someone she could call for help, just in case. Mel's grip on the chef's knife tightened. "It's just me."

"Miss Reyes—" he began.

"Mel," she said, cutting him off.

Nathaniel coughed. "Mel, I'm not sure I should be alone with you."

That probably was the smartest damn thing he could've said.

"Our professional relationship is over, so technically, I'm okay. However, I know I'm taking a risk. We're not romantically involved, and I have made it perfectly clear that you are free to leave as you wish." She threw the pan of chicken in the oven after hitting it with Abuelita's signature spice recommendation.

It turns out she knew a recipe, after all. Mel set the timer to what she thought was about right and dug in a drawer to get her thermometer, which she now realized was still in the unopened package.

"Besides," she continued, opening it up, "no one will know you're staying here, so I don't see it being an issue. My coworker always dates his former clients, and no one seems to notice him." When Nathaniel didn't speak, she paused and added, "Thank you for your concern, though."

Nathaniel stood awkwardly across from her. "Your professional life wasn't what I was talking about. I'm not sure my staying here is appropriate with you alone."

Mel frowned as she filled a pot of water and threw in some salt, like Abuelita always had. Of all the things he could worry about, she hadn't expected him to be concerned about propriety. "Nathaniel, that's nice of you, but women can live alone nowadays, and most even have their boyfriends over all the time or move in."

Nathaniel looked dubious.

"Go ahead and set your things down over there. Here…" She reached into a drawer to give him something to do. Mel held the scissors in her outstretched hand to him. "Take the tags off your clothes, and we can wash anything you have."

"That's very kind. It's too late for laundry, but maybe my undershirt—I can do it," he said quickly. Nathaniel held the Target bag containing his literal old clothes. Mel would've told him where he could burn that shirt, but she was really trying hard to be a good hostess.

"Just throw it next to the washer. It's behind the door next to the linen closet." Not wanting to touch the fabric, which straight-up reeked, she said, "Here, just throw it in there and I'll show you how it works."

Mel watched him put in the tattered cloth, which looked like fine linen. Nathaniel jumped when the lights and music came on.

Mel laughed. "It's okay, I did the same thing when I first got it. When it's done, it'll play a little song. You can watch it if you like," she said, amused when he did just that.

When the water started to pour in, Nathaniel jumped a bit and leaned in, transfixed as the machine began to spin, tossing the sorry excuse for a shirt around.

"This is incredible," he said to himself.

"Yeah, too bad they don't have one for folding yet." A hiss came from the top of the stove as the potatoes boiled over, and Mel ran back to turn down the heat.

"Does it rinse it too?"

"Yep, all automatic." She mopped up the spill, which had given the kitchen a warm smell of chicken and boiled potatoes, making her stomach growl. "Then it wrings it out, so it'll be damp when I throw it up top into the dryer."

"How does it dry the clothes?" Nathaniel asked, sitting in front of the machine, his eyes following the pitiful wet rag.

"Hot air, and it just spins around," Mel called out over the sound of the pots and pans she was wrangling. They were all stacked so high that eventually, she muttered, "The hell with it," under her breath. She threw some chopped veggies in with the chicken after she stirred and flipped it. Boom, one less pot to clean, she thought as she threw it back into the oven to finish.

With everything cooking away, she propped a hip on the counter and watched Nathaniel for a moment. He sat mesmerized by the spinning like a seven-year-old. There was a whisper of a little grin on his face that she could make out at the corners of his mouth.

Yeah, she thought, she didn't need to worry about entertaining him.

Mel tested a potato and found it soft, so she quickly set the table and tried not to smile too much because this was the first time she was eating at it. It was a momentous occasion.

"What do you want to drink?" she called over.

"I'm not quite sure what to ask for."

"Fair point, I guess. Well, do you want to try one of your sodas?"

Nathaniel tore himself away from the greatest show on earth and stood next to the table, as if unsure of what to do next.

"Soda?" she said again, holding up the cans. When he nodded, she asked, "What about ice?"

He smiled a small smile that made his eyes crinkle and came forward to see how it worked.

"So yeah," she said, handing him a can and the glass of ice, "it makes ice automatically. I think it's almost standard now, but some people still have to make it by hand. Here you go."

"Thank you." He shook the glass, hearing the ice rattle, before he began to read the outside of the can. Mel brought the pan of chicken and set it down on the table next to the bowl of boiled potatoes. She looked around to see what was missing and snagged the butter for her potatoes before sitting down and choosing a Cherry Coke.

Nathaniel was focused on the can, his eyes squinting just a little bit at the fine print.

"Do you wear glasses?" Mel asked.

"No," he said, still squinting. "I can read fine, but this lettering is so small."

"Oh, the ingredients? Yeah, it's all chemicals anyway." Mel buttered her potatoes before handing the dish over to him. "I don't know, but you might need some reading glasses."

"I can read fine enough."

"Except when it's small, though, right?"

He nodded with a furrowed brow and held the can out a little farther while he continued to labor over the lengthy list of chemicals that she couldn't pronounce.

"What about that book you were reading?" she asked, cutting up her chicken. "The history one. Could you read that okay?"

"I took my time, but I could make it out fine."

It was fuzzy, but he had been determined. Mel got it. She made a mental note to look into getting him some readers.

She reached over and popped the top of her Cherry Coke, pouring it into the glass of ice she had brought herself. Nathaniel's eyes had flicked over when he heard the pop before he looked at the pull tab of his can.

"Did you have cans like this before?"

He nodded, working to pull it up with his thumbnail. "Yes, but not this little bit on the top—" The hiss came before the pop and foam erupted from the top of the can. He swore and jumped out of the chair with the can held aloft.

Mel popped up to grab a dish towel. "No big deal," she said, mopping up the spill. She handed Nathaniel the towel, and he wiped the can clean. "To be honest with you, that happens to all of us once in a while. If you shake the can, the pressure builds," she said, making a circle with her finger in the can's direction. "That happens. It's fizzy."

Nathaniel tasted the plain Coca-Cola she had chosen for him and coughed a bit before burping. He blinked a few times and set it down. "That's"—he coughed again—"different from what I was expecting."

"You don't like it?"

"I don't know. I think I do."

Nathaniel tucked his napkin into his collar and fiddled with it until it stayed in his T-shirt before digging in and eating with almost dainty table manners, wiping his mouth frequently as he went. Mel had never considered herself a slob, but she was now having second thoughts in comparison.

He ate differently too. With every bit of food he cut, he slid his fork onto his knife before bringing it to his mouth. Almost backward from herself, but it wasn't sloppy—quite the opposite.

She took another bite of chicken and savored the flavor. While not Abuelita's—but nothing could compare to that, honestly—she had to admit it was pretty good. Pleased with herself, she ate more.

"This is far superior to what I had in jail."

Mel barked out a laugh. "So my food is better than prison cooking? Great."

Nathaniel looked at her, confused, while she giggled away.

"It is," he maintained. "I thought that food tasted good, but this is much more."

"No," she said between laughs, trying to catch her breath. "That's not really a compliment. Prison food is horrible. At least everyone says so."

"Those people mustn't have been in the army," he muttered before taking another bite.

Mel cracked up again. "That's pretty funny."

"Well, this is truly delicious."

"Thanks. I don't normally cook, but I have a few tricks up my sleeve."

Nathaniel wiped his mouth again and said, "You have many talents."

Mel smiled, but didn't answer. She felt her cheeks go a little pink. It pleased her to know she impressed him.

"You practice law, can drive, do laundry, and cook. All in one night."

"What did it used to be like?" she asked.

"Different."

"Okaaaay." Mel waved her hand in a circle to urge him on. "Like how? Okay, how did you do laundry?"

Nathaniel ate some more potatoes and wiped his mouth again. "Scrub out any stains, boil the whites, and leave out to dry. That sort of thing."

"Sounds about the same."

"It's getting the water that was the real challenge."

"Oh, yeah, I guess so. Forgot about that. What else is different?"

Nathaniel smiled and shook his head. "Almost everything."

They chatted while they finished dinner. Nathaniel helped Mel load the dishes into the dishwasher while asking her questions for which she didn't know the answers.

"How does it work? Where does the water come from? Where do the pipes come from?"

He was fascinated by everything. When she went to grab the ice cream from the freezer, he looked closer at the ice maker's mechanics until Mel handed him a spoon and the pint of Chubby Hubby.

"Enjoy," she said over her shoulder as she and Cherry Garcia headed to the couch, where she flopped down with the remote.

Nathaniel came and sat on the love seat, watching her TV with keen interest.

"So you haven't seen much besides the weather, right?" she asked, trying to fill the void and remember how to entertain someone.

"They had news," he said, opening the lid to his pint, just as she had done. It was unnerving, almost like having someone copy every movement she made.

"I like sitcoms, romance movies, and happy stuff." Mel took a bite of Cherry Garcia and tasted the sweet chocolate-cherry flavor. God, she hoped they served this in heaven.

"There are all sorts of things to watch, you know? Cop stories, scary movies, crap reality shows, but for me? I like to keep things light. Maybe it's my job, but when I come home, I'm really just looking to veg."

Nathaniel observed her, but said nothing.

"That didn't make a damn bit of sense to you, did it?"

He tried to hide his smile, but she was too quick. After all, it was her job to notice details. "My job can be tough sometimes."

"I know. It's honorable work to defend those in need."

"It is," she admitted. "That's what I love about it. Abuelita, my grandmother, always says how much more money I could make, but it isn't about that for me." She took another bite. "Anyway, sometimes the job is exhausting and frustrating, so when I come home, I just want to—"

She didn't know how to say it. Chill? Have some downtime? Watch TV until her eyes drooped in the blue light from the screen? Forget about the real world for a few hours?

"Rest," Nathaniel said, nodding. "I remember. I didn't do the same work, but I remember the profession's demands regardless of who my client was. At times, after reading and preparing for hours, all I wanted to do was rest."

Mel sat watching TV on mute. It was a commercial for a vacation package with a fake model couple dancing in the surf, clearly pretending to look in love.

"John Adams was a lawyer, right?"

Nathaniel nodded. "He defended Captain Thomas Preston and the others in the Boston incident."

Mel frowned and took another bite. "Oh, I hadn't realized that."

"You should try your ice cream before it melts," she pointed out before taking another bite. Nathaniel and she both finished their ice cream. Of course, he loved it and settled in to watch TV, absorbing everything.

Mel couldn't stop herself from yawning. "Here's the remote. You change the channel like this... Yeah, you got it. Just keep going until you find something you want to watch. I'm going to... Well, I'll be right back."

Nathaniel nodded and began flipping from channel to channel. He looked like a regular guy, almost making her panic. What in the hell did she think she was doing? This guy had just left prison this morning, and not only was it bad enough that she had purchased him clothing and driven him around, but he was sitting in her freaking apartment, eating ice cream on her freaking couch.

She tried to tell her logical, good-girl side to calm down

by reviewing the day's events and pointing out to herself that nothing threatening had happened all day and that she believed he was actually lost in time. All aboard the crazy train!

Alright, she thought, when her anxiety started to spike, it was time to go to bed. She could drop him off at the shelter tomorrow if she wanted to. None of this was permanent.

She looked back over at him, as he studied the screen intently in his blue T-shirt, and realized she wasn't afraid. She was enjoying her time with him.

"You can watch as long as you want. It won't bother me, but I'm going to get ready for bed." Mel grabbed the pillow and the spare set of sheets out of the linen closet. Returning to the couch, she made a bed and got him a blanket, taking care to smooth everything out and make it presentable.

"Thank you for making me a bed," he said quietly.

"It's nothing, really. I'm sorry, I didn't think to get an air mattress."

"Thank you for everything," he said again in an even softer voice.

"Ahh…you're welcome." She wished taking compliments and thank yous came more naturally to her.

"Nathaniel, I hate to ask, but before you change into your pajamas and go to sleep—"

He looked up, blue eyes bright with emotion, a yearning to act. "Yes? What can I do for you?"

Crap, why was this so difficult? It wasn't that she didn't trust him, but at the end of the day, she didn't know him well, and they were alone. Mel refused to feel any guilt.

"Nathaniel, I'm sorry, but I know you have a knife and firearm with you right now…"

She let out a breath of air when he nodded, but then stopped as he turned to get it.

"Here. You take them. You can keep them, as payment." Nathaniel patted his chest and looked around before diving for his old coat. "You said that old guns are worth something. And here, take the pocket watch for when you start to doubt."

"Oh, no. No, it isn't that."

"I want to pay you. I mean to really—"

"You really don't need to. I was going to ask to keep them in my room." She paused. "I think it might make me feel, ah…"—she cleared her throat, suddenly awkward, which was unusual for her—"more comfortable, I guess."

Clarity dawned in his eyes, and he inclined his head to her. "You will not need to fear me or anything while I am near you. Ever. I swear."

Mel took both from him and almost dropped the gun from the weight when Nathaniel took his hand away. "Ah—thank you," she said quietly. I'll just…" She gestured to her bedroom door. When he nodded, she laid the gun on her nightstand before coming back out.

"I have to work in the morning, so I'll need the shower."

Nathaniel nodded again and waited for her to say more.

"So if you want to use the shower, tonight's probably a good time. Oh, and I was thinking that I can drop you off at the library tomorrow while I'm at work. If you'd like that, I mean."

"That would be generous of you."

"Yeah, sure. I mean no big. It's on my way and every-thing." God, why was this so awkward?

Because she was making it awkward, duh.

"Alright, well, let me know if you need anything. The plaid pants are pajamas. Good night."

He inclined his head a little toward her with a smile.

"Good night, Miss Reyes."

Mel could hear Nathaniel heading into the bathroom as she closed the door behind her. She stopped at the edge of her bed and fell onto the pillow. As she stared at the array of Revolutionary War weapons on her nightstand and listened to a man in her shower, she closed her eyes and wondered how her life could've changed so much in one day.

The morning routine had been much like the army, though without having to tend to the horses. Mel had woken up in a frenzy and ran right into the shower. While she was there, he had walked to the kitchen and found a frying pan. The fire had taken some time to start, but thankfully, the instructions were printed right on the equipment. A leftover potato was in the fridge, along with a pack of something that looked like fatback, and a couple of eggs. Nathaniel cooked the fat first, then the potatoes, and finished with the eggs. He had been trying to figure out the coffee maker when Mel came out, wrapped in a towel, with another on her head, holding her hair.

When he saw her standing there with water droplets still on her skin, he was so stunned that he dropped the forks he was holding.

Mel crouched down and gathered them up. Nathaniel stood frozen to the spot, drinking in the sight of her shoulders and neck. "Are you good? It's gas, but it looks like you got it already. You're a quick learner. Wait, is that bacon too? Oh my God, thank you. You didn't have to cook for me."

"There are eggs and some potatoes too."

"Thank you so much. I meant to get up earlier, but the alarm… Doesn't matter. Thank you. Oh crap, I didn't even think to make the coffee." Mel reached over, still in her towels, and the smell drifted through the room in seconds.

Nathaniel couldn't help but stare at the perfect skin of her back and how her shoulders moved underneath. A dark lock of hair had escaped the towel and trailed down her neck. He could make out the curve of her hip, see her legs, feet, and toes, which were smooth and perfect.

"Cups, cups." Mel reached into a cabinet, and the towel inched higher on her slim thighs. "Alright, there we are. Let me get some plates." When she turned, the towel wrapped around her split and threatened to fall.

He couldn't take much more. "Why don't you get dressed and I set the table?"

Her dark eyes turned up to him. "Nathaniel, I can't thank you enough. I'll get dressed real quick and be right back." It wasn't until she scooted off into her bedroom and he heard the door click behind her that Nathaniel released the breath he had been holding.

Minutes later, the Mel he knew came out dressed in another black dress with her hair back, framing her face. There was something on her face that made her eyes different from before. Her lashes were darker, and overall the appearance made her more fearsome, but he had seen the fresh-faced beauty a moment ago, and wasn't likely to forget it soon. Propriety be damned. He had seen Miss Reyes with new eyes and enjoyed the view.

"Okay, you have my phone number, right?" Mel asked Nathaniel when they were downstairs getting into the car.

"Yes, I have it here." He patted his pocket in his new trousers.

"Okay, good. I'll be in the office for the morning, and

maybe in the afternoon too. I dunno. I want to go in to see some clients face-to-face, but it'll depend on whether I can get through some crap first. Alright, there it is. That building right there is the library."

It was a large building, that had more glass than he had expected.

"Okay, you won't have a card, but"—she dug around in her large black bag before handing him a card, that was stronger than paper—"here's mine, so you can get any books you want. They have chairs, and yeah, okay, I'm rambling again.

"Remember, if you need me, ask for the telephone and dial that number. What else, what else? Oh yeah, lunch."

Nathaniel was about to tell her not to worry. The food he had heated this morning was more than he had eaten on campaign on a good day toward the end, but she shoved some bills into his hand. "Look, I think there are a couple of places to get food nearby, and this will be plenty."

"Mel, this isn't necessary. I'll be interested enough in the books."

"Well, here you go anyway. I need to go; I'm late."

He got out of the car and turned to wave her off. "You're sure you'll be okay?" she asked now.

Nathaniel smiled at her concern. She was a stunning beauty with a razor-sharp wit and a caring heart. "I'll be right here."

"I'll be back later," she called out as she drove away.

Nathaniel watched her drive away while he held the money and card. He was taken aback by her kindness and fussing. It warmed him that she cared about him. He looked down and folded the money carefully before tucking it into his pocket with her card and the one he had taken from the coffee shop the day earlier.

The air felt cool and light as he walked in and looked

around. Inside the door was a board with bright pieces of paper all tacked up, advertising different events. This library, like the one in the jail, had a book club, along with a knitting club, dances, movie nights, English classes, lectures, and concerts. A bookcase filled with a rainbow of books, all different sizes and colors, sat next to the board with a sign above advertising each as twenty-five cents for a paperback, and fifty cents for a hardback.

Finally, some prices with which he was familiar. Nathaniel read the title of each one before heading farther in through the second set of doors.

Inside, the library was similar to the jail library, but it was bigger, brighter, and the shelves were fuller and taller. The ceiling stretched above him, and windows in the roof showed the clouds lazily floating in the sun's wake. Down below, stacks of books stood in perfect rows of shelves in a clean room, lined with tables and chairs. A few women sat at a desk, while others sat at screens like they had at the jail.

"Excuse me," he said to the lady with blonde hair that reminded him of Emma and a pink, flowery top, which he somehow knew Mel would never wear.

"Yes, sir, how can I help you today?"

"I've never been to this library, and I'd like to see your books on history."

"Okay. Any particular period?"

"After 1776, please. If you have it, that is."

She looked at her screen and adjusted her bright red glasses before beginning to type, as Mel had called it, onto a pad with letters. "World or US?" she asked without look-ing up.

"Both, if you please."

"Anything else to narrow it down? We have over three thousand books that meet that criteria." She looked at him now through her red-framed glasses.

"I guess introductory books, please."

Minutes later, when he walked over to the section, the librarian pulled various titles and handed them all to him. Before Nathaniel knew it, he was sitting at a large table with a stack of books he could hide behind.

Determined because, after all, there was a lot he needed to catch up on, Nathaniel grabbed the top one and opened it to the first page.

"You just get in?"

Mel looked up at Stella, who looked gorgeous as always. Stella was a beautiful former basketball player—long and lean, with hair so light it could almost pass for white. Blue eyes and a figure that wouldn't quit, matched with an impeccable wardrobe, made Stella a total knockout. All the men were in love with her, but Stella didn't notice, and if she did, she didn't care.

Stella had a boyfriend named Stan from the IT department, who was about as remarkable as a doorknob. They didn't look like a typical couple, and Mel knew the men all said that Stella was way too hot for Stan—that they couldn't see what she saw in him—but again Stella didn't care. Stan was sweet to her, and she liked him.

"Yeah, I had a headache again. Headed home to get ahead of it."

"You should do that more. You've been getting them a lot."

"It's this damn heat. Why does everyone love the summer so much? Like, what in the hell is wrong with winter?"

"It's cold and the crap snow gets everywhere, making it impossible for normal people to drive while the idiots are all out and about."

"Yeah, I know, but besides all that. There aren't allergies, and my hair actually cooperates. Plus, it isn't as hot as hell," Mel pointed out while pulling files she hadn't touched out of her bag and onto her desk.

"The holidays don't give you a headache?" Stella asked with her arms folded, leaning on the doorjamb.

Mel stopped what she was doing and pointed in Stella's direction. "Touché, but I don't have that many people to buy for."

"I like it when summer rolls around. Great beach weather."

"I can't tell you the last time I've been to the beach," Mel said, returning to slapping piles of folders every which way, trying to find the case she needed.

"Well, that right there is your problem," Stella said, not missing a beat. "Summer without vacation is a bitch."

"I agree."

"Well, why don't you go somewhere? I was so shocked I almost dropped my phone when you said you were taking a half day."

"Maybe. Hey, let me ask you something."

"Shoot."

Mel picked up a pen and flicked it around, not wanting to make eye contact. "How much does Stan eat?"

Stella arched one perfect eyebrow before tucking one corner of her mouth back into a smirk.

"How do you mean?" she asked with a quiet smile.

"Like, you know, food and shit."

"Are you going to ask me for recipes for two in a minute?"

Mel just looked at her. It was their preferred form of communication when they couldn't confirm or deny.

A slow smile spread across her face. "Nice to see you have a hobby. I'll send you an email with some, you know, to have," she added with a wink.

"Thanks." She could feel her cheeks heating with the pressure. Just coming out of her bathroom and seeing him cooking at her stove sent her reeling. He was a lot more attractive now that he was cleaned up and had filled out a bit. Of course, the normal clothes helped too. Also, she had been so nervous about dropping him off at the library. It wasn't like he was a kid who could wander off. If he did walk off, that wasn't her problem, so why was she so worried about him?

"Sure thing, and yeah, to answer your question, more than me, and he never gains a pound."

"Ass," Mel joked and rolled her eyes.

Stella sighed dramatically. "He has a great one too."

"Okay. TMI." Picturing Stan's ass under his baggy Dockers was enough to give her an eye twitch, and with Nathaniel haunting the back of her mind, she didn't need the help.

"By the way, did you get the reports I sent over?"

"Yeah, thanks. Just what I needed."

"You haven't read them yet." It was a statement, not a question.

Damn, Stella was good. Not that Mel had ever questioned her reports, but now she knew just how spot-on they were.

When Mel didn't confirm or deny, Stella's eyes sparked again as she slowly smirked and raised her eyebrow. "Must've been some headache."

"It wasn't like that," Mel muttered under her breath.

"Well, I'm happy for you. It's about time." Stella tilted her head toward the files. "Let me know if you have any questions when you read them," she tossed over her shoulder as she turned.

Mel spent the next few hours working through some new cases and prepping her other ones for court. Her mind kept wandering to Nathaniel and what he was doing. She had never found it hard to focus at work before, and this experience was a frustrating distraction. She would be reading along until she came to a word that made her think of him, and before she knew it, she was wondering what he was up to.

She was drumming her pen on her legal pad, trying not to think about time travel, when Patrick stuck his head around the corner. "Hey, there you are."

She jumped as if she had done something wrong, and dropped the pen in the move. "Hey, what's up?"

"Are you alright? I almost called you last night to check in." Patrick slid into her office again. Today, he was wearing a light-blue shirt with some sort of small pattern and blue pants. He looked good, if you could see through the cloud of cologne around him.

"Just a headache. Happens," she said, turning to log into her computer as if she hadn't been caught daydreaming. Was she really that much of a workaholic that one half day had people checking in on her? At least Tabby had responded to the email request with a polite, professional approval, that included well-wishes.

"Anything I can do to help you catch up?"

Mel shrugged and waved her hand over her desk as if the piles were evidence enough.

Patrick came farther inside and picked up her pen cup from college, studying it. "Tell me about it. My desk is covered too."

She gave him a tight smile and kept typing, mentally telling him to go away.

He didn't.

"Yeah, I'm starting to wonder what's next for me now."

That got her attention. Mel paused her typing just long enough to glance at him.

"Really?"

He nodded and closed the door before sitting down in the crap chair across from her desk.

"Been here six years." Patrick propped up his elbow and rested his head on his hand. "Longest I've been in a job. Until now, I moved every four. Kept it fresh."

"What made you stay here so long?"

"I dunno." He shifted into her chair. "The work is challenging enough. Plus, I guess the people are okay. Present company included." Patrick shot a meaningful look her way, which she did not return.

"Uh-huh."

He let out a laugh. "Worth a shot. No, I guess it's been an interesting ride, but"—he shrugged—"we'll see what happens."

"Looking anywhere else?"

"Keeping an ear to the ground with what's happening in Manhattan at a few firms. Like I said, we'll see."

She wanted to ask whose ass he was kissing this time, but thankfully it came out as, "Good luck. I hope you find what you're looking for."

"Appreciate it. You know, I could keep an eye out for you. Put in a good word and all that. I do know a lot of people who have already made partner."

"Thanks. Listen, Patrick, I need to catch up…"

That did the trick. He was leaving. "No worries, I need to catch up too. See ya later, Mel." And with that, all that remained was the lingering stench of trying too hard.

She finished up a large part of the to-do list that was starting to get away from her, and was leaving for the night when she walked by Tabby's open door.

"Hey," she said, poking her head inside.

Tabby was sitting at a desk, peering at her multiple screens. Her silver bob, normally styled in curls around her face, was tossed up into a haphazard clip with tendrils jutting out everywhere.

"Hey, Mel. Feeling better?" Tabby asked, looking up. She smiled with warmth but looked exhausted.

"I am. Thanks again for being so cool about it."

Tabby waved her hand. "You have tons of leave, and we all need to be careful not to burn out. I might need to take a day here in a bit. I'm can't tell if I'm losing my edge or my mind."

Mel could see that. Tabby was neat, and always the model of decorum, but her jacket was tossed into the guest chair, and there were piles of papers on the floor.

"Is there anything I can help with?"

Tabby sat back and took off her tortoiseshell glasses and shook her head. Everyone knew she had been pulling data and sources for months on this investigation, but she never had shared details. "You have enough on your plate already. Thanks, though, for offering. You're a real one."

If anyone was real, it was her. Tabby truly believed in the mission and wanted to help the clients they represented. She never lost her vision for the practice and hadn't slid into the temptation of larger firms promising bigger pay. Some said she had a family member who struggled with addiction and got into trouble, but no one knew for sure what drove her, and Tabby was too professional to comment on her own personal life in the office. She had an open door policy for all staff, but never passed down her own burdens. She was a true leader.

"Alright, well, let me know if that changes, and try not to stay too late."

Tabby smiled and put her glasses back on. "Will do. Go get some rest, Mel. Have a good night."

Mel smiled and left, thinking that for the first time, she was indeed looking forward to another good night.

CHAPTER 19

Mel pushed through the door of her office and was almost knocked flat by the wall of sticky heat outside.

It was later in the day than she wanted to leave—thank you, surprise meetings—and she juggled her oversized bag while digging out her car keys. Of course they were at the bottom. They were always at the bottom. Right along with the can of mace and a rogue steak knife from last night that managed to just miss her hand when she was looking for a pen.

She eyed the clock and felt crappy that Nathaniel had been waiting on her. Hopefully, he had found a book to get into at least.

Though she hated to admit it, getting through the day without thinking of Nathaniel had been impossible. Everything had reminded her of him, but then again having a man in her house for the weekend was not just new territory, it was another solar system. When she had used a pen after the near stabbing incident, she wondered what he would think of the pen. Bagels had been ordered for the meeting—a sure sign it was going to be a long one—and Mel wondered if he had heard of them, or cream cheese for that matter.

Every bit of the day had some thought connected to him. Was this what it was like for couples? Always thinking about each other? Shit, when she typed an email to Stella, her eye twitched at the thought of Stella thinking about Stan's ass. Nope. Not going there. It was too much, and besides, she and Nathaniel were definitely not a thing.

He was more like a roommate or a big puppy she had picked up on the way home.

In no time she was pulling in front of the library, which looked to be just closing. Mel pulled up and jogged in to find Nathaniel.

She hadn't been inside this branch since getting a card when she had moved into her apartment. Mel loved to read —when she had the time—but she was more of the type to buy books. She liked to own a piece of them.

In the back of the stacks, Nathaniel was sitting in a chair reading with his eyes slightly narrowed, by a little table that held a small stack of books.

"There you are," she said, both excited and relieved.

He looked up and gave her a smile when he stood as she walked up. "How was your day?"

"Ugh. It was okay, I guess. Nothing too crazy. What about you? Do you need to check those out?"

"No, I already spoke with the woman at the desk over there. They were helpful in getting me a"—he waved a hand over the mountain of books—"small selection."

"Are you a fast reader?"

"Not fast enough. Although, I'm almost finished with one."

"In my book, that's pretty fast."

They gathered up the books and left, just before the librarians locked the doors behind them. Mel fought the traffic on the way home, while Nathaniel asked her a few questions on the Civil War and then the Great Depression.

"It's hard to imagine how that much money can—" Words failed him.

"Vanish? To be honest I never understood that concept myself, but I think it has to do with inflation and people buying more than they actually could afford. Maybe on credit? Like I said, I know more about recent history."

"All of it is recent to me."

"I'm talking post-World War II."

"1945."

She really didn't want to get into more history conversations, but didn't have much of a choice as Nathaniel was brimming with his new knowledge that he had learned from the book.

Changing the subject, she asked, "What do you want to do for dinner tonight?"

"Anything you serve will be more than welcome," Nathaniel said. "Do you know a lot about the moon?"

"Uh, yeah, kinda, I guess."

"No, the astronauts." Nathaniel said the last word slowly, emphasizing each syllable as he tested it out on his tongue.

"Oh, like the moon landing? Oh yeah, everyone knows about that except the weirdos who think it didn't happen." Mel rolled her eyes. "It's crazy to think, isn't it?"

"I looked at the moon growing up as a child and always wondered about it."

Mel looked out at the setting sun on their drive back to the apartment. "I think we all did that as kids." She let out a laugh. "I still do it as an adult."

"Really?"

"Yeah, one year for Christmas I begged Abuelita to get a telescope. Do you know what that is? Okay, yeah, good. Well, I wanted one and not a toy. I wanted the real deal."

"Did you get it?"

Mel smiled to herself. "After Abuelita played me, like always. Fixed income, not a lot of money, had to give tithes to the church—why couldn't I ask for something else like a pretty dress?" She rolled her eyes again. "But Abuelita always put my education ahead of everything else. She was big on me studying math and science. Whatever I wanted to do, she was behind me."

"That's wonderful for a young girl."

"Abuelita is the greatest, but yeah… So on Christmas morning, I came down not expecting my telescope and I had even made my peace with it. Abuelita had pointed out we didn't have a lot of extra money, and they were very expensive, and one day if I saved enough, blah-blah-blah."

Mel slowed to let a woman running with her dog cross the street at a four-way stop before continuing on their commute. "So I come down the stairs, right? And there's this big box, so I get all excited and rush over, tearing the paper left and right only to find out it's new school clothes. Whomp whomp."

Nathaniel smiled at her. "But there was more?"

"Right. So Abuelita came down and was making her coffee and asked me how I liked my Christmas present, so you know I told her they were great and thanked her. So she says you're welcome and then—this is the best part—the woman goes to sit in her recliner, like a big comfortable chair that supports your legs," she added when Nathaniel frowned at the word, clearly not understanding it. "Anyway, so she sits down and goes to lean back when she notices there's something behind her and gets all upset." Mel smiled at him now. "She's such a good actor. Yeah, so she was fussing about how something fell back behind and how she bet it was the wonky angel—she has like two dozen at least that she puts on the mantel and one never sits quite right—

so she has me climb back there to look and boom, there it was."

Nathaniel was smiling broadly now. "She fooled you then?"

"It's ridiculous because she played this game almost every year while I was growing up."

"Did you always get what you wanted?"

"I don't know how, but yeah, Abuelita always made it work, so I guess all of this is to say, yeah, I'm into the moon."

"I read that chapter twice before I went up to the ladies and asked for books on the moon landing."

"Then you probably know more than me. I know the Apollo missions and about the Challenger—that was horrible, but there's a bunch more. There's a Mercury, I think?"

"I can't believe it."

"I recall saying something like that recently," Mel pointed out.

Nathaniel laughed. "I've looked at the stars my whole life, and now I'm living in an age where there are people up in space right now. Above us at this moment."

"Yeah, it's wild."

"When I saw the picture of the Earth—the one taken from the window of Apollo Eight—I couldn't stop staring at it."

"That's the one that is the whole Earth, right?" Mel asked, trying to remember which one he was talking about.

"No, I saw that one on the next page." Nathaniel paused before whispering, "I never knew how beautiful this planet was."

Mel pulled into a parking space and pulled the key out of the ignition.

Neither of them moved.

"I grew up with that picture. Saw it in my books and classrooms," she said finally. "I guess I always assumed, you know…" She looked out at the sky. The colors reminded her of a peach that was beginning to darken, but it would be hours before the stars would be visible. "I can't imagine not knowing what Earth looked like."

Nathaniel sat there and smiled. "I don't know how to explain what it was like. I guess...I guess we just wondered."

As Mel sat and watched him pull out a book and flip to the exact picture they were discussing, she came up with one heck of an idea.

The next morning was pretty chill, as Mel had slept late. She and Nathaniel had spent the night before eating spaghetti, talking about different points in the 20th century that he had learned about in his book, before settling in with Ben and Jerry's and watching *Close Encounters of the Third Kind*. After all, it was a classic, and matched the theme of the night's talks.

Mel had kept having to explain to Nathaniel which parts were fictionalized and which parts were actually reality, like all of the lost people to whom he related.

"So they all got to go back?" he had asked.

"Yep, I guess so," she answered, thinking that maybe this was a bit of an insensitive choice, since she hadn't put two and two together.

At the end of the movie and before they had gone to bed, Nathaniel had quietly asked, "Do you think there are more like me? And that I'll get to go back? That pilot came back from World War Two thirty years later."

"I honestly don't know," she said, tossing the spoons in the sink. "People go missing, and some are found, but they haven't traveled in time."

The thought had kept them both up. When Mel had said good night, locking the door with her shoebox tower, she laid down on the pillow and thought about what he had asked. Apparently, she wasn't the only one thinking because after an hour of tossing and turning, she could see the light still on in the living room, before she finally fell asleep.

Now the sun blazed into her room followed closely by the beautiful smell of coffee and breakfast. That was a nice perk, she thought, pulling on a thin college T-shirt and shorts to venture out.

Nathaniel was leaning against the countertop fully dressed and shaved, with a book in one hand and a spatula in the other.

"Good morning," he said when he saw her. "I hope it's okay, but I made more eggs because you liked them yesterday."

Because she liked them. He was so eager to please and looked genuinely happy there was something he could do for her. Maybe she should delegate dinner to him as well.

He broke out in a broad grin, before pouring some egg mixture into a hot skillet with a sizzle. "There's coffee too." He looked particularly pleased that he was able to work her machine with her quick lesson yesterday.

Looking around, she saw he had again rolled up his sheets and blanket in a peculiar, but neat way before he set them aside on the floor next to his folded new clothes as well as the bag of his other clothes, that didn't reek so much after he had asked to air them out yesterday. Not wanting anyone to see old clothes hanging out on the balcony all day, Mel had tossed the clothes in the dryer with half a box of dryer sheets, which seemed to do the trick.

He served her eggs and a piece of toasted bread onto the plate. While she had never before considered that living with a man could be anything other than a colossal pain in the ass, she now was beginning to see the upside. Mel added a few more things to her growing list of stuff to ask Stella about.

"Thanks for making me breakfast again," Mel said in between bites. "Where'd you learn to cook so well?"

Nathaniel shrugged before he sat next to her and picked up a piece of fried bread that he slathered with butter. "Army." He chewed and swallowed. "But we didn't have a lot of provisions like here. I never got to cook much back home."

"Well, you're doing a great job."

He smiled down at his plate, and she wasn't sure, but she thought there was a tinge of pink on his cheeks.

Once the plates were cleared, Mel hit the shower and thought of her little surprise for Nathaniel, who was sitting on her couch again engulfed in one of his books on space. Over the dishes, he had let her know that he already finished one of his big history books and now was getting more into the specific subjects, one of which was conveniently the middle of the twentieth century.

Boy was he in for a kick-ass day, she thought to herself and smiled as she dressed.

And that wasn't the only surprise she had in store for him. She didn't know why, but showing him new things gave her so much joy.

She watched him descend down the steps to the subway station, looking at the turnstiles with a mixture of bewilderment and awe as people went around him to the left and right, wrapped in their own world. She reached out and tugged his hand forward through the turnstile as she paid with her phone. All of it amazed him.

The signature screech of the train was the warning before a blast of hot air pushed through the station. Nathaniel jumped back half a step when the out-of-service train didn't stop.

"Don't cross the yellow," she said as an afterthought.

"Clearly."

They boarded the express A train and sat next to each other, Nathaniel's head swiveling from staring out the window to looking at the people on board, before jumping every time the intercom announced the next station.

They made it to 42nd Street and had a few blocks to walk, while Nathaniel peppered her with questions about the engineering and history, which sadly she didn't know. Disappointed with her lack of interest in the clearly amazing infrastructure of the city, Nathaniel trailed behind, almost knocking into a woman and her kid when he was staring up so much at the tall buildings of Manhattan. She knew he'd be asking her about skyscrapers soon.

"Watch out," she said, when he almost walked into an overflowing trash can, and then over a subway vent.

"You can hear it!" he said, his face full of glee.

He looked like a little kid, so excited to be making sense of the world around him.

"Only a few blocks more."

"It feels like rain."

"No, that's just the air conditioning units above you."

He craned his neck up again to look at the little boxes.

"Don't worry about that. You're going to love this," she said, grabbing his hand to walk toward their destination.

Mel could now see ahead to the telltale span of open sky as they headed toward the Upper Bay where *The Intrepid* and the space surprise lay waiting.

She walked around the final corner and sang, "Heeeere we arrrrre!"

"Where—" Nathaniel turned to see the large battleship in the water. His eyes lit up at the historic future in front of him.

"Surprise! Come on, let's get inside." She couldn't wait until he realized the space shuttle *Enterprise* was inside.

CHAPTER 20

The next morning, when Mel cracked open her lids, sunlight blinded her. God, how did she sleep so late? Maybe it was because she and Nathaniel walked all over the entire museum yesterday, twice. She had been so tired that she had barely said good night.

They had walked through the entire first floor, and he stopped to read everything, so Mel broke off to get a coffee and browse in the gift shop. Everything was new and fascinating. All of the technology amused him and was explained in such a way that the children running around with their parents could understand, so Nathaniel could pick things up easily. One such exhibit was the patterns of air over the wing of an airplane. The simple drawing demonstrated the concept of lift and made it look so obvious that he commented it was hard to think the greatest minds of his age had not yet developed it.

When they finished the space exhibits, they moved on to the WWII ship. She wandered through the all-metal halls and rooms, while Nathaniel stopped to read everything. He was so excited to tell her it had the same rooms as the British man-o'-war he and the other infantrymen had used to cross the Atlantic, but all of it looked so different. For one thing, it still boggled his mind that all of it was metal and floated. The galley was massive, and the steel barracks looked sturdier than the hammocks he had slept in. Everything was interesting, and the day had been a success, though exhausting.

Mel managed to sit upright in bed, but stayed there with her eyes closed as the seconds ticked by. The smell of coffee reached her nose, and she pried her lids open enough to get her moving. Grabbing her robe off the post and tossing it on over her nightshirt, Mel headed out to be met with a pretty okay sight that was starting to spoil her—the coffee was already made.

Not only that, once again, Nathaniel was standing wearing the other pair of jeans she had bought for him with a moss green T-shirt. There was a pan on the stove, and she eagerly awaited what was inside, even though dimly in the back of her mind, she recognized that she was supposed to be the hostess here and that she should actually get her butt up to cook.

"Good morning," Nathaniel said, meeting her eyes with a smile.

"Morning," she said before yawning and stretching out her shoulders.

Without further comment, Nathaniel reached confidently into a cabinet and pulled down a plate before piling on potatoes, toast, and eggs. He took care with the spatula to lay the over easy egg on the potatoes on the plate. That was before he cut her toast on the diagonal, taking the extra time to make sure it was perfect.

"How early did you get up?"

"With the sun. I didn't want you to have to wait."

Mel glanced at the table which was set for her. No one

but Abeulita had ever done that for her. She had never even done it for herself.

"It's pretty much the same as yesterday, but I don't know if you have the ingredients to make hot cakes."

It took Mel a minute and a couple of bites of fat-soaked potato to catch up. "Oh, you mean pancakes? I would need to get syrup, but yeah, we can pick that up next time we're at the store."

A distant buzzing caught her ear, and for a moment she considered ignoring it until—

"Oh shit," she said, jumping up. She hadn't spoken to Abuelita since Wednesday night and it was— she calculated the days in her head—shit, it was Sunday now. Mel rummaged through her bed sheets to find the damn phone before the call ended. If she didn't pick up, the likelihood that Abuelita would come personally and knock at the door would skyrocket.

Unless, Mel thought with panic, she had already left and was on her way. That was not good.

Finally, she found it and whipped the thing up to her ear before it was too late. "Hello?" she said, managing only to sound slightly out of breath.

Her grandmother's slightly shrill voice spoke in Spanish. "Melanie, are you okay? I haven't heard from you. The last time I checked, my phone number was still the same."

"Yeah, I'm—" Mel scooted back on the mattress and lost her balance, falling flat in a loud thump.

"Melanie? Is everything alright? You sound sick. I'm coming over."

"No, no, no, no. I'm sorry, it's fine. I'm fine," Mel said again. "Yeah, sorry, no, just work's been crazy."

"Are you sure? I can be over there—"

"No, I'm good. Good over here. What have you been up to? How was mass?"

For a moment, she was worried that Abuelita wouldn't be swayed, but it seemed to do the trick. Abuelita launched into her stories about the new priest who was just okay, but not as good in her opinion as the one two priests ago. Marguerite brought her son, but his shirt was messy. Abuelita could forgive that because he was at least there.

This last statement was followed by a meaningful pause during which Mel said, "Mm-hmm. So, how's the building fund going? Have they made any progress yet on that, uh... you know, that thing they have been building?" It was low-hanging fruit.

"Abuelita," she silently mouthed to Nathaniel as she walked back into the kitchen and sat down. Comprehension dawned, and he nodded before returning to his book.

Mel sipped her coffee and chatted with Abuelita, which meant listening a lot and occasionally asking a question to show that she was paying attention.

When her coffee was empty, Nathaniel noticed and, with an amused smile, reached over to grab it and refill it just the way she liked it before setting the mug back down in front of her.

"Thanks," she whispered.

The line went dead on the phone.

"Hello? Hello? Crap, I must've lost her. Let me call her—"

"Who are you talking to?" Abuelita demanded.

Sheer terror slid through her. "Abuelita! There you are. No, I'm not with—"

"So you're talking to yourself now? I'm coming—"

"No, no, it isn't—"

"Why do I not know about this person? Is it a man? It must be a man, and I don't even get to meet him? Well, fine, just—"

"No! We aren't—"

"WE? There's a *we* now? I see how it is," she spat. "I call with concern for you, but I am pushed aside when there's something new. Forgotten like—"

"No, no! He's nobody! He's nobody!"

"Ay. Well then, you bring Señor Nobody to dinner tonight, and I'll be the judge of that."

"No, Abuelita, listen—"

"Six o'clock, Melanie."

"Abuelita? Shit, pick up, pick up, pick up." But no matter how many times she called, Abuelita refused to answer.

Screwed. She was screwed.

Later that day, they were finally in the car after Mel had cycled among panic, complaining, and apathy.

"Why? Why was I so stupid? I always fall for her traps. Why does she even care? I'm not a teenager. Shit, I'm not even in my twenties! I'm a grown damn woman."

"If you don't want to go, you don't have to."

"She's my only family, and she raised me. I love her, and we look out for each other. Besides, I'll feel guilty if I don't."

Nathaniel nodded in agreement in the passenger seat beside her as they drove downtown. They had run to Target to get him another outfit, which included a collared shirt and pants that weren't actually made of denim.

Usually, she didn't dress for Abuelita, but considering the circumstances, she needed all the brownie points she could get. Over half of the contents of her closet were waiting for her on her bed to be hung back after she had tried on outfit after outfit, to send the right message.

When they were back at the apartment and dressed, even with all of the panic, Mel had to admit that he made a handsome picture. Then as she was driving, her eyes kept cutting over to see him in the passenger seat. Partly to see if anyone could tell there was something different. Partly because she liked the view.

"Okay, so act normal when we get there. Don't do

anything historic or weird. Sorry, that sounded mean. Um…
Can you believe this person? It's called a blinker, asshat!
Anyway, yeah, so how did I meet you again?"

"Through a work function," Nathaniel said, rehearsing his
lines.

"And how long ago did we meet?"

"A few weeks ago."

"What do you do?"

"I just got out of the army."

Good, this was all good, Mel thought to herself. She was a
lawyer. They would focus on the parts of the story that were
true to direct the conversation in a way that suited them.

"What do you plan to do now?"

"I'm looking for work, and you're helping me with that.
Maybe something with law or horses because I grew up
around them."

"Where are you from?"

"Easy. England." As if his voice wouldn't give him away.

Despite the blanket of sticky, stifling air smothering the
city this evening, Mel rubbed her hands together. No need to
ask him about his family because he would tell the truth—
they were all gone. Which was why Mel had been helping
him, of course.

She wasn't sure why Abuelita's approval meant so much
to her. It wasn't like Nathaniel was her boyfriend, but he was
the first man she was bringing to meet Abuelita, so the pressure was on. She had nothing to hide. Nothing other than he
was a secret time traveler. No biggie.

"Okay, here we are. God, I feel like I'm going to be sick."

"Just breathe through your mouth until you feel better.
We'll walk slowly to the door." Nathaniel reached back to the
small bouquet he had insisted on picking up for Abuelita
despite Mel's best attempts to stop it because, "It makes us
look too much like we are dating."

Mel felt she was being led to the chopping block as they ascended the steps. Abuelita had opinions on everyone else, which may be why Mel had been hypercritical of men in the past.

Instead of using her keys, she raised her hand to the buzzer and felt like a stranger standing on the stoop.

Abuelita knew how to play hardball, alright.

She buzzed them in and met them at the stairs without a housecoat. She was dressed in a light green pantsuit with a matching shell top that she normally reserved for church.

This was serious.

Abuelita didn't look at Mel, but took in Nathaniel next to her. Her gaze was absorbing his features, and for the briefest moment, Mel knew for certain that even though Abuelita's pupils hadn't moved, she was studying his clothes with an eagle eye.

When nothing was said, Mel started to panic and sucked in a breath to speak and break the awkward silence.

Nathaniel beat her to it. "Hello, I'm Nathaniel Harrington. My mother would've hated for me to show up empty-handed," he said, handing over the flowers that looked to be some sort of puffball.

Abuelita stood digesting this introduction, which apparently and thankfully must've passed muster because she said in the good English accent that she normally reserved for answering the phone and doctor's offices, "Oh, you didn't have to. Thank you, they're perfect. I have always loved beautiful plants. Please come in."

Mel stood in shock during the exchange, as Nathaniel smoothly navigated the conversation, complimenting her home and graciously thanking her for the hospitality.

Apparently, being part of the British aristocracy in the eighteenth century actually could come in handy.

"Ladies first," he said kindly, stepping back for Abuelita as he held the door. His eyes twinkled in her direction as if he were laughing at her predicament.

"Hello, Melanie, won't you come in?" Abuelita said in perfect English. She could feel the iciness.

Once inside, Mel was almost tackled by the heavenly smell of carne guisada and what she hoped were potatoes.

When they stepped into Abuelita's kitchen, the air wrapped around them like a warm embrace. The bubbling pot on the stove sent up wisps of steam, carrying the deep, earthy aroma of sofrito—the heart of every dish she made. Garlic, sweet bell peppers, and onions melded together, softened into a golden base that thickened the sauce, clinging to tender chunks of beef.

She stirred the pot with practiced ease, the wooden spoon scraping gently against the bottom as she checked the consistency. "Almost ready," she said, her voice warm, but her sharp eyes making sure no one dared to lift the lid before it was time.

Hints of cumin and bay leaf layered into the air, mingling with the subtle brine of green olives that floated among the tender potatoes and carrots. It wasn't just food —it was history, comfort, and love simmered to perfection.

A steaming bowl of fluffy white rice waited on the table, ready to soak up every last drop of the thick, savory sauce.

It was clear, though she would never admit it, that Abuelita had pulled out the big guns for dinner. Plus, the table was already set. While Mel should've been happy, she felt like an outsider, no doubt a calculated move on Abuelita's part. The woman could've negotiated peace talks in the Middle East.

"Nathaniel, would you like something to drink?"

"Water will be fine, Mrs. Reyes, thank you. You have a beautiful home."

"Thank you, and please call me Abuelita. Everyone does," she said with a casual flick of the wrist and a warm smile.

That is a lie, Mel thought, eyeing her grandmother. No one called her Abuelita except Mel.

"Melanie, what would you like to drink?"

"I can get it myself. I know where the kitchen is," she said, moving to get a glass.

"Would you also be so kind as to get Nathaniel a glass of water too?" Abuelita asked in a sweet voice that gave Mel no alternative.

Mel was grinding her teeth now. This was a trick to get her serving Nathaniel. Abuelita always had a method to her madness. The second they were alone, Mel was going to have to set the record straight about her and Nathaniel.

After Nathaniel and Mel helped Abuelita bring the rice, beans, and tortillas to the table along with the crown jewel of the meal, arranged artfully on a deep serving dish, Nathaniel waited until both she and Abuelita had sat before taking the seat laid out for him.

No one moved. Oh no, Mel thought with panic. This was the test she hadn't seen coming.

"Nathaniel, would you like to say grace?"

"Abuelita—" Mel interrupted.

"I'd be honored," he said with an incline of his head. "O Lord, we have so much to bless thee for, we must refer it to eternity, for time is too short: bless our food and fellowship for Christ's sake. Amen."

Mel sat with her mouth open for a good solid three seconds before recovering. Abuelita raised her eyebrows and nodded slowly before making the sign of the cross and offering them both tortillas, which Nathaniel graciously accepted.

"Is there a problem, Melanie?" Abuelita asked, her voice sweet like caramel.

"Nope. Not at all, actually," Mel said, tearing off a piece of tortilla.

The three of them ate, while only two talked about almost every little thing, each making the other laugh with their polite conversations and anecdotes. Mel sat and watched this little show while eating silently, only nodding and making remarks when they included her. It was clear that Abuelita had warmed up to Nathaniel and that this was no longer an act of intelligence gathering. More than a few times, she had dropped back into her standard accent until she just stayed with it for the remainder of the conversation, which included everything.

At this rate, the baby pictures and awkward teen photos would be out before dessert.

Throughout it all, Nathaniel remained pleasant and attentive to the conversation while eating with his exquisite table manners and laughing at all of Abuelita's jokes, even the dry ones.

Nathaniel had wiped tears away from his eyes after a particularly funny rendition of Mel trying to water a plant when she was young, only to end up soaking herself and the whole porch while missing the plant entirely. The story had been pretty funny as much as it pained Mel to admit it.

"Please," he said, rising with a smile, "Let me clear the table. No, please rest." He motioned when Abuelita started to get up. "Allow me." Nathaniel, ever the gentleman, collected the plates and took them into the kitchen.

Abuelita turned her direction and smiled with an impish grin that said all was forgiven. She leaned in and whispered in Spanish, "I like him."

"That's great, but we are not dating."

"I can tell when you're lying."

"Then you should know when I'm telling the truth," Mel answered with a hiss. "We are not together."

"Hmph," came the reply. "There's something you're not telling me about him. I know it."

"Abuelita, we are not—"

"Coffee?" Nathaniel said, walking in with some mugs that she knew had been on the counter waiting by a full pot.

"Muchas gracias," Abuelita said, beaming up at her new favorite person.

By the time they had finished dessert, Abuelita's signature Tres Leches Cake, the cards had come out, and Mel was beginning to wonder if Abuelita might have fallen in love with Nathaniel herself.

The game was poker, and it was going terribly for Mel when faced with not only one but apparently two card sharks.

"You shouldn't let an old woman win so much, Nathaniel," Abuelita said, dealing another hand.

"I assure you; I am not. You are winning, and fairly at that."

"Where did you get to be so good at cards?" Mel asked her. "Isn't it a sin to gamble?"

Abuelita offered another one of her enigmatic smiles and winked before dealing out another hand. "I know a few things. The ladies' church group gets together for cards once a month."

After three more hands, Nathaniel had managed to best Abuelita to her apparent amusement and mild frustration.

With the cards cleared, Abuelita called Mel back into the kitchen to put the dishes in the sink before they left.

"He's such a nice man. So neat. And such a gentleman," Abuelita said to herself, as Mel stood nearby with a dish towel.

"I'm not dating him," Mel said with her arms folded for what must have been the ninth time in their quick conversations when Nathaniel was out of the room.

"You should be."

"No, it's complicated. I'm just helping him get back on his feet."

"He likes you," Abuelita pointed out while loading the cups into the dishwasher.

Mel was stunned and took a second to catch up. She had just thought she was being comforting. Did he like her? No, of course not. "Don't be ridiculous."

"When have I ever been ridiculous?" Abuelita fired back. "You're so stubborn, just like your mother."

Okay, now this was turning into an unfair fight, Mel thought, gritting her teeth.

"I'm not stubborn and he doesn't like me, and besides, even if he did—"

"You'd still push him away?" Abuelita said, wrapping up a piece of cake for her new favorite to take home, since he had loved it so much.

"Melanie," she said with an exasperated sigh. Oh God, Mel thought when she heard her full name again. Here it comes. "I don't know what you're not telling me, but a good man is sitting out there, and you won't even give him a chance. You can be an independent woman and have a man. I'm not going to live forever, and then who will you have?"

Well, wasn't that a blow to the gut? Mel sighed. "It's not that, it's just—"

"Complicated?" Abuelita asked, now meeting her eyes. "Are you sure you're not the one making it complicated?"

"Believe me, there's way more to the story."

Abuelita nodded with understanding. "Ay, there always is in these sorts of things. Everyone has a story, but you can't let that stop you."

Mel had nothing to say, which was damning in itself. It might as well have been a confession for all Abuelita cared, because the next thing she knew, she was being tugged into a bear hug that smelled deliciously like Abuelita's signature perfume and homemade tortillas. Mel couldn't help but hug back.

"At least give him a chance. For me," Abuelita said in Spanish, still holding on to her. "Because I do like him," she declared, before adding, "and I'm too old for him."

Mel laughed and nodded, at least happy that they were back on good terms, before taking the cake to the living room, with Abuelita following. Abuelita gave Nathaniel a long, tight hug at the door and thanked him for coming, inviting him again, anytime he'd like. Mel got the same treatment, but with a silent, meaningful look.

Before Abuelita shut the door, she waved to Mel with an all-knowing, Cheshire cat smile. Mel waved back and cranked over the ignition of the Civic, considering that, indeed, Abuelita would be an excellent choice for Ambassador to the UN.

CHAPTER 21

Mel was trying not to be overly eager as she drove across town to get to the library, where she had again dropped Nathaniel off this morning before work.

She had picked up some readers while meeting a client at their bodega. It wasn't that she was looking for a reason to see him. It was just on her way. That was all.

Besides, she figured she needed a lunch out, which might as well be with him, especially since last night had gone so well. She was really starting to enjoy his company, and it had gone beyond thinking about him at work, to now missing the time they were together. Before meeting Nathaniel, she would get so into her work that she would wonder how time went so fast. Now, she was double-checking the clock, wondering why it was so slow.

As she pulled into the library parking lot, she smiled to herself, thinking that it had been good that Abuelita had liked him. Even though this wasn't going to go anywhere, it was nice to have a friend.

But much to her surprise, Mel didn't see Nathaniel

anywhere. She checked the time and frowned a little. It was still early for lunch.

"Excuse me," she said to the lady with red-rimmed frames behind the information desk. "I was supposed to meet my friend here. He was the one who had checked out all of the history books."

"Oh, yeah, we saw him here earlier." She leaned back and called to another lady on the computer in a small office behind. "Val? Hey, when did that man leave? Yeah, the one who had been sitting in the history section? She said he left about an hour ago, but he didn't say where he was going."

"Do you know where he might be?" He may have just stepped out to grab a bite, since she had given him some money. At first, he hadn't wanted to take it, but eventually she wore him down.

"Sorry, he didn't mention anything. He may have walked to grab lunch. There are a few places open about a block over."

"Yeah, okay. Thanks," Mel said as she pushed through the door and walked down the street, scanning all the windows.

It would be a quick walk, and it was lunchtime, so maybe she was just panicking for nothing. She stepped out and peeked into the closest pizza joint. A quick glance told her that Nathaniel wasn't there or at the nearby diner, but she spotted An Beal Bocht Cafe and headed inside.

Sure enough, there he was. Nathaniel was sitting facing away from her, nose in a book, at the bar.

"Hey, you! Looking for a lunch buddy?" She sniffed and stopped cold. The scent of hard liquor hit her in the face like a wall. "Have you been drinking?" She saw the glass next to him and figured that was her answer.

"What's wrong? I thought you were at work," he asked, slower than usual.

"I can't believe you're drinking. It's not even noon!"

"What's the problem?" he asked, looking genuinely puzzled.

"Are you drunk?" she asked, raising her voice.

The bartender rushed over. "Listen, ma'am, he's not being a problem. We—"

Mel had been holding on to a lot for weeks. Now it all bubbled up. All of the doubt, then suspending her disbelief, sharing her home, meeting her grandmother, and now this. This was her line. She snapped.

"You think that's what I gave you money for?"

"I didn't realize there were rules—"

"Rules? Rules?! More like common decency and self-respect. You can move out today," she said before turning on her heel.

"Mel, wait! Melanie, stop. What has gotten into you?" Nathaniel asked her when he caught up outside. "What— Why are you crying? What happened?"

"Go to hell!" The tears came hot and fast, just like the swell of emotions—deep sadness, grief, disappointment, and betrayal.

"Woah, hey, come on. What happened? Tell me."

"I was trying to surprise you and pick you up for lunch. I got your stupid glasses, by the way," she said, thrusting the bag his way. "But when I got to the library, and you weren't there, I got scared I wouldn't be able to find you."

"I'm sorry I didn't—"

"Drinking, practically drunk in the freaking morning! Do you have any idea how not okay that is now?"

"Calm down."

"Don't you *dare* tell me to calm down! I'll calm down when I damn well feel like calming down!"

Nathaniel's voice was firm and deadly calm. "I'm sorry you're upset. I didn't intend to hurt you."

She didn't answer, hating how the apology softened her

anger into something she couldn't name and didn't know how to handle.

"After everything that I have been through, I am not entitled to a drink? I'm not in my time. I'll never see my family again. I'm not even wearing my clothes on my back or buying my food. Do you know how that feels? I can't go back. I'm alone, Mel. Alone and helpless."

She sniffed. "You have me."

Nathaniel muttered a curse under his breath. He lowered his voice and took her hands in his. "And I appreciate your hospitality more than you know, but it's different. I feel like a child, like a stray dog." He looked away, staring hard at the sidewalk. "I can't do anything for myself or you, for that matter."

"You're a good cook."

Nathaniel's lips thinned, and he let out a rueful laugh. "You think that makes a damn bit of difference?" He swore again. "I didn't know that drinking wasn't permissible during the day. Men used to go to the club often in my time. I did regularly."

She stayed quiet, feeling bad about the scene she was making, deciding whether or not to tell him. Mel drew in a breath.

"It's not just that," she said, looking at the sidewalk. "My parents were killed by a drunk driver."

"I'm sorry."

"Yeah, well," she said, looking down. "I don't like to talk about it, but suffice it to say I'm not a fan."

He blew out a breath that reeked of whiskey. "I'm sorry."

Mel swiped at her tears and stared hard at the sidewalk. "Plus, I didn't know where you were, and I didn't know why, but I got worried."

Nathaniel wrapped both of his arms around her and

pulled her in. Mel didn't resist and let herself get folded into the hug, feeling his chest under her cheek.

"I'm right here now."

The cotton T-shirt was soft and warm against her skin, but backed up by smooth muscle. Mel hugged back and let the tears fall until she was able to pull it together. "Your shirt is wet." She sniffed and pulled back.

"It'll dry. Are you hungry?"

"Shit." She puffed out her breath and checked her phone. "No, I need to be at the jail now. Probably was pushing it anyway to bring you these early."

He pulled the frames out of the bag and slipped them on. "They look so…dark." When he looked up at her from his new frames, the difference was fairly shocking.

The dark, almost rectangular rims looked striking against his high cheekbones, setting him far apart from the man who had left the jail. Dressed like an average Joe, Nathaniel Harrington looked more fitted to teaching college than being on a battlefield.

"Thank you for your kindness. Your generosity is beyond measure." He bowed slightly, and Mel felt her cheeks heat a little.

"Okay, great, you're welcome," Mel said, avoiding eye contact. She went to walk back to the car, but Nathaniel didn't move until she looked him in the eyes.

"I'll be at the library at five," he said, with a smile that was filled with tenderness. "Not another drop of alcohol."

Mel blew out a sigh, and tried to figure out what in the hell had just happened to her. No one knew about her parents. No one, except Abuelita and now Nathaniel.

She pulled down the mirror and collected herself, swiping under her eyes. Mel always had healthy boundaries, and had long accepted the accident. She had been to therapy and led a healthy, well-adjusted life.

But everything with Nathaniel was different. He undid her in ways she couldn't explain.

Mel had never had a man over, but he lived with her. She never would've given money to someone, but she gladly did for him. It wouldn't have occurred to her to leave work midday to bring someone glasses, but she had for him. She hadn't cried in years, let alone in public, but today she had sobbed in his arms and let the tears fall.

She had to get it together. With a final sniff, she blinked a few times and drove toward the jail, determined to have a clear head. As much as she tried to get it together, José could tell immediately when she walked in that she had been crying.

"You good?" José asked, brow furrowed when she walked inside to security.

Mel tried to muster up a smile. "Yeah, just a little tired, and I think the pressure is getting to me."

"Take it easy on yourself, alright? Can't have the good ones burn out."

That gave her the push to try and get a grip. Her clients needed her best, not what was left over after her day.

Try as she might, though, Mel thought about him the whole day between appointments and all throughout meetings. It was unfair of her to have an expectation that she had never communicated. Didn't pirates drink all the time? Shoot, did Nathaniel know a pirate? Was that even the same time period? She didn't know any pirate history. There was a lot of whiskey in *Outlander*, and it hadn't bothered her, probably because there weren't any cars. Perhaps he shouldn't be the only one studying. When five o'clock came, though, she drove to the library with a feeling of excitement she couldn't deny.

This time, he was right where she had dropped him off,

standing with a bag of books. He smiled and waved when he saw her car. She did the same.

Later on, for dinner, she threw in a frozen lasagna and some garlic bread, which they ate with a Caesar salad kit in almost near silence, before retreating to the couch to watch TV with ice cream.

Mel flipped through channels until she found The History Channel.

In the dim light of the screen, she felt herself sliding into him. It wasn't intentional; it just felt nice. That was all.

"I'm sorry for earlier. I don't normally have emotional outbursts."

"You do not need to apologize. This is a lot for you as well."

The simplicity of the sentence said it all. It was a lot for him, but Mel's life had changed more in the past week than it had in years. They were both in the same boat, navigating a new path together.

"How are your glasses, by the way?" She may have snuggled in a little closer, but blamed it on her post-lasagna sleepiness.

"I didn't know I couldn't read well until I put them on. They've sped things up a bit."

His warm arm slid down from the couch, and its heavy weight settled onto her shoulder, side, and hip, cradling her closer.

The final thought she had before sleep tugged her down for the night was that maybe she wasn't the only one who had needed a hug.

CHAPTER 22

The days passed, and they settled into a routine. After dinner one night, Mel put the dishes in the sink and went to the fridge instead of the freezer for their normal ice cream.

"I got you something," she said with a grin.

"What do you mean?" he asked.

"It's your birthday, right?"

"August 29th, I guess it is my birthday. You shouldn't have gotten me anything. You've already given me so much, and I'm not sure how I can ever return the kindness. I've almost lost track of it all."

Mel shrugged and ignored him. "Any guesses how old that makes you?"

"Two hundred and eighty."

"Yeah, but you're the best looking two-eighty ever."

He grinned at her, and she had to look away, feeling the flush. They hadn't moved beyond sitting on the couch close to each other. There also hadn't been any more emotional outbursts, for which she was grateful, but the deepening sense of familiarity was there.

"So, I don't know when they started this, but…" She trailed off as she pulled out a small cake in the clear plastic shell. It was yellow—the only flavor worth having, in her opinion—and layered with white buttercream frosting. Mel popped the plastic cover off before sticking a red candle in the center.

"Lighter, lighter," she mumbled, reaching into the back of the same drawer where she'd found the candle. "Alright, here we go. You do know that you get a wish, right?"

"This is the fanciest cake I've ever seen."

Mel gave him a small smile and watched as he reached out and slowly touched the edge of the plate to spin it around and see all sides. She folded her arms and propped her hip on the counter to watch him. The cake was beautiful in the way ordinary birthday cakes are.

"Happy Birthday, Nathaniel," he read to himself. The red lettering had come out great.

"Do you want to take a picture of it?" she asked when he still hadn't moved toward the fork.

"A picture? Of a cake?"

"Say cheese!" she said, holding up her phone.

He looked up at her, incredulous. "What?"

"Just smile for the picture, silly."

He did so and then looked down. The picture came out great. Before thinking about what it meant, she hit the heart button to save it to her favorites.

Nathaniel leaned closer to the cake and looked up at her before he gave a smile that warmed every part of her heart. It was only then that he looked like he was still in his early thirties. Every other time she looked at him, he always seemed so much older, but then again, that was war. Not to mention, time travel.

"Alright, I got one without the candle lit," she said before she flicked on the lighter and touched the flame to the small red candle.

"What's that thing?" Nathaniel asked, his hand outstretched.

"Oh, I guess this is new for you too. This is a lighter. There's a little fuel inside, and you flick your thumb down like this." She demonstrated again and passed it to him.

"That would have been very helpful," he said, still looking at it in awe. He flicked his hand twice and studied the flame.

"You can have it. They're cheap now and aren't a big deal."

She snapped another picture and started to sing.

The tune of "Happy Birthday" had never seemed that special to her, but as she finished the first line, his reaction had her second-guessing herself.

His face had changed from shyly happy to something close to mesmerized. Mel managed her way through the familiar lines fairly well despite her audience. When she finished, he kept staring at her with a warm smile, the candlelight flickering in his eyes, the glow illuminating his face.

Mel felt the heat bloom in her chest. She couldn't look away.

"That was the sweetest song I've ever heard," he whispered.

Mel stood still, feeling awkward. "Thanks," she finally managed, her voice low.

She hadn't dated a lot, but her exes had a softness to their skin that spoke of youth and inexperience. Nathaniel's youth was long gone, along with any baby fat left over from his childhood. Whereas other twenty-to-thirty-somethings looked like kids, Nathaniel looked far more adult. He looked like a man.

"You should probably blow out the candle. You don't

want to lose your wish," she heard herself say. Her voice was barely above a whisper.

Nathaniel didn't move. He kept watching her while the dancing flame reflected in his eyes. The smile on his lips was a look of bemusement and contentment.

He blinked and drew in a breath slowly. Without looking away from her, he turned his head slightly and blew out the candle with perfect aim.

"Your wish won't come true if you tell me what it is," she said. "That's how it works."

"Okay," he said, his voice also low. "I won't tell."

Mel had to forcibly remove herself from the spot and tear her gaze away from him. "I need to get the forks."

Mel dropped her gaze then and opened the drawer too fast, breaking the tension. The cheap silverware clattered in the tray and made her jump. She dug out two forks and nudged the drawer closed with her hip as she turned back to the table.

"Well," she said, steadying herself. "Shall we dig in?"

The corner of his mouth pulled back into a smile, and he took the fork from her before looking at the cake and finally releasing her from his gaze. Mel stifled a sigh of relief mixed with regret. She felt hot all over.

"It's still almost too pretty to eat," he said, and damn if she didn't wish he was talking about her.

CHAPTER 23

Nathaniel set his fork on the table and leaned back. The cake had been the most delicious thing that he had ever eaten.

Mel scraped her fork along the plate where the cake had been and swept the last remains of what she called frosting into her mouth. She eased the fork from her lips.

He tried not to stare, but she was so different, just like that cake, than anything he had seen in his life. The women he had known were quiet, reserved, and obedient.

They wore delicate dresses. Mel wore jeans like a man, which to his eye was a big improvement.

They dreamed about marriage matches and children. Mel lived alone and practiced law.

They never were familiar with men, other than a few stolen kisses. Mel put up one in her house.

They did what they were told. Mel did everything but.

She was a force to be reckoned with. Her clothes were tight, and her hair was wild. She wore makeup, but she was also educated and was a skilled cook. She wasn't scared or shy, and it was quite clear that she did just fine without a man in her life.

He was fascinated by her.

There were two things that were very much the same. She was a woman, and she could sing.

Every lady that Nathaniel had ever met had tried to play piano or sing in hopes of entertaining young men enough for one to ask her papa for her hand. Mothers would often drag their daughters and have them perform at every opportunity, with varying degrees of success, whenever an eligible man was around.

Of all the pretty girls he had seen, and of all the forced concerts and recitals Nathaniel had been to, none of them even came close to Mel. Her voice was like a stream on a summer day, cool, refreshing, light, and tender. Maybe all of those mamas had it right. When she had sung him a simple little tune for his birthday, his world had stopped, and the only thing that had existed was her.

"Well, we had cake, so now it's time for presents!" the object of his thoughts said.

Mel got up in her fantastic jeans and went into her bedroom, where Nathaniel could hear rustling. "Hey, when did you say those jeans are from?"

"Huh?" she called back.

"Your pants, you called them jeans. When do people start wearing them?" He meant women but didn't want to ask that part lest she figure out what he was after.

"Oh, um, well, I remember seeing a show about immigrant inventors, right? And on the show, it talked about Levi Strauss and how he came over during the California Gold Rush—you've heard about that, right?"

He nodded and was happy to recognize another fact from his text.

"Right, well anyway, he made his fortune not by digging

for gold, but instead selling products for the miners, which is really an excellent idea, and he came up with these. I guess they were more durable or something. You would probably know more about that. I think it really became a popular thing, I dunno, probably around the forties during World War II and then definitely into the fifties."

Nathaniel nodded and mentally thanked Levi Strauss for his ingenuity as Mel walked back to the table.

"Alright, here you go," she said as she slid a little box across the table. "I got you a little something."

The little box was wrapped in a slick, shiny silver paper that had a bunch of shiny ribbons in every color that were curled into a small mass on top.

Nathaniel sat stunned.

"You do know what a gift is, right? Like that was a thing back then?" Mel asked, suddenly seeming unsure where to put her hands. She twisted them together in a knot.

"Well, I guess usually if my parents gave one of us a little gift, it would be wrapped in brown paper and maybe have a little twine. This is so…" He trailed off as he turned the little package over to see all of the sides.

"Futuristic?" Mel asked with a laugh.

"Yeah, like how is this held together? The bloody ribbon isn't doing anything."

She let out a quick melodic laugh that stopped him again, as she took it out of his hands. "I guess that would be a little weird. Here. Okay, I have no idea when this started, but you see this little thing right here?" She pointed to a waxy substance over the fold. "This is tape. It is sticky on one side, and it comes in a roll, so you stick it on and the pieces stay that way." She peeled a corner off with her fingernail.

He reached out and touched it. Sure enough, the top was smooth and almost clear, while the bottom was tacky and stuck to his finger.

"That's incredible," he murmured to himself.

She thrust the package back into his hands. "That's just the wrapping. Go ahead and open it."

He stared at the little, pretty package in his hands and flipped it to the side where the tape was already pulled up a little. With his fingernail, he tried to ease it up more like she had done.

"You can rip it too; it's no big deal."

Nathaniel looked at her. Mel shrugged one shoulder and smiled.

"People rip this?"

"Usually kids. When someone gives them a birthday gift or any kind of gift, they often make a big show of tearing it all apart."

He frowned. "It's far too nice to waste."

Mel rolled her eyes and laughed. "You're just like Abuelita. She takes forever to open a present. She even folds it so she can reuse it. I'm not sure she has ever bought a new bow."

"I knew I liked her," Nathaniel said, working on the package, careful not to tear the paper, which made a different sound than he was used to in his hand.

Once the package was free from its wrapping, Nathaniel ran his hand over the creases to smooth it out before folding it and tucking it away. Mel groaned across from him.

Nathaniel looked up at her. She was so beautiful. Her hair was like the ribbons, a dark curly mass, and his hands itched to touch it. Her dark eyes were laughing at him while her perfect lips turned upward in a smile.

"Thank you," he said softly.

"You haven't even opened it," she pointed out. "It could be something awful."

"I doubt that anything from you could ever be bad."

Mel blushed and looked down for a moment, and he could tell she was pleased with his comment.

"I hope I'm smart enough to figure out what it could be," he said, smiling himself. "I feel like a damn idiot most of the time here."

Mel waved her hand at him. "You're fine, and don't worry, you'll know what this is. I did think about that when I bought it, though."

Nathaniel looked at her again and, like always, committed every inch of her to memory in case he woke up back on the outside of New York under a wet tent, cold and hungry.

He opened the box to reveal a small, red, cylindrical object with a white cross on one side. Picking it up, the weight of the metal surprised him as it was heavy for its size. The cool of the metal warmed to his touch as he slowly turned it over, trying to figure it out, so he wouldn't look like the idiot he had feared. A silver ring at the top dangled as he flipped it onto its side to examine the layers of steel inside.

"Thank you, I truly mean that," he said. "Uh…would you mind showing me how it works?"

Mel's voice was tender and patient as she explained. "It's called a Swiss Army Knife. They came out after your time. It's like a pocketknife on steroids—sorry, like a super pocket knife. See each one of these layers?"

He nodded and ran his fingers over them again.

"They all fold out and are different tools. The Swiss Army designed them for soldiers to work on the rifles or guns. At least that's what the website said." She laughed. "I don't know much more about it than you."

"So I just fold it out like—" He pulled out the first layer to reveal a shockingly sharp blade. "I'll be damned. How does it not collapse back inside if you try to cut… Wait." The knife wouldn't fold back in and stayed strong despite how hard he pushed on the back of the blade.

"Yeah, I always have a hard time with this part myself," Mel said, leaning in. The scent of her was spicy and floral and very distracting.

"See this little piece here?" she asked, pointing to a diagonal piece of metal inside. "It's like a spring, I think. You pull it back and then—" She pushed on the knife and it clicked out of the locked position and began to fold in.

"I'm always scared I'm going to fold it too fast and cut my finger like an idiot," she said, laughing. "Play around with it. There are a bunch of other tools."

Nathaniel peeled back each item and studied it. He had seen something like this before. His friend Simon had owned one, but that version was only a folding knife. It had been a private purchase, of course.

On this version, though, was a corkscrew, a saw, a screwdriver, a nail file, a toothpick, a pair of scissors, and two other blades of different sizes.

"Mel..." he started. "This is a very fine gift indeed. I'm truly not sure I can ever give you—"

"Pffft," she said with a wave of her hand. "I'm just glad you like it."

"I love it. I mean that. Thank you."

Her eyes took on a more sultry look as she gave him a warm smile, all of the silliness gone. "Happy birthday, Nathaniel."

It was that moment that he made a bargain with God. He didn't know much of anything anymore, but if what had happened to him was possible, he was sure God must exist. Nathaniel prayed that if he believed hard enough, maybe God would let him stay here long enough to get closer to her.

CHAPTER 24

Mel closed the distance between her and Nathaniel. Her fingertips reached out on their own and grazed the shirt covering his chest. She could feel the taut muscle flex underneath her touch and moved her fingers along. Subtle ridges told her where his ribs were.

The pads of her fingertips skimmed upwards and traced the skin covering his collarbone. Mel pulled the collar of his shirt down and open. Under his exposed skin, she could see the cords of his muscles straining over the smooth bones beneath.

She ran her fingernail across his skin. Goose bumps shivered across the surface as he sucked in a breath and held it.

Mel looked up into his eyes and saw they had darkened, the centers dilating to almost a black pool. He was frozen where he stood. She spread her palms wide on his chest and felt his heart beat within.

"You should stop," he said, his voice like gravel.

She leaned in now and touched her lips to his chest. The weight of his head came down to rest on her crown.

They breathed together.

Arms encircled her, pulling her deeper into his embrace.

He smelled like soap and shampoo, but there was something else that she couldn't identify. It was rich and spicy.

The warmth from him radiated around her, heating her to the bone.

She closed her eyes and breathed in his scent before peeking out from under her lids to see the stubble that shadowed his cheek.

"Do you want me to stop?" she whispered, finding his nipple through the cotton of his T-shirt and running her nail over it.

He sucked in a breath and held it, not answering her question. A slow smile crossed her lips, and she looked up at him through her lowered lashes.

Her hands found the hem of his shirt and deftly slid underneath, finding the skin of his stomach smooth and tight. Another ripple went through him as her nails scraped slowly upwards.

"I think I want you," she said against his chest.

"Do you?" he said, his voice straining with control. Almost every muscle she could feel was taut with restraint.

"Yes," she answered, her voice dropping now.

He stepped closer, and the hardness in his jeans made her breath catch in her throat before sending a shot of heat down her body like she had never felt before.

His hand crept up the back of her nape and pulled her hair to the side, exposing her neck.

"Nathaniel—"

"Mmm?" He bent his head down low and ran his lips along the side of her neck, causing a shiver of her own to race down her spine. His hands opened and splayed over the small of her back, pressing her into him.

Teeth grazed along her earlobe, and the rush of air when he breathed her in sent a hot flush all over her skin. Mel's eyes closed, and she drank in the feel of him kissing the sensitive area just below her ear.

He leaned back, and Mel opened her eyes to protest right as his mouth found hers, and she gave in to him. His lips teased her own, lightly kissing, but nothing more.

Mel leaned in and kissed back before flicking her tongue lightly over his lips, silently asking for entry.

Nathaniel was more than willing to oblige. He hugged her harder now to him. He hugged her harder now to him, his length pushing against her, sending more heat down to her core. His tongue found hers and explored, faster and farther than before.

The palm of his hand now came around to her side and slid over the fabric covering her hip in a hypnotic pattern, warming her skin underneath until she was on fire from the need.

Mel arched her back, pressing her body against his so that they were melded except for the thin cotton between them. He found the curve of her breast, and the heat spread throughout her body. Her nipples craved the same attention, and a soft moan escaped her throat when his hand ran over them.

Nathaniel's hands found the hem of her shirt and teased it lightly until the pads of his fingers grazed the skin of her side. His hand resumed its pattern of stroking her side up and down, going farther each time until he came in contact with the edge of her bra.

Mel could feel him falter when he reached it, but kissed him hard to urge him further.

The burning heat rose up to new heights as he explored the edge of the satin on her chest. Mel arched her back up into his palm, so that his fingers slid under the strap and eased it down her shoulder, trapping her arm low. She reached up with her free arm to pull him into their kiss, closing any remaining gap between their bodies. Her trapped arm found his hip and tugged him closer.

Nathaniel's hand dipped into her cup and found her breast before kneading it. As his palm molded to her shape, he teased her nipple. The jolt of pleasure shot through Mel, making her knees buckle.

He reacted fast, sweeping his free arm around to steady her before he backed her against something hard, which she dimly remembered as the countertop.

"Wait," she breathed out.

Nathaniel pulled back the barest inch and looked at her through heavy lids. His lips were parted, and his breathing was heavy.

"My room," she said through gasps of her own. She led him the short distance into the darkness of her room.

"I want to see you," he said, his voice rough.

Mel paused.

"Please," he urged.

Mel waited still. He ran his hands up her back under her shirt and then slid them around to the front, covering the satin that shielded both of her breasts, while his lips grazed against her neck.

In an instant, the fire was back and stronger than before, making her melt into his arms, which she had no doubt could support her.

"You're so beautiful," he murmured against her shoulder that he had exposed with his mouth.

Rather than answer, Mel turned her head to capture his lips with her own. His mouth claimed hers again, tasting and stoking the fire that was raging within her.

Both of his hands now dipped below the satin to cup her skin. Mel covered his hands with her own through the fabric of her shirt and pushed him against her. When he began to tease and massage again, the hot need between her legs begged for more.

His ridge now rested against the back of her jeans. Without breaking from his mouth, she pushed herself into him and smiled against his lips when a rough sound escaped him.

Mel swept her hands behind her and stroked him once, surprised by the length. Nathaniel sucked in a breath, but Mel kissed him harder, pushing them both further until he pulled her so hard against him she could barely breathe.

Needing more, she pulled his hands, reluctant to leave her breasts, toward her waistband, which she quickly undid. Not needing more of an invitation, Nathaniel slid his hands underneath, exploring the lacy satin, before spreading his hands wide and gripping the skin of her hips.

Mel tugged at her jeans, sending them to the floor. She spun now and lunged at Nathaniel, who had ripped his shirt over his head, before throwing it in the darkness around them. They collided, mouths entangled, grasping at each other's skin to feel every inch of it. Mel tugged at Nathaniel's jeans before clumsily fighting with the closure until, at last, he reached down and freed himself.

His hands went for her shirt and yanked it over her head before slamming into her again. The skin covering his chest met her own, and she felt the damp tip of his hardness against her now exposed stomach.

Nathaniel tried to yank her bra away, but it held fast, and he swore. Mel undid the clasp and launched herself at him. His mouth roamed on her skin, kissing, sucking, and tasting.

They clambered backward until Mel fell on the bed with Nathaniel on top of her, the need commanding the temptation between them.

Nathaniel hooked his thumbs into her underwear and drew them down and out of the way, disposing of his own.

In the dim light from the hallway, she could see he was huge and throbbing with desire. As he stood tracing her skin with his hands as if to see her in the darkness, Mel reached out on her own and closed her palm around his thick length.

Nathaniel leaned back and hissed, before panting in time with her careful strokes. His own fingers caught up, found her core, and slid into her tight wetness before matching her pace. They were frenzied, each wild in their craving.

He grabbed her hand and guided it lower on his shaft, holding it in place, while moving his fingers inside of her, coaxing her higher and higher, bringing her to a point of chaotic energy, where nothing existed but him and her. Her thighs began to tremble against her control, but Nathaniel pushed them apart with his own and held them in place.

Mel choked out a cry from the torture of him toying with her. When her hips lifted off the bed, begging for more, Nathaniel released her hand and steadied her before lowering his head.

Mel jerked and writhed underneath him. When she thought she could stand no more, the soft, subtle texture of his tongue licked slowly up her core and sent her hurtling over the edge, blind into oblivion.

Before she could recover, with her eyes still closed, she felt him drinking her, suckling and lapping away, stoking her fires again. Mel shuddered and felt the coil of need begin to tighten again.

"Nathaniel—" she whispered, reaching out to him. When he looked up, she pulled his shoulders toward her, pleading silently.

He rose up above her. Mel reached out and gripped him again, feeling the wetness at the end of his hard length.

She rolled onto her side and bent down to lick him from the base of his shaft to the tip. He jerked and she felt his hips roll forward, begging for more, which she happily gave, driving her further and further until she could feel the strain in the grip of his hands on her shoulders.

"Mel—" he croaked out. When she stopped, he rolled her over and took less than a beat to spread her legs with his own and line himself up with her aching center. The broad velvet head rested there until she looked up into his eyes, when he thrust, invading every inch of her.

Mel cried out and rode the wave as he pummeled fast and hard, driving them both higher up the cycle again. She hung onto his shoulders as he buried deeper still and found her mouth, his tongue invading and taking what it wished.

Faster and harder they climbed until, with a cry, she came apart, and went boneless. Nathaniel pumped hard into her twice more, grunting, before heaving himself up and spraying hot, wet jets onto her stomach. With a sigh, he collapsed onto her, breathing fast and deep.

They lay like that for minutes or maybe it was hours. Mel didn't know.

A rush of fabric and cool air on her skin told her that Nathaniel had left her. Mel whimpered and tried to pull the sheet up when she felt a warm, damp cloth sweeping over her stomach. She curled toward the movement and reached out her arms. The cloth disappeared, replaced by an arm as Nathaniel lay down behind her, holding her against him. With his warm breath at her ear, Mel gave way to the pulling tide of a deep sleep.

CHAPTER 25

Nathaniel woke up later than he had in a long time. Judging by the sun, he hadn't slept this late since joining the infantry. When his eyes cracked open, not only was the sun already blazing into the room, but it highlighted all the different colors in Mel's hair that made up the dark chestnut brown.

Her lashes rested against perfect skin as she slept, still breathing deeply and slowly. He leaned up and raked his eyes over her, wanting to see everything that he couldn't last night in the darkness.

She was indeed beautiful, but that was not all. With her eyes closed in peaceful rest, she was stunning. He had been attracted to her before, but now saw past her rapier wit and easy humor. On an average day, Mel was such a force to be reckoned with that being able to see her without her determined stare that hardened her features was fleeting and rare.

Now she slept, and Nathaniel could see what had been denied him last night. Perfect lips with a cupid's bow top and full bottom were a soft pink, which he could now see matched her nipples, set on full, flawless breasts.

He craved the sight of her skin and held his breath as he eased the covers down. Something caught his eye, and he frowned.

As he pushed them just a little lower, he sucked a breath in at the sight of her abdomen.

Mel's stomach was streaked with scars going every which way, coiling around her middle and out of sight. Some were pale and stretched, while others were no more than a line on a map. Distorted and discolored against her perfect skin, there were so many that he couldn't count them with ease. It was clear they were old and had long since healed, but the signs of trauma could only fade so much.

Looking back at her face, his heart broke as he saw her now for the warrior she was. She had said her parents had died in a car accident, but never before had he considered for a moment that she, too, had been in the car. It was clear to him now why she had refused to turn on the lights before they had lain together. As beautiful, strong, intelligent, and courageous as she was, Mel was ashamed.

On impulse, Nathaniel leaned forward and began to touch his lips to each scar.

Mel shot up and grabbed the sheets to cover herself.

"What are you doing?"

Nathaniel sat motionless, watching her.

"You're beautiful."

"Please don't."

"I mean it." He paused. "Why didn't you tell me?"

"I don't know," she said again, clutching the sheet to her chest, looking around the room for something to hide her body.

"I'm not leaving."

"Please," she said, throwing a pillow at him, which he easily caught.

"Mel—"

"Don't start with me. I don't want to hear it."

"After everything we've shared, do you think that it matters to me? It only makes me respect you more." He shifted on the bed toward her. "Come here."

"I don't want a hug."

"Who said you're getting one?"

She kept her eyes on him as his arms enveloped her again and held her against his chest, settling her into the crook in which she fit perfectly.

"You're hugging me."

"Oh, am I? Apologies," he said, leaning back against the headboard, with his arms pulling her back with him. His hand rubbed her back up and down.

She wanted to stay mad, but the stupid rubbing must have been some magic because the next thing she knew, she said, "No one's ever seen them before."

"Hmmmm," he said. "Hence the lights."

"Yeah, and besides, I've only been with one other guy."

"Shall I get my pistol?"

"No, it was a long time ago, and he was an idiot anyway. Didn't take very long, and the lights were off. Just wanted to see what all the hoopla was about."

"Hoopla? I see. I hope I lived up to such a description."

Mel smiled and shrugged a little. "I mean, I guess. It was okay." She laughed when he poked her.

"I'll have to try again," he said, nuzzling into her neck.

"Maybe, if you're lucky. My average is once every ten years, so it might be a while."

"You are worth two hundred years," he said, kissing her cheek.

She laughed again. "Stop it! I need coffee. Stop." She swatted at him.

Nathaniel cupped her cheek and turned her face toward his. "I'll make coffee and give you your privacy, but don't ever think for a moment that you are less than an extraordinary beauty."

She didn't say anything and watched as he left until he closed the door behind him.

While she dressed, he carefully counted the spoonfuls of grounds like Mel had taught him on his first morning here as he poured them into the coffee pot.

Mel had been perfect, a far cry from anything else he had experienced. Everything about her continued to surprise and stir something deeper within him.

The door to the bathroom clicked shut behind him, and he heard the water turn on shortly thereafter. He grabbed the pan he had grown fond of for making breakfast and laid it on the stove, heating it and getting the butter.

When they had returned to the grocery store last week, they picked up the mix for what Mel called pancakes, and those seemed to delight her. So, Nathaniel wanted to make them today, especially after this morning. His knuckles tightened on the handle of the coffee mug in his hand at the image of her scars. He had no idea how extensive the injuries had been, but knew he had seen that her legs, at least the part exposed by her dresses, were unmarred.

While the pan heated, he grabbed some clothes and tossed them on, then came back and stirred the mixture together quickly. As he poured it into the hot fat, he watched the bubbles form and then pop.

Since he had arrived, he had gotten quite good at this cooking, but everything else Mel took care of. There was little else he could do or offer her, and determined to give something back to carry his weight, he at least found something that he was somewhat good at. As he flipped the pancake in the pan, he felt more like a maid than a man. What would his brother have said?

As much as he wanted to stay here, he knew that he

needed to leave eventually to make way for someone better. Someone from her own time, like the man she had been with before. He surely had money of his own.

The thought pierced him, and he slapped the pancake on the plate with a grimace at the idea of Mel sharing her life with someone else. Nathaniel poured in more batter and propped himself up with his hands on the counter as he glared down at the bubbles, but this was the only thing he had to offer her, and—

The bathroom door opened. Mel walked over in a towel and gave him a heart-stopping, dazzling smile before standing up on her toes and kissing him straight on the mouth.

"Good morning. Oh, pancakes! My favorite," she said, ogling the pan. "Let me get dressed. I'll be right out."

As he watched her slink back to her bedroom in just a towel before she closed the door, he let out a sigh, before swearing under his breath. The irony was cruel. He had traveled through time and met the most incredible woman, and yet, she deserved so much more than he could ever hope to give her.

CHAPTER 26

"Alright, let's roll," Mel said, grabbing her purse and keys the next day.

Nathaniel was still fascinated with cars, and the way Mel drove with such confidence attracted him to her even more. Though considering the last two nights had been the best of his life, Nathaniel didn't know how much more he could be attracted to her.

"Where are we going today?" he asked. It had been an assault and whirlwind of new information since he arrived, but he was finally enjoying every second and trying hard to commit everything to memory, just in case he woke up and it was all gone.

"Boy oh boy, do I have a surprise for you," she said.

"That sounds big," he said.

"Yup."

Nathaniel glanced over at Mel, who was driving while singing along to the radio. Her world was so different from his own. Looking out the window, he chewed on his cheek and wondered when he would start to fit in. So far, the only thing he had done to try and be a man and impress her was warm her bed and cook her breakfast. Not that he minded either, but he didn't have a penny to his name. He couldn't drive, work, or even politely refuse her charity.

It was a hard pill to swallow that the clothes on his back were from her, and he had no way to repay her.

They were in the car and had listened to three hours' worth of music before pulling off the road and into what she called a parking lot. Lines of different cars of all shapes and sizes littered the field. Men and women in waistcoats and matching shirts directed her and the other cars into a new line that was forming.

"Alright," she said after putting on the brake and killing the engine. "Let's go."

She hopped out and slung her bag over her shoulder. "Did you lock it?" she called back.

"Yep," he said before opening the door and hitting the switch she had shown him earlier.

They followed the people in front of them as they crossed the field.

"Are you going to tell me what this is?" he asked.

"You'll see in a bit," she said.

"Is it a fair?"

"Kinda, just wait."

As they climbed a small hill, Nathaniel began to hear music, but not Mel's kind. Fifes and drums. He stopped immediately.

"What's wrong? Come on, we're almost there."

Nathaniel grabbed her hand and yanked her back. "Can you hear that?" he asked. Dear God, he had just started to get comfortable. He couldn't go back now.

"Ow, Nathaniel! Yes, silly. I hear it too." She tugged on her arm, but he wouldn't let go. If he lost her now—

"Mel, I don't wanna go back. I can't."

A shadow of concern drifted over her face. "Nathaniel...

Sorry, excuse us." She pulled him under a tree. "Listen… Dammit, I should have thought of this." She ran her hand through her hair, pushing it away from her face. "Look, this is a Revolutionary War reenactment. I thought you would like it."

"A what?" He knew he looked suspicious, and didn't care.

"It's a reenactment. Everything here is pretend. It's for people to see what it was like back then—" She must have seen the look on his face.

"Crap, no, not like really. It's pretend, allowing families to learn about the battle. See?" She pointed to a husband and wife with a toddler and a little girl who looked to be about seven. All of them were in jeans.

"It's okay," she said. "Nothing bad is going to happen. The worst thing that happens at these kinds of things is heat stroke and heartburn from too much food."

"Why would anyone want to know what it was like?" he said. He was still suspicious, but felt like a foolish idiot for being scared of something a child was excited about. So much for impressing Mel.

"It's just for them to learn. Come on." With that, she tugged on his hand and led him toward the music and over the hill.

At the crest, a sea of white tents and a field beyond lay in a small valley.

"Wait, look at all the tents. They're just like—" He paused, drinking in the familiar sight. "Not the bright big one, but the others."

"Yeah, that's where we get our tickets, and then we can go exploring. We got here way early for the battle."

"Battle?" he asked.

"It'll be okay. I promise." She squeezed his hand, and although it made him feel young, he squeezed back.

They walked into the first tent, and Mel talked to the

woman seated at a table. She paid and got two tickets and a map of the grounds.

Nathaniel tried not to stiffen when she pulled out her wallet, and renewed his resolve to find something to make money. He was still getting used to the idea of a woman doing everything Mel could do, but he certainly didn't like her paying for everything and didn't think he would ever be used to it.

Once they were past the gate, she turned to him and said, "I don't know about you, but I have a hankering for some good fair food. C'mon, you'll feel better when you eat."

"Wha—" But before he could finish his question, Mel was charging ahead toward a small stand that smelled like fat and sugar and had a line at the two windows.

"What is it?" he asked.

"Delicious. That's what it is."

The woman in the window waved them over, and Mel stepped up to order.

"Hi, two funnel cakes, please." Mel passed over the money and grabbed a fistful of the paper napkins, similar to the ones he had seen at her apartment, before pulling him to the side.

"Look at that." She pointed to the menu on the side of the truck. "Fried candy bars. Obscene, isn't it? Just nuts. Maybe on the way out—"

"Is this lunch?" he finally managed to ask.

"Nah, this is just a mid-morning treat. There's barbecue over there that I'm planning to head to next, but seeing as it's the morning, I wanted a little boost to my day. Funnel cake is practically a doughnut anyway," she added with a wave of her hand.

"We didn't eat this well in the army." Was this how they taught about war?

"Yeah, but no one would buy anything from a gruel stand. It's just for the crowds."

Their order came out of the small window, and Mel went over to collect it before thanking the person inside.

"Bon appétit!" Mel pulled off a chunk with her fork as she balanced the plate on her lap. To avoid getting covered in the white substance, which was a fine sugar, Mel leaned forward, giving him an excellent view of her chest. She leaned back to swallow and closed her eyes in absolute bliss. The column of her neck was slender and taut. A small moan escaped her just like the night before. Nathaniel coughed and had to focus on the food in front of him while he discreetly adjusted himself.

"Mmmmm, the first bite is always better than I remember," she said in a reverent whisper, her eyes still closed as she savored the confection.

Nathaniel looked at his funnel cake in front of him. The plate it was sitting on was about two sizes too small for the cake and was already weak from grease. White sugar covered the entire top. He moved too quickly, and it sprinkled all over his lap. Mel saw it happen.

"Don't worry, it brushes right off," she said before taking another mouthful.

Nathaniel swept himself off and tore off a chunk just like Mel. The cake was so light that half of it was gone before he realized how much he had eaten.

"It's so sweet it hurts my teeth," he said, wiping his fingers. Mel nodded in agreement and took another bite.

There was a bit of sugar at the corner of her mouth. Nathaniel reached over and swiped his thumb over the spot, but before he could take it back, her pink tongue darted out, licking him.

A zing of pleasure shot straight down his spine. Mel's eyes twinkled as she laughed at him before lowering her dark lashes to continue to eat in pleased silence.

"Alrighty," she said, consulting her map when they had finished eating. "Where to, soldier?"

"Uh…well, what do they have?"

"According to the map, there's Sutler Row here, and then there's the British camp here. The Continental one is over here, and uh…it looks like there is a living history section here." Mel kept pointing things out on the map while he looked around. The tents did look like the ones he was used to, but they were too clean. He couldn't help but tense up when two men dressed as colonists walked by them.

They both wore blue regimentals with red facings, hats, and each had a canteen swung over their hip, bouncing with each step. Neither looked to be older than twenty, and neither looked as though they had walked for more than a mile.

"Is it weird for you?" Mel asked softly, following his eyes to the boys.

"Very," he said.

"Well, let's go explore the Sutler thing first, and you can tell me what you think about everything."

He let her lead him while he looked around in wonder. He saw a few more soldiers walking around, followed by a few ladies dressed either too nicely or too drab to be correct.

"Pretty, huh?" Mel asked. He turned and saw her watching him with a wry smile.

"Not quite my type," he said.

"I meant the dress. You think I'd look good in something like that?" she asked, looking at the confection flounce trailing in the dust.

"I think you'd be the most beautiful thing here."

"My, my, sir, you do flatter me so," she said with a flourish and an accent to match his own, before she grabbed his hand and tugged him along.

They walked into the first sutler tent, which was by far the biggest one. Nathaniel looked up at it as they stepped inside, feeling the once-familiar stifling heat that resulted from the lack of ventilation.

"This is a hospital tent," he said.

"A what?"

"The size. It's for a hospital."

"That's kinda small, isn't it?" she asked, looking up.

"It would probably fit twelve men, twenty if they needed to."

"Jesus," she said under her breath.

A rather jovial-looking man, sweating through a wool waistcoat, walked over to them. "Good day, folks, do you find yourselves in need of some provisions?"

"Um, I guess we're just looking around," Nathaniel said, unsure of how this was supposed to work.

"Well, you just lemme know what I can do for you. These here are the best prices you'll find around." His eyes, keen for a sale, shifted away from them then to the couple that came in behind them, before he stepped around to assault the newcomers.

Mel caught his gaze, and she raised an eyebrow as she smirked. "Come on," she said. "You can show me what all of this is."

They walked through the heat of the tent, which made Nathaniel realize how much he had enjoyed what she called the A/C, and took note of all the various items for sale. In the first section, regimental coats, hats, waistcoats, and breeches were hung in neat rows. An apple box of socks lay on the ground beneath them. Picking one pair up, he ran his hand over the knitted material and showed it to Mel.

"This," he said, holding the pair up, "is probably the most useful damn thing in here next to the muskets."

"So then, all the history about wearing through socks that fast is true?"

"My feet will never be the same." He let out a long, low whistle when he saw the price.

"Inflation's that bad, huh?"

"I made fifty-five pounds a year in the army."

Her mouth fell open.

The hearty salesman swung back into their path now. "You look like a strong, strapping lad. Allow me to interest you in a nice coat."

Nathaniel paused, and the salesman's eyes lit up, and quick as a flash, he pulled down a wool coat and ushered him into the sleeves. "I have a keen eye for sizes, and yes, this one is perfect. You, sir, are a perfect forty-four."

While he prattled on, Nathaniel caught a glimpse of himself in the mirror the man had staged at the end of the tent. He had to walk forward a bit to see for himself.

The civilian coat was darker than his own, probably because it hadn't been faded by the sun. The weight of the fabric felt the same, but it was stiff and unused. While he hadn't been in the habit of studying himself in a mirror during his former life, he did now and found that he looked like his old self. A fear and sadness swept through him, and again he sent a silent plea up to God that he could stay here a little longer.

"Well, sir, I must say that you make a fine presence in that piece. Shall I bring it to the counter, or would you like to wear it around?"

Nathaniel had to shake himself free of his reflection before he said softly, "Thank you, but I, uh…I already have one."

The salesman adjusted his tactic quicker than a frog on a fly. "A fine British gentleman like you? I'm not surprised, sir, as you have the highest quality of taste. Perhaps you need a new shirt or some breeches? Allow me to pick out a few pieces."

Mel stepped onto the Persian rug, which looked like the one his mother had in the foyer of their old house, and stared into the mirror with him. "What's more comfy?"

Nathaniel considered her question as he took in his appearance again. "Well, it's familiar, but I like the clothes you bought me. They're softer. Not as itchy, you know?"

She rubbed her hand over his arm and chest to feel the fabric, and it made his heart beat faster.

"Aren't we quite the pair?" she asked, looking into the mirror.

He looked like his true self now, but she, with her mass of dark curls and tight jeans, looked better than ever. Quite a pair indeed. They stood together with her hand on his arm, each from their own time. His hand covered hers, and he tried to commit this sight to memory in case he should be robbed of her. Just the thought of it made his heart squeeze in his chest.

A brown wool tricorn flew onto his head from behind, as the salesman swooped around, breaking the moment. He must have taken note of where Mel's hand was because the next thing he said was, "You two do make a fine couple if I may say so, sir. Miss, regrettably, I'm afraid I don't have much in the way of ladies' furnishings, but my associate two tents down has just the things you may need."

Mel withdrew her hand immediately, but the warmth lingered.

"Thanks," she said, but the salesman was already talking about this and that to Nathaniel.

Nathaniel's brain caught up with the situation, and he tried to figure out a way to extract himself from this before the salesman got too far down the road. He mentally added up all of the totals for each item the man had brought over and found the number staggering.

He eyed the man in his breeches and waistcoat, with the

shirtsleeves rolled up. "Sir, I appreciate you taking the time to offer your suggestions, but I am afraid I have several of these items already." Before the salesman could voice a protest, he continued. "I know that you carry quality pieces and that your price can't be beat, but I could not possibly part with my own in favor of new, as they have seen me through many a skirmish and the occasional battle. I'm just here to show…"

He wasn't sure what to call Mel, but clearly, this man appreciated a good show of his speech, and she had said that this was all about pretending how things used to be, so he went with what his mother would want. "Miss Melanie, here are items similar to those of my own. I do thank you for your kindness."

Whatever the man had been expecting, it wasn't that. "Well, of course, sir, do walk around my humble establishment and let me know how I may be of assistance to you."

"Wow," Mel said when he walked off.

Nathaniel shrugged. "That's the first time I've felt close to normal, well, you know, since—"

"Yeah, that's kinda what I was going for when I thought about bringing you here."

He smiled at her. "Thanks. It is like mine, isn't it?"

"I can't tell the difference, but I mean, this smells better."

Nathaniel barked out a laugh.

Still in the coat and hat, he walked around the tent with Mel, pointing out different items and explaining what each was for.

It was hard to see some of the so-called relics for sale, such as the buttons and the box of shrapnel lying in the corner, but they did at least feel familiar.

He shed the coat and hat before thanking the salesman, whose name had turned out to be Chuck, who had handed him a card in case he wanted to make a purchase.

"It is my proudest duty to help out any young man engaged in fighting on behalf of his King. Please swing back around if you want another look at something," he called out after him.

They peeked in a few more tents as they walked through Sutler Row. There was a blacksmith, a lady with knit woolen caps, the tent full of women's things, and a few authors and artists. Smaller tents filled the gaps where there were more hats, books, and civilian men's clothing, which he found to be of good quality and most familiar with what he knew and had seen. Again, the only notable difference was the prices, which Nathaniel didn't think he would ever get used to.

CHAPTER 27

"Alright, so do you want to do living history or go to the camps first?"

"Living history sounds interesting," he said with a wry grin. "Sounds like me."

They walked over, Mel stopping to talk to some women who were cooking over a fire, while Nathaniel meandered through the tents. She wrinkled her nose at the sign that said, "Refugees and Hospital."

"I'm too squeamish for this. Can we skip it?"

He hesitated, not wanting to miss anything. Ever sharp-witted, Mel noticed and asked, "How about you look around and I'll grab some more food for you to try. The smoke is starting to get to my asthma anyway. Do you want to meet at the stands before the battle? I can grab us a spot in front."

"Are you sure? I'd hate to leave you."

"I wanted you to see all of this. I thought it might, you know, mean a lot to you. I'm good for movies and snacks, but maybe you can talk to them," she waved her hands in the air. " About all of this."

Nathaniel squeezed her hand before pulling her in for a kiss.

"You know me better than anyone."

She grinned and wiggled her fingers. "Have fun!" she called out as she moved on down the row of tents.

Nathaniel agreed and headed in.

The hospital tent near them was like others in that it was shockingly clean, to the point where he was nearly blinded by the sun. A small flap was folded back through which he ducked inside and immediately wished he hadn't. It was divided into two sections. On one side was a hospital, and on the other was a group of women cooking.

The sights and the smells made his head swim with memories.

He turned and noticed the civilian entertaining a family in blue jeans a few paces away near another hospital tent with the flap open. A small sign that read "Refugee Living History" was next to them.

"Are you really gonna eat that?" a little boy asked the woman sitting on a camp chair.

"Carter!" his mother hissed.

"Of course we are. This is our lunch!" The women were both wearing linen dresses.

The younger woman got up and pulled an oak log from a generous wood pile before throwing it on the fire. The older woman stood up and stirred a pot on a trivet over coals, turning a roast tied to the spit.

Behind them, a table sat with white china, two loaves of bread that looked a far cry from what he had seen referred to as bread in the past, a few apples, eggs, and a half-finished sock on the kind of needles his mother had used with points on both sides.

The boy must have wrinkled his nose because she said, "Oh, come now, it's not that bad! These are hard times with the taxes and Boston Harbor being closed. We must be thankful for what we have, and this"—she gestured with her hands at the food—"this is a feast!"

It was indeed.

"See, honey? Back then, there wasn't enough to go around like we have today," the mother said to her son, who remained decidedly unmoved by the stew bubbling away.

"What if you didn't like it?" asked the little boy.

"The food?" the woman asked. "You didn't have a choice! It was this or go hungry." The woman said that a little too jauntily for Nathaniel's taste, but it seemed to shock the little boy, which was her desired effect.

"Yeah, can you imagine not having dinner tonight?" the mother asked her son, rubbing his back.

The little boy's face was solemn as he shook his head no, and Nathaniel couldn't keep the sad smile from his face.

"Good day, sir! Come forward and take a look at our items here. We are happy to answer any questions you may have."

Nathaniel looked around him and found no other man in the area.

"Yes, you! Come closer if you'd like. We're just making our lunch and keeping an eye on dinner tonight."

He inclined his head slightly and stepped forward. "Hello."

"We are patriot refugees from New York. We've fled from our homes and have taken up near the British camp."

Nathaniel took in the abundance and opened and closed his mouth twice before he could form a sentence.

"Refugees?" he finally said. If they had thought he might be dim-witted before, then surely they were convinced of it now, though he couldn't help it.

Images flashed through his mind of the day after the battle. In a crowd of people all leaving town, one woman with nothing but a sack slung over shoulder, so she could carry her infant, while a toddler pulled at her skirt, crying.

"Mama, I want to go home. I want to go home, Mama. Mama—"

The woman had marched slowly through the mud of the street, oblivious to her daughter's cries or the state of her filthy skirt—one in a crowd of many forced from their homes, carrying only what they could. The cries turned to wailing a few yards away. The child's screams and pleas echoed off the damaged, empty buildings as she spoke for every adult and soldier present. Those people had lost almost everything.

"Sir? Excuse me, sir? Do you need some water? Here, why don't you sit down for a minute?" The woman pushed one of her camp chairs toward him.

Nathaniel, ripped out of his memory, shook his head. "No-no, thank you, ma'am. I apologize. It uh…it must be just the sun getting to me."

The sturdy woman eyed him carefully, clearly expecting him to collapse any moment.

"There's a water station in that direction on the way to the British camp, if you need to cool off," the mother said next to him.

"Thank you, I might do that." He turned to leave and swayed, gazing at the hospital.

Empty white cots lined in rows filled the space, and in the middle stood a makeshift table of two boards on barrels with a variety of instruments that he would rather not see again. The surgeon had his shirtsleeves rolled up and wore a stained apron. He stood behind the table, holding a tourniquet in one hand, while talking to a family.

Turning to leave, Nathaniel noticed something. It held his feet to the ground as sure as if they were stone.

It was a good thing the man and his wife, who had a child

strapped to her back, were turned the other way so they wouldn't see the blatant shock on Nathaniel's face.

The man's left leg was like his own, but it was the right that had him staring.

Although it was the same shape as the other leg, it was decidedly not made of flesh. The bottom part resembled the barrel of a musket, and instead of the calf, there was a thicker section covered in images of what he now recognized as the United States flag.

The man folded his arms and shifted his position as a normal person would. If he had been wearing trousers, Nathaniel was sure he wouldn't have been able to tell.

The man posed a question to the surgeon. "So, walk me through a knee disarticulation back then. What were the options?" His voice was clear and steady.

The surgeon tilted his head to the side. "Well, there wouldn't have been a whole lot, but it does depend on the nature of the injury, of course."

"Well, mine was outside of Baghdad, we were in a convoy, and my Humvee went over an IED, so extensive bone damage from shrapnel." His voice was matter-of-fact.

The surgeon nodded once and said, "Thank you for your service."

The veteran nodded in return, but said nothing, waiting.

"While not as common as in later wars, the dangers of artillery wounds were still very real. Cannon fire could tear through ranks, and exploding shot or splintered wood from nearby trees and fences often caused devastating injuries. At battles like Bunker Hill and Saratoga, surgeons reported men torn apart by flying debris or grapeshot—wounds that were brutal and often fatal." The surgeon began pulling out various glass vials and bandages, laying them out.

He held a clean bandage up. "In the field, medics would first dress the wound before helping the wounded to get to the hospital. In a situation similar to the one you described, the surgeon would probably take the leg off at the hip joint."

As the surgeon went on, Nathaniel's vision swam. Sweat was trickling down his back.

Screams of men in delirium begging for death or mercy filled his head. Blood-red socks lay in the mud before him. The hot stench of rotting flesh and fresh blood filled his nose. His head was spinning.

There were men everywhere. The hospital was full. Makeshift beds, ripped from nearby houses, were scattered. The wounded lay all around him. Some lay on the grass, some crying out in thirst, blind with pain. Others quietly died alone in the chaos, forsaken to their injuries deemed too extensive to save. He saw Benny's face in front of him, the red at his side.

The sweltering heat bore down on him. The smells, the sounds. All of it. Someone screamed. The surgeon was running toward him now. Someone grabbed him. He turned to leave, desperate for air, when he fell into darkness.

CHAPTER 28

When he woke, a rhythmic sound, low and humming, reminded Nathaniel of a fiddle string being plucked without expertise. There was something cool on his head and under his arms. He reached to take it off, when a hand stopped him.

"Take it easy. You passed out," a woman's voice said.

"Mel?" he said, but it came out as a croak. He tried to sit up.

"Woah, easy now. Yeah, that's right, you just lie back down. You're in an ambulance. My name is Katy. You were overheated at the living history site and fainted. Take it easy. Is there someone we can call for you?"

Nathaniel looked around now, finally able to take in the room around him. He was on a thin bed with metal railings on either side, in a small space with metal cabinets that held various wrapped packages, which he could see through a glass window. The woman in front of him, who must have been something like a nurse, sat waiting for a response. The fine lines around her brown eyes spoke of experience, as did the strands of gray in her short, black hair.

She eyed him and held out a bottle containing a shocking yellow water.

"Here you go. This will help get some fluid in you and restore those electrolytes you've been neglecting." She raised it again, nodding for him to take it.

Nathaniel took the medicine she was handing him. The bottle felt cool to his touch.

Nathaniel was now looking at the bottle in his hand and twisted open the top, just as Mel had taught him. He cleared his dry throat. "Is this medicine?" he asked.

The nurse sharply looked at him, and her eyes narrowed. "It's Gatorade. Never had it?" She raised an eyebrow and put the pen she was holding down when he shook his head no.

"It'll help. They say it tastes like lemon-lime, but that's a pretty big stretch if you ask me." The nurse returned to writing her notes and engaging in small talk. Nathaniel eased the bottle to his nose to take a sniff and found that she was right. There was a vague tanginess. He took a small sip and found the taste to be strong, yet refreshing.

"Good, thank you, ma'am."

"You're welcome. So finish that one—oh, good, you're almost done, well, finish it. Your vitals are strong, but I want you to still hang out here for a few more minutes. I'll have another bottle for you to take with you. How much water have you had since you got here?"

"None, ma'am," he said.

She glided back on the stool, which Nathaniel didn't realize was on wheels. "Annnnnnd here's the bottle of water you're taking with you too." She opened another cabinet and grabbed one, then handed it to him. "The sun is stronger than it looks out there. You need to drink water to prevent this from happening again. Do you want me to call someone for you?"

Nathaniel shook his head. He couldn't remember Mel's

number and hadn't brought it with him. It still surprised him how everyone needed to know where everyone was at all times. He didn't think he'd get used to it anytime soon.

The nurse didn't look too pleased with him, but resigned herself to his answer. "We'll be here all weekend, so if you start to feel lightheaded again, you need to make your way here before we're called to come and get you." A steely gaze pierced through him until he nodded in understanding like a child who had the good sense to recognize a higher authority when he met one.

"Good," she said, satisfied. "I'll need you to sign a waiver saying that you've understood what I'm telling you here."

Nathaniel thanked her and was back out, walking with his water bottle, looking for Mel, when he spotted a paper sign pointing the way to the camp over a heavily trodden path through the grass. As Nathaniel walked forward, a few more young British-looking soldiers passed him, presumably on the way to go shopping. One had a clean haversack over his body, and the other held a wooden canteen in his hand. Neither looked to be older than twenty-five, as their beards hadn't even fully come in yet.

A camp on the edge of the woods came into view. The familiar smell of black powder, smoke, and men hit him hard. The little white tents were all very clean and arranged in small groups, each around a fire.

Another soldier was walking toward him now, looking down at the grass. He was wearing a full knapsack, with a hatchet tucked into the straps, and carrying a musket. Nathaniel considered that he looked too young in demeanor, but otherwise resembled one of his brothers on the campaign.

Blue eyes met his, and he saw a soft mouth that no man ever could have.

"Morning," a woman's voice said.

Despite the shock, Nathaniel nodded out of pure habit and watched as the woman marched past him uphill at a good speed.

He had heard a few rumors about women fighting, but had never seen it for himself. At the time, he'd had his doubts, but seeing her charge up the hill as good as any man made him consider that he might've been wrong.

Wouldn't be the first thing he was wrong about.

As he turned back around and headed for the camp, he thought that Mel would've made a damn good soldier, provided that she thought the commanding officer wasn't an idiot. The issue, of course, would never be her ability, but how much of a distraction she would have been for the other soldiers.

Tents set up in rows now surrounded him. A few men lounged by their fires. The smell of smoke and black powder couldn't compete with the smell of coffee, a mix which he hadn't smelled since he had come here.

A few men were playing cards. One was asleep, his head resting on a pack, with a cap over his eyes. As Nathaniel walked through, he took note of the familiar sites, which paid testimony to how seriously these young men were about recreating the past. He saw a few pictures of ladies in varying stages of undress, love letters, newspapers, and twisted ropes of tobacco, all from his own time or at least appearing to be exact replicas. There were a few things out of place, though.

There had been one of the coolers Mel had pointed out earlier in the day. A blanket had covered it up, but a corner was peeking out and had caught his eye. In a tent, he had seen a different type of blanket that looked like black silk, appearing to be stuffed with something soft, poking out from underneath the familiar old, scratchy wool blanket.

A few young men began to fill cartridge boxes and check

the hammers on their muskets. Mel had the schedule and the map, but he could tell the time for the battle must be getting close.

A horse whinnied nearby, and by instinct, he turned to the sound. On the edge of the woods stood about a dozen horses tied to the highline, saddled and grazing.

His legs walked over there before his mind caught up. A large gray gelding looked up at Nathaniel as he approached before deciding the cool, shaded grass was more appealing.

The horses were so close to what he remembered that he thought for a brief moment he might be a ghost visiting his men after his demise.

"Pretty, isn't he?" a voice asked behind him.

Nathaniel turned around to see a corporal walking toward him.

"His name's Portland," the young man said.

"He yours?"

The man nodded. "Yeah, he and I go way back. I've dragged him to a bunch of these, but he seems to still get a kick out of it."

"I didn't know they had horses here," Nathaniel said, looking around at all the horses.

"Oh yeah, a bunch of us come here. It's an expensive hobby, but what the hell, my ex-wife can't have all my money, can she?" The corporal let out a rueful laugh.

Nathaniel smiled even though he wasn't quite sure what he meant.

"Are you a horse person? Most people are put off by his size."

"Yeah, I've been around horses all my life. I had a chestnut, but, uh…" He cleared his throat. "Lost him recently."

"I'm sorry to hear that. I'll be a mess when Port here goes. Since you're interested, I'd like to walk you around before the battle starts. A bunch of us are over there." He inclined his head to a group of tents with a small fire a little ways up the line of the woods. "I'm Tom."

"Nathaniel," he said, shaking the outstretched hand.

They walked toward a camp too similar to the one he had left behind during the storm, and a fiddle somewhere nearby began to play a song he hadn't thought his ears would ever hear again. A voice began to sing:

"Here's forty shillings on the drum, for those who'll volunteer to come, to 'list and fight the foe today, over the hills and far away."

He smiled and started to sing along. The smell of pork fat and smoke filled his nose, and once again, he wondered if this was his purgatory.

CHAPTER 29

Nathaniel waved Tom off when the time came for them to saddle up and get into position for the battle. While he still wasn't sure what to expect from the so-called battle ahead, he headed toward the stands he had seen before, as that's where everyone was congregating. He hoped he could find Mel there and that she hadn't been waiting for him too long at the blacksmith. He hated to worry her.

Tom's unit was the 33rd Regiment of Foot, and Nathaniel had gotten on so well with him that he had his phone number tucked in his pocket. Having met someone else aside from Mel made him feel more anchored. It helped that Tom and his friends were familiar to him and what he knew.

Maybe this is what Mel had wanted. He was eager to find her and tell her the plan had worked.

People trickled into the area while fanning themselves with various programs and maps to find some relief from the unrelenting sun. Several children in the crowd were wearing tricorns, while their fathers and mothers wore hats of a different style. Almost every person was wearing black glasses that must have shaded their eyes.

Nathaniel followed the crowds of people who were ambling in that direction. A voice as loud as God himself was echoing off the distant trees. As he walked closer, the words became clearer.

He could only pick out a few words and phrases. Drawing closer, he approached the large metal stands and walked up alongside them, while listening to the announcer describe the events leading up to this battle.

"Ladies and gentlemen, what you are about to see is a representation of the Second Battle of Saratoga—also known as the Battle of Bemis Heights—fought on October 7th, 1777. By the end of the fighting on October 7th, British forces suffered heavy losses—nearly six hundred men, with over one hundred and fifty killed, nearly four hundred wounded, and dozens more missing in the confusion of retreat."

Missing.

According to the records, Nathaniel was missing. Were there others like him who had gone missing during the battles?

"There you are. I've been looking everywhere!"

He whipped around to find Mel walking up behind him, carrying a bottle of water and a small brown bag.

A cannon sounded off in the distance and made her jump in surprise, as did most of the audience. The announcer continued to outline the movements of troops. On cue, the hairs on his neck stood on end, and his heart began to pick up speed. Another cannon answered the call of its mate.

"You okay?" she asked. Mel had recovered quickly, but it was clear she'd been taken aback by the sound. She still looked a little uneasy with the noise and worried about him. Nathaniel was touched.

He reached out and held her hand.

"They sound different," he said, leaning in so she could hear him over the charges and the announcer.

"What do you mean?"

"They're empty. Not as loud. No metal, I think."

"Let's hope so," she answered him.

They walked forward and selected a spot on the ground near the stands, which were filled with families. Over the field, several British units came into view as they crested over hills, marching in a long column that shifted into a line of battle. There were flags speckled throughout the group and companies riding alongside in formation.

"The British forces, led by General Burgoyne, are advancing down the hill, attempting to break through the American lines near Freeman's Farm. Among them were elements of Fraser's Advance Corps, including British light infantry and grenadiers."

The steady beat of the drums sounded off behind the flags waving over the men while the announcer continued. Horses began to trot forward, and the first volley of musket fire was discharged.

A ripple of unease danced across his skin as he felt the familiar mix of nausea and adrenaline pump through his veins. His body urged him to move and answer the call of the drums to advance. He jumped when her hand touched his arm.

"Is it like it was for you?"

"No," he said, looking out. "But it is just as well. The sounds are close, but it's not the same."

"How so?" Her warm breath was hot on his cheek when she leaned over to ask the question. It was his tether to this time and place, and he clung to it in his mind so that he did not lose himself to his memories.

Infantry on both sides now had marched out and were starting to fall to their apparent death.

Nathaniel drew in a breath before he said, "There's no screaming."

"They're yelling."

"That's not screaming." He was grateful she didn't know the difference.

Men were lying on the battlefield now, and a scattered few were limping away from the fight.

As the infantry units continued to square off, a few charged, and in response, the announcer outlined their movements to the crowd. Smoke started to drift across the field in great white clouds, creating a mystic fog that Nathaniel knew only too well.

Another fife's call and drums propelled the units forward under their various flags. Pops and volleys of empty muskets filled the air along with the smell of black powder. The cannons continued to boom sporadically, some leaving perfect smoke rings.

A whinny caught Nathaniel's ear, and he caught sight of Tom and Portland moving over the hill toward the opposing troops. Tom had his Colt Navy drawn and took aim, firing two of his six shots. A dozen other troopers from the thirty-third moved with him.

The Colonial troops moved to the back, and the announcer boomed overhead.

"To the left, you'll see Colonial riflemen from Daniel Morgan's corps beginning to flank the British position—one of the turning points in this battle."

As the announcer went on, Nathaniel watched the fight, his eyes tracking Portland first and then the other horses and soldiers Tom had introduced him to. Some had better seats than others, and Nathaniel could pick out more than a handful who didn't live in the saddle, though a few rode very well indeed.

The Colonials surged forward, and flashes of light bounced off steel when the soldiers pulled their swords from their scabbards. The horses pounded toward the British, who had followed suit with their swords quickly.

Audience cheers could not drown out the clang of steel as the two forces met. Clouds of dust rose from the ground under the hooves of horses trying to get their footing. Revolvers discharged, and horses fought the reins as their mounts clashed again and again.

A nearby cannon sounded, and several horses shrieked with panic. A young British trooper pulled his reins too far back as his horse skittered in fear. The eyes of the animal roamed around for relief as he tossed his head and leaned back onto his hind legs.

"Give 'em his head! Give 'em his head! God, he's gonna get thrown," Nathaniel said to no one in particular.

The skirmish went on and only spurred the already frightened horse more. As the soldier fought to regain his seat, he pulled the reins back, almost choking the horse. The horse's ears went back flat, and another nearby cannon fired.

All hell broke loose.

A panicked whinny was the only warning given before the horse bucked the young soldier off. He fell to the ground, protecting his head while he rolled away from the hooves. The kid clambered to his feet, trying to calm his animal.

Soldiers shouted and moved their mounts to try to shield the spectators from the frightened gelding, but to no avail. He broke out of the group, snorting and biting, as he kicked his way closer to the people.

People started screaming in the stands, only scaring the poor animal more. Nathaniel tore off running, heading straight for the horse.

The young gelding was still kicking and crazed. Desperate for a way out, his fearful eyes rolled in their sockets, showing the whites.

He was going to break out into a full gallop any second, right into the crowd or the battle.

Nathaniel whipped his shirt off over his head and bounded toward the animal at a full sprint. He had moments unless another cannon fired. The gelding was shrieking and kicking more now, with the screaming spectators around him.

He aimed for her shoulder, hoping to avoid the flying hooves lest he take one to the head or gut, and threw out his shirt one-handed over the animal's eyes. The head was everywhere, flailing to get away from the sights and sounds.

Nathaniel grabbed the other end of the shirt and managed to pull it tight around the scared horse's head and eyes, before using his other arm to try and hold the neck as he talked into his ear.

It was like wrestling a bear, but the moment he was blinded and realized Nathaniel's presence, he felt the fight go out of the big boy a little. The animal kept trying to free himself, but now he was only tossing his head and stomping his feet as opposed to kicking.

Nathaniel didn't pull, but held on, applying a constant, firm pressure like the stable hands had taught him a lifetime ago.

"Easy. Easy now. I know, I know. Up, up… No, settle down. Settle. It's okay. You're okay." He kept talking and stroking.

The horse answered with a series of disgruntled and unsure snorts, but had the good sense to listen.

Even though all apparent danger was over, a woman kept screaming her fool head off in the front of the crowd while shielding her sons, who, though they were much larger than she and old enough themselves to fight, cowered behind their mother. He fought the urge to yell at her to shut up.

Fumbling around with the hand that was stroking, he

caught the reins and tried to bring them around to lead the horse away from the field. A gray nose appeared on the other side and let out a chuff.

Nathaniel looked up and nodded at Tom, who inclined his head in return before leading the way with Portland.

"Come on, Kettle. It's okay. That's a good boy. Let's go."

Nathaniel kept talking into the horse's ear as he gripped the makeshift blindfold tight and led the horse alongside Portland's shoulder away from the ongoing battle and spectators, back toward the British camp.

"How's the rider?" Nathaniel finally asked when he thought Kettle was calm enough for conversation.

"Lucas took a fall, but he's okay. His buddies took him over to the medical area to get checked out just in case, but he's a tough kid. New to reenactments and horses in general, but a good guy."

"Do they know we have his horse?" Nathaniel asked. The last thing he needed was to be charged with theft.

"Yeah, believe me, everyone saw you run out there like an idiot. I offered to help take him back. Port here has seen it all. He's good at calming the other animals down. Doesn't spook hardly ever."

Nathaniel could see that for himself. Portland looked almost bored with the exchange and unruffled with the ongoing battle. That was a ringing endorsement for Tom, regardless of what his ex-wife might have thought. Horses all had different personalities, yes, but a calm horse typically had enjoyed a quiet environment where they didn't want for much.

"Nathaniel!" Mel called out behind him.

Kettle flinched a little and gave a nervous whinny.

He shushed him and resumed talking into his ear while he strained to make eye contact with Mel, since both of his hands were full. She ran up alongside him.

"Holy shit!" she hissed when she reached him. "What the hell were you thinking? You could've been kicked in that thick head of yours! The announcer was going crazy. Didn't you hear him?"

"Not really," he said, now murmuring occasionally in Kettle's ear.

"Not surprising," Tom spoke up. "For the record, I just called him an idiot before you showed up."

"Thank you. I'm Melanie, but everyone calls me Mel. I happen to be this idiot's friend."

"Nice to meet you, Mel. I'm Tom. Takes balls to run out there like that."

"Didn't give it much thought," he muttered to Kettle.

"Clearly," Mel said only for his ears. Her hand reached over and stroked down his exposed back, which, much to his embarrassment, was wet with sweat.

He didn't want to look over at her and focused on the grass ahead of them until he heard her say, "Hey."

Meeting her eyes, he saw the mix of worry and relief in their warm, brown hue. She drew her perfect lips into a thin line and looked somewhere between mad as hell and exasperated.

Nathaniel released the blindfold so that Kettle could see Portland and held the reins in his hand. He reached down and held her hand before giving it a squeeze, which she answered with one of her own. He was grateful Tom was on the other side so that he couldn't see, and that he didn't seem to be in the mood for conversation. With the warm sun beating on his back, he grasped Mel's hand until they reached the British camp.

CHAPTER 30

Patrick hadn't liked history. Ever.

The only reason he had volunteered to help with this reenactment was to get close to Steward, an investment banker who lived in the same building. He had tickets to an exclusive golf tournament, and Patrick wanted in. He only ever invited those who donated or volunteered. Patrick had overheard the doorman ask about it and had lingered to express his interest.

He loved how golf was one of the few remaining exclusive spaces. Being invited made it special.

So it was settled, a Saturday for a Saturday. Well, almost. He was woefully late today, but hey, it still counted, right? He wasn't about to give his whole Saturday up to the nerd fest.

It hadn't been too taxing. He had checked people off, handed them maps, and waited for the battle to begin.

When the battle began with the announcer's booming voice, Patrick followed Steward and the others to watch. That's when he saw something interesting. He had to do a double-take when he first saw her, but that was Mel, all right.

She was walking next to the stands and looked great. It

had been too long since he had seen her in anything but her work clothes, and those jeans she had on fit every curve like a glove. He had always liked her in and outside of the courtroom. He had asked her out a couple of times, but she had given him a cool pass with an excuse about work or her grandma, which was okay. At least she was trying to be nice-ish about it. After a while, he gave up asking her directly.

He asked around plenty, though.

No boyfriend—or girlfriend, for that matter—to speak of, currently. She mostly kept to herself and focused on her job. He tried to lend a hand from afar. Sending her Chinese the other week was a stretch, but she said thank you, so he felt good about it. It might take a while, but someone as hot as her was worth the chase. Besides, she was so smart, it made it more of a challenge. Patrick had always loved hard-to-get things. Again, it made it special. Women who threw themselves at him just because they learned he was a lawyer were a casual entertainment. There was no thrill, and he became bored with them faster than the bed cooled.

It was funny to see her here. He didn't know she had an interest in history or anything that wasn't her job, for that matter.

Mel approached the battlefield and—

A frown came across his face before he recognized what he was seeing.

She was talking to some guy.

Mel put her hand on this dude's arm and was saying something into his ear.

Oh…

His lips lifted upwards in a sly smile as he read more in the body language. So she did have a life. Meant there was potential. How could this guy compete with him? He didn't look like anything special.

A cannon fired, and a horse screeched. The crowd

murmured and started to rise, pointing in that direction. Mel's man took off running and whipped his shirt off straight for the horse, who had thrown his rider and was out of control, heading for the stands.

People in the lower part of the stands started yelling to get out of the way, and all rose like a tide in a sluggish attempt to flee. People grabbed babies, kids, and tugged at disengaged teens. A woman was screaming somewhere and needed to shut up.

The man flung his shirt over the animal's eyes and was calming it down. A few of the reenactors on horses rode over and were talking with him. Patrick's eyes tracked to where the fallen soldier had been and saw him being helped into a gator to be taken to the ambulances. The man seemed to be pretty good with the horse. Others rode over now, and it looked like they were taking the animal back to wherever it had come from.

Crisis averted, but the show went on.

Mel caught up to the man and looked somewhere between raging pissed off and terrified.

Patrick stepped back out of view and watched as Mel ran her hand through her windswept curls before grabbing the man's hand and holding it as she walked with him next to the horse. They both looked at each other, and she leaned up to whisper something in the man's ear before he looked down and said something that made her laugh and wrap her arms around him in a hug.

Patrick had to know more, which is why he followed behind at a discreet distance.

Professional courtesy, after all.

CHAPTER 31

José Gutiérrez never forgot a face. It came in handy while working at the prison and served him well outside of his job. He always wondered where people came from, where they were going, and what could drive them to do what they did. The face gave so much away.

He wasn't afraid to run into anyone outside of work, since he didn't deal much with the prisoners directly. When he did, he was always professional. Didn't get too close. Didn't push their buttons. Just here doing his job. It made it easier to sleep at night. That, and that the crazy ones weren't getting out.

Still, he paid extra close attention on the occasion when he did see a former inmate.

He had picked up extra shifts as security for significant events, and the Battle of Saratoga reenactment was only a few hours away. With the baby coming, any little bit would help. He had saved up enough leave to stay home for two weeks, but his paternal leave was unpaid, as was his wife's twelve weeks of leave. Just because they could legally stay home didn't mean it was easy or that they could afford to.

José had almost avoided this job because it was so far away, but when his wife saw the event pay, they agreed to do it as long as she stayed in bed and didn't go into labor.

"Don't have a baby until you return. Got it," she said, giving him a thumbs-up from the couch when he left that morning.

It had been a very easy day. He had walked around, keeping an eye on crowds and pointing people toward registration or the bathrooms. Briefly, a little boy had gotten separated from his family, who had come running a minute later when they saw him. He complimented the kid on handling it so well and coming to an officer, before telling him to stay close and waving the grateful parents off. He hadn't even had time to get the kid's name and say it into his radio.

It was a fun day of work, riding around and offering water while seeing the camps, demonstrations, and reenactors. Made him feel like he had traveled in time—wild stuff.

The main event was the big battle, and he sat and chatted with the other guard while watching the stands fill up with spectators and the reenactors take their positions. He was enjoying the announcer's explanation and thinking about when he could bring his wife and baby back next year, when the cannons went off right before the soldiers started marching.

His radio squawked to life from where he and the other security sat in the gator. On the other side of the stands, there was a commotion as the cannons fired. One horse went crazy and was hopping all over the place with no rider in sight. It tore through the tape separating the spectators from the field.

"Oh, shit," said his partner for the day, firing up the engine. They took off toward the horse and soon spotted the rider lying in the grass. A few other reenactors had ridden over to contain the horse.

They focused on the man, or rather, the kid. He barely looked old enough to be out of high school.

His white face was all sweaty and pale as he panted out of control.

"My leg! It's in my leg!"

Sure enough, somehow, a sword had nicked the side of his thigh. It had missed the important bits, and thankfully didn't seem to have hit a major artery, but still, it wasn't good.

"It's not in there anymore. Just got you a bit. Let's get you to medical," he said, and loaded the young redcoat onto a stretcher and into the back of the gator.

"You'll be okay—just breathe. We got you," he said in his soothing voice, hopping in the back to hold his hand while the driver took off to the ambulance.

That's when he looked up and saw not one, but two, familiar faces. Mel and her client Nathaniel were standing near the crazed horse. His shirt was off, and he was stroking the animal to calm it down, while she stood back warily watching him.

Their outfits were casual. She looked from him to the animal and back. Worried. He was calm and determined. He glanced down at her and smiled. That was when she reached for his hand and hugged him around the neck.

Oh boy.

CHAPTER 32

Mel walked with Nathaniel and Kettle and watched when they reached the camp. Nathaniel moved in a complicated and graceful dance with the animal, anticipating his moves while he removed the equipment.

If she was honest, the animal freaked her out. It was huge, and having been raised in the city, there was never much exposure outside of a middle school field trip to a pumpkin patch.

Nathaniel was different.

When the animal moved one way, he moved the other in a seamless ballet that suggested they were communicating in a way that none of those watching were privy to.

Nathaniel reached for a brush without comment and began brushing the foreign animal down with the gentleness and care that she knew by instinct that he would have treated his own horse with.

His horse.

He had mentioned one, but hadn't asked about the fate of his horses. It hadn't even occurred to her that they could have a bond like the one she was seeing, but then again, why would it have? She had never been around them or had a dog. Or a cat. Or a goldfish. Shoot, she hadn't even had a plant.

Ouch. Talk about married to the job, she thought.

Nathaniel ran his hand along the animal's coat, which now gleamed in the sun. His lips kept murmuring soft nothings as he checked and rechecked the hooves and legs for any injury before leading him away back toward the others.

"He's a good one, isn't he?" Tom said, making her jump. She could feel her cheeks warm with the embarrassment of being caught staring.

"Yeah," she said. "He's better than me. I can tell you which part of the horse is the back end, but that's about it."

Tom smiled next to her. "They're just like people. Some are fussy, some are quick to get pissed, and some are super relaxed. You can tell a lot about someone when you look at how they are around horses."

Great. So he probably thought she was high-strung and super stressed out. Well, if the shoe fits…

Nathaniel walked over. "I tied him up, and he seems better now. Grazing over there. I didn't see any food, and wasn't sure—"

Tom raised his hand. "Don't worry about it. It's probably in the trailer, but it's okay. Lucas will be back soon enough to check on him."

Mel looked at Nathaniel, but didn't see any indication that this information was new to him. Instead, he stuck out his hand, which Tom heartily accepted.

"It was good to get back around some horses," Nathaniel said.

"Glad you came today. Not sure Port and I could have gotten to Kettle as fast," Tom said with a smile.

Nathaniel inclined his head. "Thank you for showing me around. I was glad to have the company."

"Let me know if you ever want to come back around. I have some authentic gear I can let you borrow to dress out in."

Nathaniel smiled at that, and Mel knew what they both were thinking. If Tom could see what Nathaniel had at the apartment, he would be deeply impressed by *his* authenticity.

They said their goodbyes, and Mel walked with Nathaniel back toward the parking lot.

"You shouldn't have run after him like that. You could've gotten hurt," she said to him, feeling weird as she said it.

He squeezed her hand back and pulled her into another hug. She closed her eyes, feeling the warmth of his arms around her.

"It's alright. I'm fine."

"I got so scared when I couldn't find you."

He shushed her like he had just done for the horse, and embarrassingly, it worked.

"I know. I'm here now. Though that does seem to be a theme with us."

They walked hand in hand toward the car, as Nathaniel filled her in about the nurse with the yellow drink, which made her worry, even though he assured her it was a momentary thing.

"I wanted today to be nicer than it was," she said, with one hand on the wheel and one arm leaned up against the door, her hand propping up her head.

He turned toward her and frowned. "Do not say that. This is the most useful I've felt since I've been here. Well, other than fainting."

"Don't say that. You're useful!"

"Not in the way a man should be," he said again, a note of bitterness in his voice. "I should be taking care of you, not the other way around."

Mel sat up a little straighter. "I told you; it's nothing. It's not a big deal. Things are different now."

"It is important to me. I want to provide. I want to care for you, and I don't just mean in your kitchen or in your bed."

Mel cracked a smile, but didn't say anything when she realized how serious he was.

"I want to provide for you. I want to be of value. I want to be a man. Not some pet. That's what men do. They earn, protect, and provide for their women."

"Their women?" she asked, with a glance toward him. Wondering, not for the first time, what that made them.

"Yes, you are brilliant, and so independent—"

"You should stop there."

"But how can I ever be happy if I'm not doing something for you, for myself, for anyone?"

The harshness in his voice echoed in the silence.

"You don't have to do something to have value," she said, her voice quiet as she reached over to hold his hand. "You're allowed to just be happy. You make me happy just by being here."

"I wish I felt the same way," he said, choking the words out one at a time.

Mel withdrew her hand from his at this confession and put it back on the wheel.

"I don't know how I ever can be happy again without a purpose."

That night, Mel heated leftovers before they ate on the couch, this time watching *Titanic* since Nathaniel had reached this part of American history.

She rested her head on his shoulder and breathed in the smell of him. Clean soap, with a hint of smoke and gunpowder underneath from the time at the camp.

"I know it's hard for you, but I don't think I've been this

happy in years."

He turned to look down at her. She shifted so her eyes met his. "I want to make you happy."

"You do," she said, her voice low.

"I wish I could make you even happier. Make your life easier. Take away your worries."

"Then what would I do all day?" she asked, serious. "I need a purpose too."

"I guess we're in a jam."

"Guess so," she said, as he leaned down and kissed her.

They took their time, exploring, tasting, savoring. This time was less fearful and bolder, driven by the desire to connect soul to soul rather than just new lust.

Clothes were on the floor, and they used the couch in ways she had never thought possible outside of books.

He ran his hands down her back and pulled her into straddling him. They deepened the kiss as he pressed her chest into him, and she worked her body against his in a slow thrust that deepened her pleasure to a place she hadn't previously known. This wasn't fast or hurried, but a slow savoring of him. Gone were any fears about her body or scars. It was just her and Nathaniel coming together as one.

While she held the back of his head, he pressed his lips to her neck and down her breasts, making her moan with pleasure as she tossed her head back in abandon. Right as she lost her breath with waves of pleasure, he let her crumple against him and stroked her back as her head rested on his shoulder, murmuring soft things in her ear.

He waited until she stirred then carried her to the bedroom, where he laid her down reverently onto the bed. Again, she didn't reach for the sheet or turn off the light as she usually would have. Nathaniel was drinking her in with a mixture of hunger and awe, and she didn't want it to end.

"You deserve everything I could give you in this life and my last one," he breathed in a hoarse voice.

"I just want you as you are." Her voice was low, a whisper, as she watched him come over and worship her with tender kisses starting at her foot, then working his way up her calf, thigh, hip, breast, and neck.

By the time he reached her ear, she was squirming with pleasure coursing through her, eager for more.

She reached up and pulled him down to her mouth as she pleasured him, reveling in each moan. He said her name like a prayer and held her like a treasure.

Nathaniel withdrew from her and pulled her to him, thrusting in deep again, and riding her into oblivion before he crashed with waves of pleasure over her again.

They held each other in the dark. Their hearts beat in unison as they breathed in sync. Yin and yang, they lay perfectly matched in each other's arms.

Nathaniel sat up and looked down at her.

"I will be forever grateful that I exist at the same time as you."

Mel felt her eyes water, and she blinked away tears, afraid of the depth of her feelings for him.

He kissed her with such tenderness that it was like a warm breeze, before pulling her against him as they slept, arm in arm.

CHAPTER 33

It had been a day, Mel thought on Monday morning as she shut down her computer and shoved her papers back into her bag. All the time spent with Nathaniel was really starting to cut into her work, and the tasks she needed to complete on other people's cases were adding up.

Even Tabby had noticed and stopped by to check in on her recent progress, or lack thereof. It hadn't been more than a quick doorway check-in that ended with a kind, understanding smile, but Mel still felt the pressure.

Mel hadn't realized how much work she did off the clock until the time had been filled in different ways, including the best sex of her life last night.

Going to the jail today could've gone better. Seeing a client's hopeful face reminded her of the importance of her time. That meeting for her had been one item on her too long to-do list, but for her client, it was the only item on his.

She wanted to wrap things up and go home to Nathaniel, but she tried to stay focused. Of course, her dirty mind and wanton body betrayed her by revisiting the memories in incredible detail. Details that meant she was uncomfortable in her clothes for most of the afternoon in the office.

"Hey, lady," said a smooth voice from the doorway.

Mel jumped as if she had been caught doing something bad, even though there was no way he could've known what she had just been thinking about.

"Hey Patrick," she said, clearing her throat, which somehow only made her seem more guilty.

"All caught up?"

"Hardly," she said, waving a hand over the case files on her desk.

"Yeah, I had noticed you weren't working as late as you used to. Got a hot date I don't know about?"

Mel tried to hide the bubble of panic that stirred in her chest by putting a mask of steel over her features.

"When do you finish all of your work? I can't believe your case load is so light, you have time to visit."

"I like to come visit you."

"Well, I was just leaving," she said, making a show of packing her bag—that was going to eventually give her back problems—and swinging it up onto her shoulder.

"I see that," Patrick said, still standing in front of her door, blocking her exit.

"Did you need something?" she asked, getting annoyed.

"I need a drink and some dinner to wash it down with. You free?"

"I—"

"You know all work and no play makes for a dull day."

That about did it for her. She hated being interrupted and had had enough of his behavior.

Mel drew herself up to her full height and, in her court-room voice, said, "Patrick, I'd appreciate it if you stepped out of my way."

He raised his eyebrows and didn't move.

Mel looked him dead in the eye. She didn't want to make an enemy out of him, but if he insisted…

Patrick stepped back, but not by much. She didn't have a choice and recognized what the bastard was doing.

With as much poise as the small space allowed, she walked through the door and shut her office behind her. He had moved enough to let her by, but in doing so, her arm had to graze his shirt.

"Mel—" he started.

"Have a good night," she said without stopping. He wasn't the only one who could talk over people.

"If I'd known you had someone at home, I would've sent more food the other night. You'll have to let me know their Chinese order."

The icy dread dripped down her spine. There was no way he could know about Nathaniel.

"Good night, Patrick," she said, not turning around to give him any evidence. First rule of being accused of something: Shut up. Second rule of being accused: Don't act guilty.

She didn't stop moving until she was around the corner and heading straight for her car, which was only parked a street away.

"Hey Mel!"

"What the hell did I just— Oh, sorry."

José Gutiérrez took a half step back in the parking lot, his brow dipping in confusion.

"You alright? Something happen?" he asked, concerned.

Mel rubbed her hand over her face. José had always been a nice enough guy.

"Shit. No, sorry. I thought you were someone else," she said.

"Maybe this isn't a good time."

"It isn't, but what's up anyway?" she said.

"I'm worried about you, Mel."

"You too?" she asked with sarcasm.

He paused and looked at her. "I saw you at the reenactment with your client."

That stopped her cold. Mel felt an icy nervousness fall over her body now. Is that how Patrick knew about Nathaniel?

Thoughts came flying into her head with questions like how, when, and what he saw. She remained silent.

"I was working the event," he said, filling in the information that he correctly assumed she needed. "Saw you and your client." He let that sentence hang in the air between them.

Shit.

The fact that José wasn't getting into the nitty-gritty meant he knew what was up.

Double shit.

"I'm allowed to counsel—"

"Mel. Don't give me that."

Mel clamped her lips shut and waited to see what he was going to do with his new information.

José looked around him in the parking lot before leaning in. In a low voice, he said, "Listen, maybe with the baby coming I'm getting the protective father vibes, I don't know, but I've always looked at you like a sister. I don't want to see you get hurt, by him or anyone else. You don't know this guy. None of us do. I don't need to tell you how much is at stake here."

Mel wanted to dissent, but decided that if he knew something she didn't, that would only make matters worse.

"If you need help with something, let me know. I'm here for you. Okay?"

She nodded and turned toward her car.

After fumbling for her keys, she popped the door open

and slid in, giving her shoulder a welcome break after the Olympic-sized bag had been on there for two conversations.

José tapped on the window, which she rolled down.

"The fact that you haven't bitten my head off is worrying me more."

Mel sighed. "Thank you, José. I mean it."

"Are you okay?"

"I will be."

"Promise me?"

Mel looked at him again, and her heart broke a little. She hated lying to him. He was such a nice guy and genuinely cared for her as a friend—the complete opposite of Patrick. Lying didn't come easily to her when it came to him.

"I promise."

"And for the record, I don't like the other lawyer either."

"Patrick?"

"Yeah, no bueno."

"Thanks, José. I appreciate it."

"You have my number." It wasn't a question.

Mel cranked the engine over and waved to him as she pulled out. She really didn't want to believe he could be right. She knew Nathaniel and that he was a good person with a complicated story, but was he good in her life with the relationship out in the open?

She needed to think about that. It was one thing to have the best sex of her life, but it was another to build a life with someone with no paperwork, credit, or job. He had told her he wasn't happy without his own agency. She had tried to assuage him of that, but now it was starting to sink in. What kind of relationship could it be if it was so one-sided?

She'd figure that out later. Right now, she was rattled and needed to see him. Earlier that morning, she had offered him a lift to the library as usual, but he said he wanted to walk and make his way there.

Mel parked the car and hustled to her apartment. Her bag landed with a thump on the floor under the old photograph of her parents.

"Hey!"

Silence answered her.

"Nathaniel?" she called out again.

A hollowness bloomed in her chest as she looked in all the rooms and confirmed he was indeed gone, though his belongings were left behind. Good, he meant to come back. She breathed a sigh of relief and disappointment.

Mel moved throughout her small space. In the living room, the coffee table was bare except for her neglected novel, and the throw sat folded on the couch. Gleaming stainless steel greeted her in the kitchen sink as opposed to the usual heap of dishes.

There was a note on the counter. Mel's first thought was that his handwriting looked different from any she had seen before. Like a stream of music notes on a score, the letters were long and thin, with their base being smaller.

———

MEL,

Gone in search of a job. Will return soon.
N.

———

THE TENSION GONE, her shoulders slumped. She held the note in her hands.

Looking around, Mel cast her eyes over the apartment. She had lived here alone without being lonely, but today, she couldn't remember what she used to do to fill her time. For the first time, a feeling of loneliness settled into her chest. It no longer felt like home. It felt empty.

Mel set the letter down and tried not to worry about the potential legal logistics of Nathaniel trying to find work, navigate the area, or make his way back. Fingers fumbling for something to do, she headed toward the bathroom to get comfortable.

As she passed through the living room, she turned around and saw the classified section of a newspaper lying in the recycling bin.

No school like the old school.

CHAPTER 34

Will Rackford made his usual way over to the Riverdale stables like he had for the past forty years, and pulled out a cigarette when he was far enough from the farmhouse that his wife wouldn't see.

Of course, Martha still knew.

She was smart, which was half of what had made their forty-six-year marriage work. The smell on his clothes gave him away, but she wouldn't fuss at him for things she didn't see.

That policy was the other half of what had kept them married for forty-six years.

It had been another scorcher and he was damn tired of it already. The heat was fine for summer evenings, but afternoons were exhausting to live through. The path from the house to the barn was only a quarter mile, but the damn thing seemed to grow every year. It also got hotter every year, and surely that had everything to do with global warming and not the fact that he was fifty years older than when he started. Hopefully this new hire was worth a damn because even though it pained him to admit it, he needed help. Good help, that was so good, he could rest easier knowing he was training his replacement, and not going behind some city kid that wanted to do this for a summer before leaving for college.

Will took a drag on his cigarette before flicking it on the ground and stubbing it out with his yard boot. A pop came from somewhere as he bent down to slowly retrieve the butt.

Lying low meant no evidence. Ever.

He tore off the wrapper and stuffed the filter into the pocket of his old jeans for safekeeping until he reached his secret place of disposal.

Even though it was harder, he still loved being out here. Barn sounds reached his ears and calmed his soul like the smooth balm that every horse owner knew. The soft snorts of his thoroughbreds greeted him. Several were snoozing in their stalls, but a few gave him a welcome nicker. During the heat of August, Will kept his animals inside during the day. They'd be turned out for the cooler night once his appointment got here.

It was, after all, his favorite interview technique.

Tess, one of his favorite broodmares, nuzzled his outstretched palm.

"You'll let me know what you think of this one, won't you?"

The deep brown eye blinked.

"Good girl." He patted her neck and moved along the rubberized floor.

His grandfather had built this barn, but it hadn't had the nice features his father had added to it. Will had continued the tradition and was working through his inheritance to keep his horses in peak condition. It had been a long time since they had won a big one, but racing was still good money, and every now and then there was a pot that was worth a damn. Thank God for the ponies and for parents of local kids who would pay for rides and lessons and Van Cortlandt Park.

Ask any true horse person, though, and they would be happy to tell you that the money wasn't the goal here at all. There was something about these animals that got into your blood and stayed there all your life.

Friends of his had lost everything in their portfolios, but they still fed their horses top-shelf feed, and rightfully so. It was a bill they shouldn't—and wouldn't—miss. In a perfect world, the horses could help pay for their expenses, but Will had lived on this rock long enough to know that the world was rarely perfect.

Anytime the opportunity came up to take in a retired animal, he always jumped at the chance. Horses retired from Central Park or the NYPD mounted unit had all spent their final years at these peaceful twenty-one acres. Veterinary bills, medicine, and food all cost money, and the older horses only had companionship to give in return. A good return on the investment, in his mind.

Will wasn't a particularly religious man, but he knew something was up just from a few things he had seen in his life. Somewhere deep inside, he hoped that maybe taking care of a few horses somehow would balance out everything he had done when his time came to an end.

He picked at the filter in his pocket between his fingers.

A few of the horses' ears twitched with the crunch of gravel that Will had been waiting to hear. His lips turned down as he hadn't heard a car and wondered if he was finally starting to lose it.

Will made his way to the end of the barn in time to see a skinny man walk up. Looked like he was in his thirties, so hopefully not a college student, but young enough to handle the workload and was looking for a long-term position. It was hard to find people content with hard, simple work. Everyone was always in a rush to move on these days.

Good. One check so far.

Thoroughbreds were way too valuable and temperamental to have a young kid take care of, and he had learned his lesson the last time—

"Good evening. I'm looking for a Mr. Rackford?" The voice was calm and confident, yet not overly so. British and sounded educated.

"You must be Nathaniel," he said, taking the outstretched hand. Firm, calloused, and a good solid handshake. Old school. No extra fancy shit.

Good. Two checks. So far, so good.

The last two guys hadn't made it this far.

"Alright, well, let's get to it." Will led Nathaniel into the barn and talked shop, pointing out where a few of the essentials were.

"I'm just about to turn them out." He let his sentence hang in the space between them.

"Yes, sir, I can do that. Which paddock?"

Will indicated the one by the house that had the best grass this time of year and went to his corner where he kept his stool.

Taking a load off, he sat and leaned against the wall his grandfather had built. There was a lot of history, tradition, and money invested in this building, and he'd be damned if he wasn't going to give the job of farm manager to just anyone, even if Nathaniel did have a recommendation from Tom, who Will had known for years. Horse people usually ran together, and word traveled fast if someone was no good.

Will watched as Nathaniel patiently talked to each of the horses and got a feel for their personalities. He attended to Tax first, who was restless and ready for dinner, which was a good sign, although almost anyone could've picked up on that vibe.

Before leading every horse out, Nathaniel inspected and spoke to them, treating each one with the level of care it needed. Some, like Tax, were easy to read. Others like Tess, not so much. But Nathaniel had read every horse right and proven in Will's mind that he had grown up around horses and knew how to take care of them the right way. Tess was still, which people often mistook for easygoing, but she scared easily and had a mind of her own. Nathaniel reached up to let her smell him, and watched her ears and head, not engaging further until she relaxed. Only then did he open the door to let her out. As she walked past Will, she swung her head in his direction and shook out her mane before continuing outside.

Nathaniel came back into the barn, and unbeknownst to him, into the final stage of the interview. He didn't make eye contact with Will at all—he didn't even hesitate—but instead went right for the shovel and proceeded to begin mucking out the stalls before getting the broom to sweep out the main aisle.

It was dark now, not that Will minded in the slightest. He always was on the lookout for an excuse to hear the peepers and smell the hay in his stables. It was the chicken soup for his soul, or what was left of it at least.

When he finished, Nathaniel came and stood right in front of him, waiting.

"I've heard a little bit about you," Will started, still leaning the stool back. "Mainly heard there's not much to hear."

He had hired undocumented workers before and treated them well. As long as they worked well and were good, he didn't mind helping out another man. This one was odd. He acted educated, but clearly didn't have a thing. Will had been watching him like a hawk for any signs of dependence and found none other than him being a little underweight. He would look better if he ate more, but his muscles were clearly strong.

A lifetime of horse breeding and racing had given him an eye for those types of things.

Nathaniel hadn't responded yet, but hadn't broken eye contact either. "What would you like to know, sir?" he finally asked.

"I don't need to know much more than I've already seen. I was at the reenactment this weekend and I saw your fool ass run out there after that kid got thrown for tugging."

Nathaniel didn't say anything, but nodded once.

"Anything I should know before I find out on my own? I never liked surprises."

"I've been arrested for having a weapon in a park without a permit but I'm out now."

"What kind of weapon?"

Nathaniel's mouth twitched. "A flintlock pistol and a short saber sword."

Will's mouth also twitched. "That's interesting." He stood and straightened, feeling another pop somewhere in his back. "This whole property has cameras in places you wouldn't believe. Don't bother trying to find them all. You'd do well to remember that. The farm manager's house is the white building around back. If these next few weeks work out, you can stay there. Bring your family if you have one. Keep it clean and tidy. I can pay cash."

"Thank you, sir."

"We'll go over the details of each horse's diet and plan, though they're all written down somewhere around here. Personally, I like my notes with me at all times." Will tapped his temple. "Lessons are mostly in the afternoons, and you don't need to do much for that since the teachers come in. We have a ways until the race season, but my trainer will be here during the week. I'll be down too when he's here. "

Nathaniel nodded again.

"When can you start?"

"Tomorrow, sir."

"Good. Don't be late. Horses go out at sundown."

Nathaniel nodded and stuck out his hand again, which Will accepted and shook. With that, Nathaniel turned on his heel and began walking back into the night.

He liked to consider himself a hard-ass, but what stopped him was Nathaniel's back. It was straight as rebar.

Will headed back toward his own home on foot and smiled to himself in the dark. He had always been a fan of the old ways.

CHAPTER 35

Mel had finally come out of the shower and was lying on the couch with a T-shirt under her robe and a towel wrapped around her head, trying to get some work done with her Cherry Garcia ice cream. It should've been a perfect night, but she couldn't settle.

She had thought about calling Abuelita, but knew better. The woman had an uncanny ability to tell when something was on her mind.

Because she had been alone, there was no excuse to go out for food or pick up something more substantial at the grocery store, so the little plastic tray that had claimed to be Chicken Parm sat empty on the coffee table.

A soft knock on the door had her off the couch in a run and looking out the peephole.

She whipped the door open.

Nathaniel—who had gotten a little sun—stood there in his blue jeans and the red T-shirt she had bought him. She didn't know if she wanted to strangle him or leap into his arms. She opted for the latter. She hadn't felt right until his arms circled her again.

"I apologize. I thought I'd be back sooner."

"Where did you even go? I saw the paper. I mean, do they even have jobs that you can get without ID and stuff?" She stepped out of the door to let him pass.

Nathaniel slid out of the sneakers she had picked up for him when he had first gotten out. "Well, not many, but there was one, and I had a hunch. I called Tom before I went over and asked if he had heard of this guy. The ad was for farm manager at a stable in the park."

"And?" she said. This was a hell of a shock. She had been certain that there wasn't anything he could do without documentation.

"He hired me. Honestly, he reminded me a lot of the way things used to be back when…well, you know," he finished.

She was stunned for a few seconds before she blinked a few times to get her brain back online.

"That's great… I mean, wow. Congratulations! When do you start? Will you need a ride in?"

"No, I walked. He also said he would prefer if I moved into the house on the property."

That information hit her like a lead ball in the stomach.

"What?"

"He wants someone there full-time to manage the property and be there with the animals through the night. It's an old house, small, but it will be my responsibility."

"So there's no paperwork, nothing? And you're okay with this? You trust him?"

"What choice do I have? But yes, and as far as him trusting me, Tom vouched for me, and Mr. Rackford said he trusted someone the horses trusted. Believe me, I never thought I'd be a stable lad, but I have to stand on my own two feet in this new world, and this is where I can get a foothold on this world."

"It sounds perfect," she said, her voice sounding foreign to her ears.

Except it wasn't. She should be happy for him, but her heart cracked open.

"It won't be without you."

Nathaniel closed the gap between them, and strong arms encircled her in a hug. She felt the weight of his head rest on hers as she rested her forehead on his chest. Mel breathed in the scent of hay and a saltiness that wasn't unpleasant, but told her he had been working.

He released her and leaned back to look into her eyes. "Thank you for all of your help. You're still helping me, and you don't even realize how much. I want to be better for you."

"Yeah, I think everything will go through. I'll talk with Stella about your documents, and— So he didn't even want an I-9? Are you sure this guy is okay?"

"I'll be fine, and no, he didn't seem to care about whatever that is."

"How's he paying—"

"Cash. Mel, I'll be fine. I have to make this work. I can't keep staying here like a pet. It's not fair to you."

"Don't be ridiculous. You're not a pet, and I told you before, there's nothing wrong with a woman paying for stuff."

He placed one finger over her lips, stopping her with gentle pressure. His eyes stared into hers. "I want to be the one to care for you," he said in the patient voice she hadn't realized she had come to rely on. "Who I was and everything I knew was wiped away. I need to rebuild. I need to do this for me because of you."

Mel nodded and blinked away tears while letting out a long sigh. "At least José can get off my case now. Ugh."

He frowned. "What do you mean? Who's José?"

"He's a friend who works at the jail." She waved her hand at him as she pulled out the milk and poured herself a glass. "Anyway, he stopped me as I was coming out of work. I was already in a bad mood, so I kind of yelled at him."

"Why were you in a bad mood?" he asked now. Concerned confusion deepened the lines in his forehead.

"It's nothing. I should have established a boundary with a coworker a long time ago. It's my fault." Before he could respond, she kept going. "Yeah, so apparently José saw us at the reenactment together and was worried."

"Mel—"

"I don't want to hear it. It's fine."

"I should have left sooner, so you're not in this position."

She waved him off. "It's whatever. We haven't done anything wrong."

"Mel, attorney-client relationships—"

"Stop. If Patrick can sleep with his clients, then—"

"Sleep with his clients? What do you mean?"

"It's just a hunch, but still…" she said with a shrug.

"This is serious. I need to leave. I don't want you to be hurt or judged in any way. I won't have that on my conscience. I promised you I'd never do anything to hurt you."

"It doesn't matter. Things are different now. We're not client and attorney. That relationship ended with the court date."

His shoulders sagged, and he shook his head while staring at the floor.

"What? I'm not in the mood for another lecture."

"You keep saying things are different now, but not as much as you think. I'm a man; you're a woman. People notice."

Mel studied the pattern of her Formica countertop and

noticed for the first time that there were little flecks of red interspersed throughout.

"God dammit," she said to herself.

"I'm going to grab my stuff and can leave tonight. I'm sure Will won't mind if I ask."

"No. If anyone sees you leaving—"

"Do you think the morning would be better?"

"No one has seen anything other than the two of us at the reenactment together. That's it."

"Hmph," was Nathaniel's response.

"Just stay tonight. I'll drive you over with your things."

"I appreciate that, but I don't mind the walk. It's about seven miles from here."

She looked up at him then. "I'm sorry, did you say seven miles?"

"Yeah, it didn't take me too long to do it."

"Nathaniel, it must've taken at least two hours?"

He nodded and just looked at her. "That's all I know. If I didn't have a horse, I walked. Though I do enjoy taking the subway."

"Nathaniel, you can't be serious." But Mel could tell that he was. "Okay, listen, it's late and I needed to be in bed..." She looked at the clock on the stove. Crap.

Nathaniel moved toward her to rub her shoulders. She would miss that.

"You're tired."

She shook her head despite yawning again. "I'll drive you over in the morning before I go in."

She could feel him ushering her to her bed, and once there, he sat her down. Wet locks of hair thumped down around her head as Nathaniel took away her towel. He returned a few minutes later with a brush from her bathroom and began to comb out her locks of hair, starting at the bottom. It would've felt like heaven if it didn't feel like they were breaking up.

Mel's shoulders dropped, and her stress slowly melted away with his hands. Rustling sheets woke her from her doze as Nathaniel folded down the duvet and smoothed the sheets before she leaned back and slid in.

While the stress was gone, the sadness wasn't. Through her lashes, she watched as Nathaniel turned off her light and left her room to go and sleep on the couch, shutting the door behind him.

Dimly and through the haze of sleep, she wished he would have crawled in with her.

CHAPTER 36

The next morning, Mel had to get up with her alarm, which sucked even more than usual because her alarm was set for earlier than normal. They loaded up the car, neither of them saying much.

Nathaniel had calmly put his items in her Civic before offering to help carry her purse, which was too big. Of course, she had refused, and the two of them set off. It probably would've been good to eat breakfast, but then she hadn't had much of an appetite this morning.

Nathaniel pointed the way to a farm that she had been by but hadn't paid much attention to.

The gravel driveway was long and lined with a black four-rail fence and old trees.

A small farmhouse she had been waiting to see came into view, and looked out of place this close to the city. It was quaint in a country sort of way, and looked like there should be a pie on the windowsill or something. She knew she should be happy for him, but the sight of it made her want to cry.

"Wow. Nice place," she said, gripping the steering wheel even tighter to keep from falling to pieces.

"You should see the barn," he said and pointed her onto another drive that went around the house through a few garden beds. They were beautiful with a few flowers in bloom, even this late in the season.

A red-and-white barn was set back a bit from the house in a shaded part of the yard that sloped down. It looked inviting and calm, even in the summer heat that was insisting on making September feel like August.

There was a covered porch running alongside the long wall of the barn—or was it stables?— that had doors with a few copper-colored horses visible inside.

Mel navigated her car on the wildest ride of its life over the pea gravel around back to a little house painted in the same colors as the barn. A rocking chair sat next to the door on the small, covered front porch. The house looked older, but it had a fresh coat of paint that she could see. Next to a large oak tree, the scene was picturesque and quaint.

She let out a rueful laugh. "I never would've believed this could exist in the city, but then I didn't believe a lot was possible a few weeks ago."

Nathaniel let out a laugh and reached for her hand, squeezing it.

Mel blinked a few tears away from her eyes. "I can't think of a better place for a time traveler to live and work."

"I couldn't believe it either," Nathaniel said and hopped out. He crunched his way over to the door and waved her over. "Keys were in the lock, and the door was open. I guess that means I'm welcome."

They walked inside and were standing in a small living room opposite a fireplace with windows overlooking the porch. A couple of brown chairs and a small love seat circled a coffee table. All of it was of an older style, but it was clean and didn't appear to have been worn very hard. The walls were painted a cheery, soft yellow and decorated with folk paintings of horses and jockeys. Mel walked back into the kitchen that had an eating area with a table and chairs. White cabinets lined the wall with a black countertop. A coffee maker and toaster sat at the ready next to a crock full of cooking utensils. The fridge, although not a high-end model, was humming away next to her. She pulled open a cabinet and found a neat array of white dishes and some coffee mugs.

A staircase separated the two rooms on the main floor, and as she walked up, she found that there were two bedrooms. One was set up as an office, and the other had a full-size bed with a white-and-gray checkered comforter and white sheets, all of which smelled clean.

"This is much nicer than I was expecting or needed."

"Maybe it's set up for families?"

"He didn't tell me about the previous manager. The bathroom is nice too. I'm still getting used to that."

"Remember to shower every day," she said absently. "It's what we do now."

"Seems like a luxury to me."

"It is, but you need to fit in," she said.

He looked back at her and closed the distance. He was so handsome, and if you didn't know any better, he looked perfectly normal, like he had been here for his whole life and was looking forward to caring for these animals.

Nathanial wrapped his arms around her and snuggled his face into the side of her neck. She did the same, holding on for as long as she could, breathing in his scent, trying not to cry. He had needed her, but now it seemed the shoe was on the other foot.

Mel didn't want to leave. She knew she needed to go, but the idea of getting back in her car made her stomach twist into a knot. Was this what it was like? No wonder every girl in the movies was a mess after a breakup.

She watched as Nathaniel brought in his bag of clothes and set them on the bed. He took out his pistol and laid it on the bedside table along with his wallet that she hadn't yet seen. The brown leather looked worn, like Abuelita's checkbook. The style was different and had a few symbols stamped on the top for decoration.

Mel wrapped her arms around his chest. Nathaniel looked like he was at home here; she could already see him looking out the window at the stables and knew she needed to leave so he could get to work, whatever it was that he had to do.

"If you need anything, you know how to contact me." It wasn't what she meant. She wanted him to say this was a mistake, and he would miss her. They could jump back in the car together. She wanted him to fall to his knees and beg her to move into this little house with him. She wanted him to call her the second she left and not hang up until they both fell asleep, only to call back in the morning. She wanted him to want *her*—to *need* her, just as she needed him.

Nathaniel pulled her closer. Mel closed her eyes as she could feel his hand going up and down her back. God, she didn't want this to stop.

"Well, I'd better let you get to it," she said, pulling back even though every molecule of her body screamed against the decision.

"Thank you, Mel. For everything. I'll find you when I can pay you back."

Her throat too clogged with emotion to speak, Mel shook her head and looked at him, blinking tears away. She had always prided herself on being independent, and now she wished he wanted her more than his independence.

The irony wasn't lost.

The eyes staring back at her were filled with anticipation and an eagerness to get back to himself and form his own life, one he could understand and make meaning of. His lips were stretched into a thin line, and a small muscle worked in his jaw.

Maybe he was having just as hard a time with this. But then again, he had never said he loved her. He had never talked about their future. How could a man out of time do so? He never knew if he would wake up and still be here. She was the one who had gotten her heart all tangled up, and here was the result.

She drew in a breath and tried to get a grip. Nathaniel walked her out and said he would call on her soon. She couldn't remember what she said, but didn't think it was much. Mel slid her key into the ignition, cranked the engine, and drove away from the little country house, the large oak tree, and the person she wanted more than anything else. She was sobbing before she knew what had happened.

Looking back into her mirror, she saw him standing there watching her go, bathed in the light from the morning sun, until the tears blurred him out.

Mel had been miserable for days. Work had been crazy with several late nights and tough court days.

She hadn't spoken to Nathaniel, who thanks to the eighteenth-century norms, had no idea you were supposed to call now every day. He thought that you could go away for months and still be fine in a relationship. She would rather die than be clingy, but this archaic way of communicating was killing her.

Mel needed a break. Being in her apartment was too much. Everything that had once been hers now reminded her of him, so she had packed her bag and planned some much-needed time with Abuelita this weekend.

Good food, good sleep, and a familiar routine would do her a lot of good. Hopefully, she wouldn't ask too many questions about where Nathaniel had gone.

So she finished up her work and drove to Abuelita's, fighting the urge to check her phone at every stoplight. She needed to get a grip. It wasn't like Nathaniel was going to call her just because she wanted him to. They were adults from opposite ends of almost every spectrum. She had helped him, and now he was doing fine. Great. The situation had turned out perfectly, so she could stop this middle school routine of waiting by the phone to see if he called. Her life was going by.

Mel hit the gas pedal a little harder than usual when the light turned, feeling the rush of cool air through the windows. She turned on the radio, and when she heard it was the beginning of "All You Had To Do Was Stay" by Taylor Swift, she turned it up and started belting out the lyrics. The tears flowed quickly.

It was a good cry, cleansing to let out her emotions and clear her head. Funny, a month ago, she had never felt this deeply about anything. There were a lot of positives one could draw from this experience if she tried. She was a more balanced person. From now on, she was going to be positive and have more than work to fill her time.

If Nathaniel had taught her anything, she had learned that she didn't want to go back to life just focusing on work. She needed something more. The Civic flew into the night toward Abuelita's with Mel singing the whole way.

Once there, Mel slid into the parking spot. She grabbed her bag and jogged up the stairs, excited and pumped with the beat of the music still in her blood. She skipped up the steps and had her key ready, only to find she didn't need it.

The apartment was quiet and dark—it was late for Abuelita—but the door was cracked.

Odd. Mel felt a tingle go down the back of her neck. Comfortable in one's own home was one thing. Leaving the front door open at night was something else. Abuelita was never afraid in her own home, but she had never done this before.

Mel pushed the door open and flipped the light switch. Everything in the hallway looked normal. The fan in the living room was off, and so was the A/C unit, so the house was quiet.

"Abuelita?" she called out.

Nothing.

"Abuelita?" she called again. Her heart picked up speed, and Mel dropped her bag to go inside. The living room was trashed. One glance at the kitchen and she saw it was the same. Grocery bags were still on the counter. One had fallen, and the eggs inside were broken all over the floor.

Had she fallen while putting away her groceries? Had a heart attack and couldn't get to the door? Maybe it was open for the paramedics?

"Abuelita!?" Mel scrambled down the hall. The bedroom doors were all at different angles. A few of her pictures were broken and lying trampled on the ground.

Her breathing was so fast, as visuals ran through her head of what could've happened, until she saw one of her worst fears.

"Abuelita? Abuelita?! Oh my God!"

Abuelita was lying face down in her bedroom, where every drawer had been dumped. The back of her gray hair was covered in blood. Mel screamed and rushed down to turn her over.

She was unconscious but breathing, thank God. Mel tried to shake her, but she didn't respond.

Through the panic bubbling up, she snatched out her phone and dialed 911, answering the dispatcher's questions.

"We're sending a unit now. Please stay on the line. We're experiencing heavy call volume. You're doing great."

Time ticked by as she tried to talk to Abuelita. There was so much she didn't know. She didn't know how long she had been like this. Didn't know if there were any secondary injuries. She didn't know what medications she took now that she had moved out.

What she did know was how frail Abuelita looked. When she was conscious, she was so full of life that it was hard to imagine her as anything but a force of nature. Now, she looked older, smaller, and weaker.

Minutes ticked by. The dispatcher was nice, encouraging, and kept walking her through the breathing assessment.

Time was a funny thing. When you wanted it to do one thing, it did another. Minutes spent with Nathaniel were too short, and weeks had gone by in a blur. Now, each second felt like an eternity. She needed help now, and help was coming, but far too slowly for her taste. There was nothing to do but sit in the moment, hope, and pray. Nothing would make it go faster than the uncomfortable position of waiting in the unknown.

"Okay, they're coming up to your block now. Can you go down and open the door?"

Mel looked back and forth from the door of the apartment to Abuelita, torn. There was no other choice. It was just her. She was alone there.

"Yeah, I can run down."

She ran down the hall and pushed through the door just as the ambulance was pulling up in front, double parking in front of her car.

She waved them in as they grabbed their gear and walked inside.

They ran through vitals, asked questions, and loaded Abuelita onto a backboard before lifting her out.

They told her comforting words that she had trouble focusing on, but she nodded and felt herself being ushered into the back of the ambulance.

I could lose her, she thought. It had been the two of them for as long as she could remember. Mel held her hand, which was usually strong and warm, and for the first time, she noticed how the arthritis had misshapen the joints.

When they arrived at the hospital, the EMTs rushed Abuelita to the ER, where a nurse spoke to Mel in a quiet voice.

A doctor came out and sat down next to her, introducing herself as Dr. Nicole Hitch.

"She's going to be okay."

Mel let out the breath she hadn't realized she was holding.

"She has some bruising and a sizable hematoma on the back of her head—likely from blunt force trauma or the fall. But her CT scan came back clear—no internal bleeding, no skull fracture. We're admitting her for observation for a couple of days, to be on the safe side. She'll be sore, probably have a bad headache, and if she's concussed, we'll know more once she's awake. For now, she's stable, and we'll manage her pain and monitor her closely."

"Okay, thank you," Mel managed before she burst into tears again. The good doctor's arms came around and held on as sobs racked her body.

Minutes later, the same soft-spoken nurse brought Mel some tissues, while the doctor excused herself and promised to check in later.

"Is there anyone we can call for you?" she asked.

There was only one person Mel wanted to call.

CHAPTER 38

Nathaniel didn't hesitate at the price of the fare when he paid the driver at the front of Jacobi Medical Center, even though it was most of the cash he had made in the past few days. He jogged into the largest building he had ever seen and approached the desk in the lobby where a woman sat. She called for an escort who walked him over to a metal set of doors she called an elevator.

Minutes later, he was trying not to lose his stomach in an small room heading up. The doors opened to reveal a set of two double doors and something like the radio in Mel's car, into which his escort spoke his name. They stood outside the double doors for some time before they opened to reveal Mel on the other side, sitting in a hard chair and hugging her arms around her chest.

Tears had plastered strands of her dark curls to her cheeks. She looked worn down by worry, and the sight broke his heart. Nathaniel strode forward. When she saw him, she stood up and gave a weak smile.

"Thank you for coming."

He enveloped her, pressing her against his chest as if

somehow he could be strong enough for both of them, so that he could take her pain and worry away. Her dark, tangled curls shook with sobs that shed tears onto the fabric of the T-shirt she had bought him all those weeks ago.

"I came as soon as I could. How is she?"

He had just finished working with the horses and had come into the house to read his history book when he heard the phone ring. He wasn't used to the sound and had jumped. It was the first time he had used a phone, and he was grateful he had watched the librarians do it.

As he heard from the nurse on the other end, Nathaniel dug around for the card for a taxi service he'd picked up when he and Mel got coffee the first time. After he found it, he dialed the number with shaking fingers.

"The doctor said she's stable, but she hasn't woken up enough for me to talk to her," Mel said, wiping her eyes on the sleeve of a crinkled, black shirt she usually wore to work. That would've been hours ago. She hadn't changed or slept. Nathaniel wished he could drive to get her something to eat. Instead, he swiped his fingers over her cheeks and took away the tears.

"The doctors know a lot more now than they did before. I'm sure they're doing everything they can. Did you find her at her apartment?"

Mel closed her eyes again and nodded as more tears fell. "The door was open, and I guess she was unpacking her groceries when they came in behind her. I couldn't find her purse, but I didn't look very hard."

Their home would never be the same. The devils who stole money as well as peace of mind would surely rot in hell.

"I don't know…" She broke down again.

Nathaniel didn't hesitate. He wrapped his arms around her and rocked back and forth, just as his mother had done for him. "We'll sort it out." It felt so right to have her against his chest again. He hadn't stopped thinking about her for a minute since the last time they had spoken.

Mel muffled something against his chest.

He leaned back a little. "Hmm?"

Mel sniffled and leaned back to look at him. "Can you stay?"

"I called my boss on the telephone and explained."

Mel nodded and then frowned. He could almost see the fog of worry clearing. "Wait. How did you get here?"

"I called a taxi."

Her eyes widened. "Nathaniel, that must have been a huge fare. I'll pay you back."

"It was money well spent."

"I feel bad—"

"I'm ashamed it took me that long. If I could drive a car, I would've been here sooner."

Mel smiled and hugged him again hard.

They stayed like that with his arms around her in the hallway. He rocked back and forth with his chin on her hair as he hummed a few tunes he knew from his old life.

He could've stayed like that forever. In truth, it wasn't only Mel who was being comforted. He, too, was worried and anxious to see that Abuelita would be fine.

Mel pulled back after how long, he didn't know. He would've kept going until next morning if she needed him to.

Her face was red, along with her eyes. "Sorry," she muttered when she looked around for something to wipe her nose.

A box of those throw-away handkerchiefs was on a large desk in the center of the ward. Nathaniel grabbed one and brought it to her. They both sat on two chairs in the hall.

"Can I bring you both some water or tea?" the woman behind the desk asked. "The cafeteria is still open downstairs, if you're hungry."

"No, thank you. I don't want to leave in case she wakes up," Mel said, wiping her eyes and blowing her nose.

"I understand. Just let me know if you change your mind."

"Let me go and get you something to eat." He didn't know a damn thing about hospitals, doctors, or nurses, but he knew Mel looked weak from the ordeal and he had to do something. "I'll take care of it and be right back, but I won't go until you say it's okay."

She reached for his hand, which he gave willingly.

A man in a white coat walked in and spoke with the nurse at the desk, who pointed in their direction.

"Are you both here for Ms. Reyes?" he asked after coming over.

"Yes, I'm her granddaughter." They stood, neither letting go of the other.

The man smiled in a warm, quiet way. "I'm Dr. Washington, taking over for Dr. Hitch. Her vitals are looking good. We're going to wake her in a few hours and run some tests. Would you like to be in the room for the exam?"

"Yes, thank you," she said, looking at Nathaniel. The exhaustion in her face broke something further in his chest.

"Of course. I'll let you know if something changes before then," Dr. Washington said before Mel thanked him, and he nodded and headed back through the double doors.

"Let me bring you some food. I'll be back," he said, and squeezed Mel's hand, not letting go until she nodded.

Nathaniel headed to the lady at the desk to get directions. Ten minutes later, he was trying to get the hang of the tongs while he picked through every tray of food, from the fruit to the meat, and selected the best of each for Mel.

CHAPTER 39

"*Ay no!*" said Abuelita when the nurse tried to check her breathing.

Mel hissed at her and jabbed a finger in front of her lips.

In Spanish, Abuelita said, "She didn't even know how to warm the metal, so how can she possibly know about a good heartbeat?"

"My grandmother wanted me to thank you for all of the hard work your team is doing for her here. She really appreciates your time," Mel said, beaming a warm smile at the young RN.

"Awww! Gracias!" the young RN said brightly in an American accent with a big enough smile to make Abuelita feel a little guilty.

Abuelita smiled at the nurse and slowly turned to narrow her eyes at Mel before laying her head back to rest her eyes.

Go ahead and be mad at me, Mel thought. I can wait it out. Abuelita had woken up this morning and was almost back to her usual self. She couldn't remember much about what had happened at the apartment, but that could all be sorted out later. Right now, she needed to focus on healing.

In the silence that followed the nurse's departure, exhaustion was beginning to take hold. Mel sat in the chair and could feel the slump of sleep weighing her down when the door across from her opened.

Nathaniel had come back carrying another tray of what looked to be enough food for an army, even though he had already fed her twice from the cafeteria. Mel stood to go to him, but then Abuelita sat up and studied her face.

"Is it him?" Abuelita said.

"Abuelita—"

"Don't just stand there, come in and let me see you!" she called out from the bed, her view of the doorway just out of her line of sight.

Nathaniel pointed to himself silently, and Mel nodded. He crept into the room and laid the tray down before going to her.

Abuelita's face melted with affection, and she waved him over.

He leaned over the bed when she stretched out her arms to embrace him. Nathaniel enveloped Abuelita's petite frame, his light hair against hers that seemed more gray than Mel remembered. Mel couldn't hear what Abuelita murmured to him, and Nathaniel's reply was even lower, but she stood and watched.

Mel felt her shoulders drop and hadn't realized they'd been tense until now. Watching Nathaniel murmur and reassure in his calm, strong way made Mel breathe easier for more than one reason.

With him around, she didn't need to always be strong. For many years, Mel had kept everything bottled up inside. All of the feelings, worry, stress, everything, because if she let her hold go just for a moment, she was scared all her emotions would sweep her away. Never once had she trusted someone enough to lean on them for her own sake. Abuelita had been the only rock in her life, but Mel couldn't tell her everything, and now, with Abuelita in the hospital bed in front of her, it was clear how fragile that rock actually was.

Nathaniel crouched down alongside Abuelita in the bed, nodding as she recounted everything she had told the police. He was dressed in jeans and a heathered green T-shirt that was begging to be hugged. A muscle worked in his cheeks that had a dusting of stubble over tanned skin as he listened to Abuelita's retelling of the very few details she knew.

Through the story, Abuelita seemed more relaxed now too. Nathaniel wasn't just a calming presence for Mel, which was something she hadn't expected. With him here, a balm had spread over the room, smoothing down raw edges and healing them.

"Then the police tell me they took my purse," Abuelita said, raising her hands in disbelief. "The wallet, I understand, but the purse…" She shook her head, trying to comprehend. "I just got it earlier this year!"

Mel couldn't help the smirk, and even from a bad angle, she could tell Nathaniel was trying to hide one of his own.

"You can get a new purse," Nathaniel said.

"Yes, I know I can, but it is the principle of the matter! What do they want with an old woman's purse?" Abuelita threw up her hands again. "What is this world coming to? Take the wallet, leave the purse. Or at least demand the money first, and let me have a chance to give it over like a proper mugging. It is common decency." She leaned down and shook her head in disgust. "I don't understand."

"I'm just glad you're all right."

"Pffft," Abuelita said with a wave of both hands as if to shoo away the attention, though Mel knew damn well Abuelita was loving every minute of this. "I am fine. Young people worry too much. Now you two go. Leave me. Your food is getting cold."

"Abuelita—"

"Go. I need my rest." Playing the grand dame, Abuelita had them leaving the room without even moving from the bed. She even leaned back onto her pillows and closed her eyes as if resting. With no other choice, Nathaniel picked up the tray and headed for the door, but Mel waited until Abuelita cracked one eye, winked, and then closed it again to lie in repose.

Typical.

"I don't know what I'm going to do with her," Mel said when they were in the cramped visitor room, eating.

"You don't want her to go back."

Mel shook her head. "She's lived there almost her whole life. How do I move someone who has been there for over fifty years? That place is a part of her."

Nathaniel took a sip of his coffee and stared into it. "She'll make her own space somewhere else. Have you talked to her about it?"

"No, I don't want to upset her. I guess I should move back in to help her and keep an eye on things."

"Is that what you want?" he asked.

"I want her to be safe."

"Of course. Though I do not enjoy the idea of you in the same place where she was attacked."

"You don't think I'm tough?" Mel tried to smile at him, but it didn't land.

"I care too much about you and her for something like this to happen again."

Mel didn't know what to say, so she looked down at her food and poked it with her fork. Hospital food wasn't supposed to be good, but Nathaniel had found the best of everything. Mel ate until she was stuffed, even taking a few more bites when he urged her to eat more.

"Okay, seriously, I'm done now. No, I can't eat another bite."

His blue eyes looked at her and studied her face. "You should eat more."

He kept watching her before lowering his lashes and taking some of the food for himself. Mel watched him eat delicately as he had in her apartment. Her thigh brushed up against him, and she felt the familiar solid warmth. Acting on their own, her eyes traced the skin of his forearm, taking note of the smooth, graceful muscles under the skin. His fingers were slender, but with a certain roughness that she knew would be gentle on her skin. Mel wanted him to reach around her and take her into his arms again. Her body ached to curl up into the crook of his arm and rest her head on his shoulder, where she knew it would fit.

"I couldn't stop thinking about you," she said.

He sat up and pressed his lips to her forehead, cradling her head with his hands, breathing in deeply. "I am always thinking of you."

Mel smiled, pleased to know the feeling was mutual.

"I've missed you. Thank you for being here today. I—I don't know what I would've done."

"I've been wanting to call on you. I was hoping we could go out for a meal, or you could come to the house and I could cook for you. I want to do something nice for you, so I've been saving my money until I had enough."

Mel smiled and had to blink away tears again. He was saving for her because he wanted her. "Oh, Nathaniel, that's so sweet of you, but you don't have to do that."

"Of course I do. I told you I need to work to be worthy of you because I have fallen in love with you."

She blinked, stunned. He said it so matter-of-factly, she wondered if she had heard him right.

"I pray every night when I sleep that I wake up still here

in this time so I can see you again, and if I don't see you, I know you're somewhere in the city. I can't tell you how happy just knowing that we exist in the same time together makes me."

Mel's lungs emptied in a rush. He loved her. He meant it. That's why he was so determined to find a purpose and a job. That's why he had wanted to move out, to get closer to her, to provide for her. He meant every word. She had thought it was just pride. She hadn't realized it was this.

"I love you too."

Nathaniel beamed back at her, his smile so wide that his eyes crinkled at the corners. It was the first genuine smile she saw on him, and it was stellar.

"But I don't want to wait that long. I want to be with you all of the time."

"Would you live with me? You can bring Abuelita."

The suggestion was so shocking that it was one she had never even considered. "Is that even allowed?"

"Mr. Rackford is eager to see me settled so he can retire. He had mentioned that families were encouraged, as he lived there with his children. Now they are hoping to move to a place closer to their daughter. I think they're tired of the little house in the park."

"I'd love that, but I don't think she'll ever leave."

"Why?" His voice was gentle and tender, instinctively knowing it was a complicated matter.

"She has kept that place like a vigil ever since Abuelo died, and then even more so after the accident with my parents. My dad was raised there, and so was I. She says there are too many memories. I think it helps her stay closer to them, like she's stuck in time. Well," she added, glancing at him, "maybe not stuck, but she feels like it keeps them closer to her."

"I understand the power of place, but times change."

"I know, but I don't think she'll leave, and I can't leave her." Mel blinked away tears as she said it.

"I understand. You're a good granddaughter," he said, and reached over to hold her hand in his own.

"I know you have to go back to work, but can you come back tomorrow? I need to go to the apartment, and I don't want to go alone."

"I'll be here." Nathaniel leaned over and gave her a kiss that was longer than perhaps appropriate in public, but still too short.

He stood and hit the button next to the elevator, nervously waiting for its approach. If you didn't know any better, you almost couldn't tell it was only his second day using one. Mel watched him until the doors closed on his blue gaze. She missed him immediately.

CHAPTER 40

Nathaniel wasn't the only one who had to return to work. Mel had spent the rest of the day sitting with Abuelita before finally agreeing—after much insistence by Abuelita—to go home for the night and get some rest in her own bed.

On the way into the office, Mel had called and learned Abuelita was doing well and would be released the next day, provided she was stable on her feet.

Mel still hadn't started packing her stuff up. Every time she came home, she noticed how empty it felt and simply ran out of steam. It needed to be done, but she just hadn't been able to get there. Tonight she would have to pack up her essentials, and deal with the rest later.

"How is she?" Stella asked when Mel got in.

"Hopefully, she'll be released tomorrow." She puffed out a breath. "I still can't get over it."

"She's tough and so are you," Stella said without missing a beat.

"Thanks. She's way more badass than I ever will be, that's for sure."

"Good morning, ladies," Tabby said, coming around the corner. "Mel, can I interrupt for a sec?"

"Let me know what you need," Stella said as Mel left to follow Tabby.

"I'm so sorry to hear about your grandma," Tabby said. "Please have a seat."

Tabby, wearing a black pencil skirt and sharp gray jacket, walked around and sat at her desk, which held evidence of all of the cutbacks in the mountains of case files that were stacked around her computer. She leaned forward on her arms and looked at Mel.

Tabby sighed. "It has come to our attention that you have been fraternizing with a former client of yours."

Her stomach sank and an ice-cold feeling set up shop in her chest. She drew in a careful breath and spoke, trying hard to keep her voice steady with the knowledge that she had done nothing wrong.

"Any personal time spent with a client was after that client was released and our professional relationship was dissolved."

Tabby drew her lips into a thin line. "I know. I was waiting for you to say that." She clasped her hands now and looked at the desk calendar that was drowning under the clutter. "I know you didn't do anything technically wrong, but ethically, we're in a gray area, and we can't have this."

"Tabby, what are you saying here? I was helping out a former client after our professional relationship ended," Mel said.

Tabby sighed again. "I'm between a rock and a hard place here, Mel."

All of the emotion from the past few weeks vanished under a cool tidal wave of logic, reason, intelligence, and law school. She was a damn good lawyer, knew her rights, and there was no reason to panic. She hadn't done anything wrong. It was time to stop acting like she had.

"I'm sorry, Mel. I wish there was another way, but if it causes this much of a scene in the office, it's not appropriate. We're all adults here, but we also need to be professional."

The bubble of panic in her chest popped and she had an idea so brilliant she had to hide her smile. Professional. Of course.

"Am I allowed to know who exactly has brought this to your attention?"

"They requested to remain anonymous."

"I see," Mel said with understanding infused into her voice. "I'd like to request a few days for me to address it with the person who I suspect brought it to your attention and see if I can resolve this matter myself, as I believe it has been misrepresented to you."

Tabby smiled. It was slow, but grew across her face like a proud teacher watching a star pupil. "I would like that very much."

"Great, thank you."

Tabby nodded once. "Oh, and of course, if there is anything you learn that you would like to share with me, please know my door is always open."

That's when Mel realized what was going on. Tabby knew about Patrick, and though he had gotten to her first, she had been counting on Mel to respond.

She spent the rest of the afternoon working in her office, contemplating her next move. She knew her chance would come and worked later than normal waiting for the moment.

She had almost given up hope, when she heard someone come down the hall toward her office.

"Mel, I just heard about your grandma. Oh my God, are you okay? I came as soon as I heard," Patrick said in a rush.

She put her phone down on her desk and ran her hands

over her eyes. "Thanks, I'm still processing it. She'll be okay, but they're still keeping her for observation. Hopefully, tomorrow she can come home."

"Jesus, Mel. That's terrible. I'm so sorry that happened."

"Thanks, it's just been a shit day over here," she said, leaning back into her chair, feeling the exhaustion as she slumped.

"What's wrong? Is there anything I can do to help?"

"No, Tabby talked to me today and said someone had complained. Kind of took the wind out of my sails a bit."

"Hey, hey," he said, coming in and sitting on the edge of her desk. "Let me talk to her. Maybe I can smooth some things over? You know?"

"Listen, I appreciate it, but—"

"Mel, let me talk to her." His voice took on a different tone. One that was devoid of sympathy. Her skin prickled. "I tell you what, maybe if I do, we could spend some more time together in the future?" He paused now, watching her, making no attempt to hide his eyes as they skimmed down her body.

An icy chill spread through her chest and down her spine. "Patrick, that is quid pro quo."

He threw up both hands. "Woah, woah! I'm just trying to help."

"I know exactly what you're trying to do here, and I'm not interested."

Patrick grinned a little and leaned toward her. "You know, we're both adults here. Tabby likes me. I'm sure with a word from me, any little misunderstanding would be easily cleared up."

Mel drew in a steady breath and stood. "Patrick, please leave. The answer is no."

He held up both hands again before shoving them into the pockets of his tailored slacks. "Fine, fine. Hey, I'm just trying to be friendly." He cocked his head to the side. "By the way, do you really think being a bitch is becoming? I mean, I find it fucking arousing as hell, but it might be tough to get a job. Sounds like you should work on that soon, sweetheart." He winked as he headed for the door.

Mel felt fury burn off any fear left, as her hands clenched into fists at her side.

"Fuck you."

Patrick spun around on his way out and gave her a cold smile. "Oh, don't you wish, honey. Too bad you missed your chance. I would've fucked you like the bitch you are, and you would've begged for more. I hope you get fired for fucking that criminal."

White-hot rage spread throughout her body. She could feel her body shaking. Mel lunged for the open door and slammed it shut in his wake.

Mel threw the lock and reached for her phone to stop the recording before pressing send to Tabby.

CHAPTER 41

Mel had a skip in her step the next morning as she walked into the hospital, balancing a full pastry box for the nurses. Tabby had answered her email last night with a formal apology on behalf of the firm. Patrick was immediately put on leave while an investigation was underway. Tabby called again to check in on her and say she believed the investigation would be short, swift, and result in termination. She also thanked Mel for her help. It turned out that Tabby's special investigation had been an internal review on Patrick, but she had lacked concrete evidence to back up her suspicions until Mel came forward. Sweet justice had been served.

The nurses all thanked her for the pastries. The charge nurse took a turnover out, thanked her again, and said, "She's doing great. We're hoping to start discharge once the doctor finishes the rounds."

"Oh, that's so great to hear. Thank you so much for all you guys do."

"She's such a treasure," a male nurse with red hair said. "Spicy, but you can tell how sweet she is underneath."

"I know, she never misses a beat."

Mel waved to everyone and walked inside Abuelita's room, excited to see her sitting up, watching the weather with a cup of coffee on the table.

"Good news, I think you're getting out of here today."

Abuelita smiled, but then narrowed her eyes. "Did Nathaniel have to go back to work?"

"Yes, but he said he'll come by later this week to help me move back in."

She narrowed her eyes even more. "Move back in with who?"

"You," Mel said, putting her stuff down and pulling over the chair. "I haven't been by to clean up, but I'm going to do that tonight. I had to work late again last night."

"Melanie," Abuelita started, her voice soft, "you do not need to move back."

"I want to. I don't like the idea of you living alone. Neither does Nathaniel. Besides, I work so much that I'm barely at my place to begin with. It'll be good, like old times."

Abuelita sipped her coffee, but didn't say anything.

The red-haired nurse, whose name was Matt, came in to check vitals.

"Alright, well, there's no swelling or any other sign of infection, Mrs. Reyes. You might have some lingering headaches, but Tylenol and rest should help at home. How's your pain level today?"

Abuelita shrugged. "I don't know numbers, but less than before."

"Okay, we had put a five, does three sound good? Still feel it, but a mild discomfort or a dull ache?"

"Yes, very mild ache."

"Alright, let's take a look at your blood pressure. Don't want you getting dizzy and falling on us."

"I never fall."

He smiled in an exasperated sort of way to Mel, who could sympathize. "I know, I know, but we have to check. I want to make sure you're good to go. Will your grand-daughter be staying with you?"

"Yes, I'll be moving back in," Mel answered before she could respond.

Abuelita glanced at her and didn't say anything.

He pulled out a penlight and flashed it in front of her eyes. "Still clear, excellent. That's good; it's important to have family." He clicked off his light and went over to the computer to begin charting.

"The doctor is going to check in with you before we release you, so it will be a few more hours, but everything looks good. Can I get you anything else?"

"No, no. I'm fine, but you should try that sazón on your chicken. You will like it."

"Will do. Thanks again for the tip." He nodded his head and slipped out.

"Making friends?" Mel asked.

"Saving him from bland chicken. It was almost as pale as him. No flavor in this hospital at all."

"No one cooks like you," Mel said, settling in to watch the weatherman go on about what would be the last heat wave of the season.

Abuelita sipped her coffee and put the cup down. "Melanie," she started, her voice gentle, "do not move in with me."

"We're not discussing this," Mel said.

"Do not. I forbid it."

"Abuelita, what are you talking about? Of course, I'm moving back in."

She shook her head. "No."

Mel shifted in her seat, irritated now. "Don't be ridiculous. You were attacked. You shouldn't be alone."

Abuelita shook her head and looked down at her mug, as if she were lamenting about the rising temperatures predicted for this weekend.

"What did Nathaniel say about this?"

"Of course, he understood that you shouldn't be alone. I told him I would never leave you, and he understood."

"*Ay,* is that what you told that man?" She shook her head again before looking over to face her. "Melanie, you have your whole life to live."

"And you are the most important person in my life," she said, reaching out to hold her hand.

Abuelita squeezed it back. "I know, and I love you, but I will not always be here."

"That's why I want to spend as much time as I can with you," Mel said, not liking the way this conversation was going.

Abuelita gave her a patient smile. "I have lived a full and wonderful life with my family, then Abuelo, your father, and then you. I want you to feel that kind of love. The kind I knew."

"But it was painful for you. I know it was."

"Of course, losing anyone you love is pain, but the love that was there was precious. I want that for you. I see something in Nathaniel—"

"Abuelita, he isn't—" Mel interrupted.

"Miracles happen every day."

"Yeah, but this—"

"We are not meant to understand everything. I have prayed novenas for years to the Blessed Mother that God would deliver a good man who would love and cherish you above all else. Who would work for you, care for you, and never stand in the way of your dreams. God has answered my prayers."

Melanie puffed out her breath. "He isn't from here."

She scoffed, "I know."

"No, I mean this time. He isn't… It's hard to explain." Mel eyed her purse that still held the golden pocket watch.

"I don't care what it is. This man is heaven-sent. I know it in my heart. My prayers have been answered. Please, go to him. Be happy. I want someone to love you when I'm gone."

Mel was blinking away tears now. "But what about you? I don't want you staying in that apartment alone."

Abuelita sighed, and the sound of the weariness broke Mel's heart. It was a sound she knew so well, but not from Abuelita. It was one that clients and their families made when they had been strong for too long, and Abuelita's shoulders had gone heavy.

"You should pray more and think less. Listen for the answers. That's what I try to do. The answer comes eventually."

Mel drew in a breath. "Nathaniel moved into a farmhouse near the stables in the park. He invited me to live with him, and said you could come too."

"What did you tell him?"

"No. I told him you wouldn't leave and that I couldn't leave you."

Abuelita looked up into Mel's eyes and patted the bed next to her. "Come here." Mel sat. Abuelita pulled her in and wrapped her arms around her, cradling her like when she was a child.

"You are so beautiful and so strong, and I am so proud of you."

"It sounds like you're buttering me up."

Abuelita's warm hand ran down Mel's cheek. "I guess I'm old now."

Mel let out a laugh. "I don't think so."

"Ay, yes, I know I am. I never felt old until this morning,

and"—she paused and drew in a breath with her eyes closed —"now I do."

Mel leaned in and wrapped her arms around her grandmother tightly.

"That's where I lived with your Abuelo and your father. When they died, I just felt like if I left, there would be too many memories gone. Like, somehow, by staying put, I could keep them with me and keep things as stable for you as possible. I've always wondered if I could've done better by you if we had left. Gone to a better school."

Mel smiled. "You did a good job. I never wanted to leave."

"Is that why you didn't look at other schools or jobs?"

"Yes, and you, of course."

"Melanie, you're loyal. I've spent my life keeping a vigil for our loved ones. You shouldn't tie yourself to the past when you have so much of your own life left."

Mel thought of Nathaniel. He had moved on. Here he was in a foreign land, in a new time, and had to rebuild everything on his own, hoping she would be with him as part of a new family, but she had said no.

"You should be the one moving to bigger things. I can stay behind with the past. I don't want to be in the way of your future."

Mel sighed and felt a tear slide down her cheek. "I love you. You never will be in the way."

Abuelita chuckled. "I love you too."

They stayed like that for a while, next to each other in the bed, with so much said, and so much still unspoken. Each of them watched the commercials as they filled the void.

"What if this is heaven-sent for both of us? What if God wants you to move on too?"

Abuelita was silent. She must have been almost stunned because several seconds went by before she smiled and asked, "When did you get so wise?"

"I don't feel wise."

"The feeling comes with age, or you just stop caring and tell people what you think anyway."

"Okay, here it goes," Mel said, sitting up and facing her from the edge of the bed. "I want to live with Nathaniel, and I want you to come with us."

Abuelita sighed. "It's hard to change a lifetime overnight. That place is a part of me. I'm a part of it. I just don't know what I'll do anywhere else. I've only lived in two places—that apartment and with my parents in Puerto Rico."

"We'll be together. That's what matters. We can take it a day at a time. We can even keep the apartment for a time just in case it doesn't work out."

Abuelita was silent. Somewhere down the hall, they could hear an intercom. "Is this the only way you will go to him?"

"I cannot choose between my past and my future because you both are here in the present."

Abuelita sighed again. It was long.

Mel made one final plea. "Please."

"I'll need to get my things."

Mel smiled. "I can get them for you."

"Good, that is good," she said, almost to herself, her voice quiet, as if making the decision had tired her. "Have Nathaniel help you."

She looked like she was going to continue, but stopped herself and leaned back on the pillows to rest her eyes.

"Of course," Mel said, slipping out of the bed and patting her hand as Abuelita fell asleep with a peaceful smile.

CHAPTER 42

S*ix Months Later*

———

Spring in New York had always been one of Mel's favorite times. The brutal snow and ice of winter broke, and gray skies gave way to blue. Typically, most people flooded the parks on the first pretty weekend after being shut inside their apartments through the holiday season. For Mel, this winter had looked a lot different.

They all moved in together when Abuelita was released from the hospital. She had sublet her old apartment to a dear friend from the church who was going through a hard time and was grateful for the support. This meant Abuelita could still visit it for nostalgia anytime she wanted, and she liked her more spacious bedroom, which had a few large windows overlooking the barn and small garden.

The farmhouse had a big kitchen, and Abuelita quickly made herself at home. Since they had the space, she hosted Thanksgiving for friends at her church who lived far from family. The Riverdale farmhouse was bursting with two dozen people, including the priest from St. Elizabeth's, and everyone ate their fill.

It had been the same at Christmas, where she delighted in her first large tree since Mel was a child. Mel and Nathaniel both joined Abuelita at midnight mass and exchanged presents the following morning. Mel gave Nathaniel an iPad so he could look up all of his ongoing questions about infrastructure and engineering. For Abuelita, she got a new recliner for her bedroom, where she prayed every morning.

Nathaniel gave Abuelita a new gold rosary, which became her favorite one. He gave Mel her own pair of brown leather riding boots for when he took her on a ride around the property. While she still wasn't confident about riding on her own, she loved—and was scared—when he got Tess up to a full gallop, and all she could do was hang on to her and Nathaniel.

Abuelita returned the favor by gifting Nathaniel a proper winter coat and a new work bag for Mel to replace the tired, oversized one she had been carrying since college.

It was the perfect gift because Mel had a much better work-life balance. She'd invited Stella and her boyfriend over for dinner so they could meet everyone, thrilling Abuelita, who was eager to always have new people to cook for. Mel also had made time to see José, his wife, and their new baby, who was adorable. They had even made plans to come out to the farmhouse to let the baby meet Abuelita once it warmed up a little more.

Today, the temperature was a cool sixty-two degrees. Nathaniel had cleaned up from breakfast and gone out early to check on the horses, while Mel had caught up on work. When she finished, she came down from their bedroom, where she kept a small desk, and found Abuelita on the porch, tending to her increasing collection of potted plants.

"All finished with your work?" she asked with the watering can in her hand.

Mel sat down in one of the rocking chairs. "For now. The plants look good. What's that one?"

"Si, they do. That's rosemary, and this is mint. It's too early to bring out the tomatoes, or the marigolds, but the seedlings popped up today in the laundry room."

"I had no idea you knew so much about plants."

Abuelita smiled and walked over to the other chair and eased down before rocking back with a smile. "In Puerto Rico, my father had a big garden because my grandfather was a farmer. I had forgotten all about that until now."

"A lot of memories," Mel said.

"Mm-hmm. Good ones."

Abuelita chatted about family whom Mel had never met and what the compound was like in Puerto Rico. Before, in the apartment, she had only talked about Mel's parents as a way of keeping that connection. It was nice to hear more of the family history and Abuelita's childhood.

The crunch of gravel sounded Nathaniel's arrival. He was dressed for work, but had his riding boots on under his jeans.

His face broke into a smile at the sight of them both.

"Ladies," he said with a slight bow of his head, which always gave Abuelita a thrill. "It's a beautiful day for a ride. Would you like to join me?"

"The day I get on the horse will be my last," Abuelita said, as always.

Mel rolled her eyes. "It is kinda fun."

"Oh, no, no, no," Abuelita said, with a wave of her hand and a shake of her head.

"I understand, which is why I've spoken to Mr. Rackford about getting a carriage to train drivers, and offering rides.

He liked the idea. It could be good for people who find riding uncomfortable."

Abuelita raised her eyebrows. "Maybe then, we'll see."

"Alright." He turned to Mel and smiled. "Want to go for a ride?"

Minutes later, she was letting Nathaniel help her up into the saddle before hopping up behind her. He wanted her to try riding Tax, the dramatic, but gentle giant, but she wasn't ready for that yet. Besides, she liked being near him. Nathaniel liked it too.

They trotted toward the trails and open paddock, before he urged Tess on into a full gallop over the green hills. Mel laughed and gripped the pommel, not used to being in the front while going this fast.

They reached one of their favorite spots where Mel noticed a blanket spread out under a cherry tree that was beginning to flower with pretty pink blooms.

"Did you plan a surprise picnic?"

Nathaniel winked at her. "With Abuelita's help."

"She's always so crafty."

"Indeed, she is," he said, unpacking a full spread of sandwiches, chips, and soft drinks.

They chatted about the stables, horses, and Nathaniel's next reenactment. He had joined up with the regiment they had met at Saratoga, and all of his friends were quite impressed with his extensive knowledge about the British Army and all things 18th century. Tom was even encouraging him to start talking on social media or write a book, which Nathaniel was considering.

When they were finished, they wrapped up the lunch and lay together watching the clouds on the blanket.

"I never thought I would be under a cherry tree watching the clouds," Mel said with her hand on his chest.

"Yes, how difficult it must be to imagine living in a park instead of an apartment in the same borough."

"Is that a joke I hear?" she asked with a grin.

"Perhaps."

"Do you miss it?" Mel asked, which had become her usual question whenever he hinted at his past.

Nathaniel thought a bit, as he always did. "No. My family, sometimes, but no."

"You're just saying that because we have hot water and Internet."

Nathaniel chuckled. The sound was deep and low in his chest. He rolled onto his side and looked at her.

"I've been blessed to see two times, and I'm so thankful I get to wake up in the same year as you."

"I love you," Mel said.

"A fact I'm grateful for every day because I love you too," he answered.

"I'm sorry about your family."

"Thank you. I've found a new one." He leaned over and kissed her, a tender, gentle whisper of his lips on hers, which never failed to give her a thrill.

"Want to head back to the house? Abuelita will be going to adoration at the church soon." This meant they had the place to themselves, and could enjoy a bit of privacy as a couple.

He nodded, with a slow grin that made her toes want to curl with anticipation.

They stood, and he wrapped up the blanket, while she walked over to Tess.

He came up behind her and put the bundle in the saddle-bag, and then he reached for her hand.

Ready to get up, she went to put her foot in the stirrup when he pulled her away.

When she turned around, Nathaniel had dropped to one knee, a small velvet box in his hand.

Nathaniel smiled up at her. "Melanie, would you be my new family…forever?"

Mel gasped, stunned as he opened the little gold clasp on the green box and revealed a gold ring with a single brilliant diamond in the center.

"Oh my God, are you serious? You know, we don't have to if you don't want to. It's not 1770-something," she blurted in a rush.

He nodded, looking up at her with a quiet, knowing smile.

"I can't imagine being here without you. I want to be with you forever."

She blinked fast, trying not to cry. "Oh my God, yes. Yes, I love you, yes."

He stood and she wrapped her arms around him, as he picked her up and swung her around in the field right as the breeze started, and petals from the cherry tree swirled around them both.

Mel was crying. There were tears on her cheeks, and she couldn't stop smiling.

"I can't wait to tell Abuelita. She's not going to believe—Wait, did you already tell her? Is that why she packed the picnic?"

Nathaniel smiled and helped Mel into the saddle.

"Yes, I did, and you know, she wasn't surprised at all."

Mel shook her head as Nathaniel nudged Tess forward.

"She'll say that she prayed for this all along."

"Thank God for that," he said, and held her against him as he pressed a kiss to the side of her neck.

Mel squealed in delight as Tess took off into a full gallop, happy and grateful for all the mysteries and love in the world.

ACKNOWLEDGMENTS

As always, there are so many people to thank, but *The Last Loyalist* would not exist without my husband, Kevin. He gave me his twenty-five-year-old screenplay based on a unit from Maryland set in the Civil War. After a year of on-site research, my first version, *Gunpowder Falls*, sat as a manuscript in my desk drawer for another nine years. After nearly a decade, Kevin's suggestion to change the story to the American Revolution was the missing piece to make the story complete.

I am also grateful to Parneet Gosal, who encouraged me to dig deep and revisit other works that had been lying dormant. Without her fearless encouragement and inspiring determination, this story would still be sitting on my desk, untouched.

I'm also profoundly grateful to my dear friend and fellow historian, Jenn Gosselin, who has been with me throughout this journey, back when I was first writing it in 2016. A loyal thought partner, she helped encourage this project at every stage.

I always owe many thanks to Ann Suhz and Ann Riza for their attention to detail, which helped edit the story and cross-check the research. I learn so much from their invaluable feedback and constructive criticism.

A huge thanks to Kirstin Barrett for her dedication and creativity in bringing this cover to life. Her creative eye and insightful expertise were essential in designing the perfect cover.

To my readers, I am continually humbled and grateful for your unwavering support. Your love for my characters and stories is a constant source of inspiration for me. None of this would be possible without you.

Lastly, I want to thank all of my former students. In my twelve years of being a Social Studies teacher, it was my honor to teach about early American history. Thank you for letting me share my love of these time periods with you. I cherish the memories we shared in class, and I hope you do too. Thank you.

ABOUT THE AUTHOR

Kathryn K. Murphy writes action-packed, romance novels bursting with emotion. If you want to know when Kathryn's next book will come out, please visit her website at www.kathrynkmurphy.com, where you can sign up to receive email updates.